NAKED

NAKED

stacey trombley

Entangled Publishing, LLC
2614 South Timberline Road
Suite 109
Fort Collins, CO 80525

Entangled Teen is an imprint of Entangled Publishing, LLC.

Visit our website at www.entangledpublishing.com.

Edited by Stephen Morgan and Elizabeth Vail
Cover design by Kelley York
Photography credit Woman (c) Byelikova Oksana/Shutterstock
Interior design by Jeremy Howland

Print ISBN 978-1-63375-007-4
Ebook ISBN 978-1-63375-008-1

Manufactured in the United States of America

First Edition July 2015

10 9 8 7 6 5 4 3 2 1

CHAPTER ONE

Sometimes being interviewed by the police is like a game.
It's kind of fun, keeping them from the truth. At least until they get pissed and start hitting, bruising, breaking. Then it's not so fun anymore. But until then, I have to keep my head up or I'll never make it out alive.

I shift in the metal chair, uncomfortable, and lean away from the cold table.

Hiding the truth is easy when no one knows anything. What sucks is when the police know more than you do. If they catch you in one lie, the whole web collapses.

Good thing the woman in front of me isn't a cop. She hasn't *said* she's not a cop, but she doesn't have to. The way she smiles at me with the kind of innocence I used to have, it's pretty obvious.

"What's your name?" she asks. As if we're just normal people having a casual conversation. As if she doesn't know how dangerous that kind of information is for someone like me.

"Exquisite," I say.

"That's very pretty." She says it so sincerely that for a moment, I think she believes me. Maybe she really is as naive as she looks.

In my world, naive might as well mean dead.

"My name is Sarah," she says.

Why in the world would she think I care what her name is?

"Okay," I say.

"How old are you?"

"Nineteen." The word slips out before I even think about it. That's my go-to answer, a lie I've told so often I almost believe it.

"Hmm, you don't look nineteen."

Funny that in all the times I've been in police stations, a hundred set of handcuffs cutting off my circulation, my age has never been questioned. I'm nineteen. They know I'm lying— my seventeenth birthday is still months away—but they don't care.

No one cares.

"Yeah, I get that a lot."

A creak grabs my attention, and I look to the door. There's a small window where the asshole cop watches us. My black eye throbs, even though it wasn't him who gave it to me. Someone else gave me that black eye, with the same hand he used to hold against the side of my face as we fell asleep together.

I'm pretty sure I've got better luck with the woman in a suit than the man behind the window. The way he shakes his head every time he sees me, it looks like he wants to hurt me—he'd enjoy it.

"You don't like the police, do you?"

My attention shifts back to the woman.

"Nope," I say honestly, despite my minor surprise.

"Well, it might help you to know that I'm not a cop." As

if her being a cop was ever a possibility. "And I'm not here to get information and leave. I'm here to help you. If I can." She smiles, like she's trying to put me at ease. Yeah, good luck with that. "You're sure you're nineteen?"

"You calling me a liar?"

She smiles. "No. It's just, if you are nineteen, there's nothing I can do for you. You'll go to jail, or go back to that life out there, on the streets. I don't want that. And somehow, I don't think you want that, either."

"Why would you think that?" Now I stand. She thinks she knows me. She thinks that she gets it, thinks she gets me.

Her eyes soften, they grow…sadder somehow.

I don't let myself show her any change in my expression. My walls keep the nightmares away. The second they fall, I'm screwed.

"I'm sorry," she says. "But I can usually tell if I can help someone. And I think I can help you."

I blink. My walls almost fall then, nearly crash down and crumble all over my feet, but I catch myself before it's too late.

I make my face blank, impassive. Don't let her see beneath my mask. It's a trick I learned for when guys pay for me. An hour. All night. Never let them see how I really feel.

It's more important than ever that I keep strong, keep this woman from getting to me, seeing too much.

"But if you were, say, sixteen," she says, "I could help you. Give you a new life. No jail, just hope."

I sit back down and look down at my hands. I don't like how much she knows, suspects.

"What do you think you can do for me?"

She stands and walks slowly around the room. When she

walks behind my chair, my heart pounds. I hate not being able to see her. I don't care how kind she seems. I'm in a police station. I'm not safe.

"I really wish you'd tell me your real name."

"Why?" I ask, just as she finishes her round and faces me once more.

"Because I don't feel right calling you Exquisite, and I'd like to be able to have a real conversation with you."

I roll my eyes. "I know better than to think you care. No one cares."

She faces me again. Her eyes are a pretty brown, surprisingly firm for how soft she seems. "Do you really think that no one in the world cares? Or just no one in a police station? No one in the city? It's not possible that someone out there would want to help you, somehow, someway?"

I think about this for a moment. "Some people want to help, but that doesn't mean they can."

"Well, then we've established that I want to help. So can't I at least know your name?"

At least she's trying something other than broken ribs and swollen eyes. But if she's really as innocent as she seems, then she's not in a position to help. Anyone who knows the truth will hurt me. Anyone who doesn't know the truth is better off believing the lie.

"I told you my name," I say.

Her shoulders deflate like she's disappointed, and she tucks a loose strand of brown hair behind her ear. She takes in a deep breath and pulls out a file from her briefcase. "Will you at least tell me why you're here?"

"Doesn't that file already tell you why?"

She looks down. "There's not much here. It says you go by the name Exquisite."

"I told you that."

"The police seem to think you're a prostitute."

Of course they do. Other than the smeared lipstick and six-inch heels—clue number one—they've seen me in here before. "People make lots of assumptions," I say.

"So it's not true?"

I don't respond.

"Who gave you that black eye?"

"A man who also thought I was a hooker," I say. Sometimes I impress myself with my ability to spin the truth to my advantage. Sure, the cop thought I was a hooker, because I am. Or was. Or something.

This is one truth she'll never get out of me.

Her eyebrows rise. "So, a man sexually harassed you, you refused him, and he hit you?"

I shrug. Sounds like a pretty good story to me.

"If that's the case, why haven't you made a phone call? A few statements and you're free to go."

I blink. She's got me there. I search for a lie here, something to tell her, some excuse about why I haven't called anyone, why I still can't. Instead, I give the kind of answer I truly hate: an honest one. "I don't have anyone to call."

The only person I can call, the person who would usually bail me out, is the person who put me here. Sort of. I mean, I kind of put myself here. It must not say it in the file, but I pulled a gun on the cop when he stopped.

Sometimes emotions are too strong to control. He's just lucky I didn't pull the trigger.

But Luis is the reason I was on the street with a black eye. Luis is the reason I had nowhere else to go. And now I don't think I can ever go back.

Once broken, some things never heal. With him, I felt as close to whole as I could get in that little apartment. He found me. Saved me. Loved me.

But now we're broken, too.

Sarah watches me for an uncomfortable moment like she's contemplating something, then puts the file down. "Can I show you something?"

My eyebrows pull down in what I'm sure is an unattractive way. "What kind of something?"

She stands and smiles to reassure me. "Follow me."

Still very confused, but curious, I follow her. The creepy cop is gone now, and we walk down the hall freely. No handcuffs, no guards. I've never been this free in a police station. We get to the main entrance, where there are glass cases of posters. A few wanted posters to the right, but the entire left side is covered with about fifty missing person posters.

"Thousands of kids run away each year. Did you know that? With nowhere to go, they often end up in prostitution." She says it like a teacher or something, talking about a subject we'll have a test on later, not like it's something I've lived through.

Does she know I've experienced this firsthand? Or is this a game, too? A test to see if I'll slip up and reveal something?

She says, "Those kids don't realize that their parents still look for them. Some parents never give up."

I look over all the posters, all the missing children. What kind of lives have they found on the streets? Did they end up like me? Selling themselves for the hope of a new life? How many of these kids are already dead?

Then I see a set of familiar dead eyes staring back at me from one of the posters. The name reads Anna Rodriguez. I look at all of the posters with the same casual indifference, but the image from that one is seared into my brain.

The girl is young, innocent. Her skin is a pretty olive color, dark enough that most people wouldn't guess she's only half Puerto Rican. She wears a ponytail with wisps of unruly curls falling into her face and a simple string of pearls around her neck.

I'm surprised this is the picture they chose—it's not perfect enough. Those curls would drive my blond trophy-wife mother crazy.

I almost laugh thinking about what she'd say of my ratty hair now. Or how about the running makeup, split lip, and rose tattoo on my ankle?

"Recognize any of those girls?" Sarah says.

I shrug. "Nope."

She seems to believe me, which is good, because I mean it. I never knew that girl, and neither did her parents.

I don't dare look her in the eye again. Without another word, she takes me back to my cell and I'll admit, I'm a bit relieved.

"Just hang in there a little longer," she says.

I don't have the energy to ask her if she's done with me, if she plans on questioning me again.

All I know is I cannot let her know the truth.

The fact that my parents still have missing person posters up, are still looking for me… I'm not sure what to think of it. If they knew where I really was, what I was really doing…

The things my mother would say would be bad enough. But my father? He'd disown me. I'm sure of it.

I pace in my cell. Back and forth, back and forth.

Life would be easier, I suppose, if I were that girl. Normal. Worrying about homework, choir practice, and who would take me to homecoming.

That girl wouldn't have a bruise forming on her upper arm from being held down, stolen from the one person she loved. That girl wouldn't be sitting in a cold cell, wondering how the cops will hurt her next.

Anna Rodriguez.

The name rings in my head, a ghost from a past I've tried so hard to outrun.

But what I ran to…was it really better?

Guess not anymore.

Good little Anna. Pretty little Anna.

That's what my parents thought I was. They dressed me up with their expensive clothes, did my hair up in pigtails and curls, put pearls around my neck. Then they expected me to smile and pretend that was what I always wanted—to be just like them. Perfect.

But I'm not. I wasn't then, and I'm certainly not now.

No, perfect isn't even close to what I really am. How about dirty? Ruined? Tarnished? Yes, that's the word my mother would use. Tarnished, like her heart necklace. Once shining with a bright gold sheen, now rubbed and used, its real value exposed. What it always was to begin with.

Cheap.

CHAPTER TWO

The streets of New York are a whole lot more than taxis and tourists and Broadway lights. I learned that the hard way at thirteen years old.

How did pretty little Anna go from Westchester suburb brat to New York hooker? Now that's a story, one I'm not sure I completely understand myself. There were reasons, there always are, but I don't expect anyone to get it, especially the innocent social worker lady who keeps trying to help me.

I wake up what must be hours later when Sarah comes back to get me. I fell asleep against the cold bars, and my skin sticks when I pull away.

Sarah has dark circles under her eyes now, like she never slept.

My old life is still floating through my head, and now Sarah just makes the memories even more vivid.

Would the thirteen-year-old me be happy about where I am now? What I've done? Who I've become?

No.

But would I go back and change my decisions?

I don't know, but that doesn't really matter now. I can't go back. I just have to learn to live with myself.

There's nothing even Sarah can do to help me with that. Right now what I need is a new future.

"Hi, Anna."

I nod at her but say nothing. I'm not much in the mood for talking now.

"Are you ready for a visit? There's someone here to see you."

I blink. "Who?"

"Not who you'd expect."

I didn't call anyone. There's no one to call. No one to come get me, no one who cares.

Is it possible Luis sent someone for me? That he came for me himself? And if he did…do I want to see him? Because even if he cares enough to come for me, I can't go back. Not now. Not after what happened.

I nod to Sarah anyway. If I don't take the visit, I'll always wonder who wanted to see me and why.

Sarah smiles, a sad smile now, and leaves the room.

The door doesn't open up again for about twenty minutes. A guard comes in and escorts me out. He barely looks at me. No nasty comments or wiggling eyebrows, no "accidental" push into the concrete wall. It's almost like I'm not a hooker.

We walk down a long, echoey hallway, and then into a new room. There are tables and steel walls. A few guards stand around, but otherwise no one is here. It's empty.

The guard leads me to a table, and I sit.

I face the way I came in, the entrance that leads back to my prison—literally. Behind me is another entrance, where footsteps tap closer.

I don't turn my head, but my heart pounds. Finally, the person walks around and stands in front of me.

My stomach drops. No, it doesn't just drop, it disappears. As much as I didn't want to see Luis, I expected to see him.

But it's not Luis.

My blood runs cold, looking at a face I never expected to see again. A face I never wanted to see again.

My father.

Everything stops, like time is frozen or something. He stares at me; I stare at him.

His facial hair has never been so long, but otherwise he looks exactly the same. Like a Hispanic politician. He's not really a politician; he's the CEO of some big company that I never understood, and he has a lot of influence in a lot of places. Anyone with money does. And he has money, though I never knew where it went. Probably toward that shiny Corvette of his.

He looks older, bags under his eyes.

His skin has always been dark like mine. Put us next to each other and it's clear I'm his daughter.

"Anna," he finally says, hard and gravelly. He frowns, looks away, and after a moment, turns around.

I don't even know how to describe this feeling. Like horror and heartbreak at once.

The last time he saw me, I was that little girl with unruly curls and pearls. Now I can't even imagine what he sees. A street-scum teen with matted hair, ripped clothes, and yellowing bruises around her eye.

I'm not even sure how he recognized me.

But he did. It's no wonder he doesn't turn back around.

I squeeze my hands together and watch as my fingers twist, trying to quash the desire for him to look at me again. To see those brown eyes so much like my own. Because I can't want that.

I always knew how he would feel to know where I've been, what I've been doing. He'd hate me more than he ever did before. He'd wish I were never born.

Was it his choice to put up those missing person posters? Does he regret looking for me? Is that why he's ignoring me now?

My father leaves without another glance back. When the door opens, I see my mother in the hallway, waiting for him, waiting to find out if the girl in this room is the daughter she lost.

The daughter she never fought for.

Of course she didn't come in herself. Ever the dutiful trophy wife. Even when things were at their worst, she never stood up for me.

A long time ago, she and I were close. She sang me songs to sleep. I told her everything. Good. Bad. But the worse things got between my father and me, the more she pulled away.

She doesn't look toward me as the door closes, like she's afraid of what will happen if it's really me. What she'll have to acknowledge.

I'm a ruined child now. Not even worth looking at.

I always knew that, so why do their reactions bother me? Why do I want them to want me so badly?

Maybe because I need someone to.

Anyone.

Luis used to call me his diamond in the rough, after he'd saved me from the street. He'd cup my face in his hands like I was something precious. But eventually *precious* started to mean *valuable*, something to be traded, sold, used.

And then thrown away once the value was gone. I wasn't even valuable anymore.

I stare at the table in front of me and listen to their muted voices coming from the hallway. Guess I wanted out, and I guess this is one way to do it. I won't have to return to the streets that ruined me. The man who loved and betrayed me.

But if it means going back to the parents I'm sure will hate me forever…

Back to the impossibly perfect movie life in the suburbs…

How can I, Anna Rodriguez, hooker, go back to any of that? I didn't belong before, and now?

No, I'm better off staying in jail.

Sarah comes back into the room. I sit silently at the metal table.

"Do you know what will happen now?" she asks me in a near whisper.

I close my eyes and think. Of all the things that could happen, this wasn't something that I ever thought possible.

I open my eyes and nod. "They'll take me back to prison."

Sarah looks confused. "Your parents are going to take you home."

"Yeah, that's what I mean."

Is it strange that I've come to like her? I shouldn't, I know I shouldn't. But she's the only one in the world who believes in me right now. I don't want her to give up on me, not yet.

Sarah sighs, so light I'm sure she didn't expect me to hear it. I look up. She blinks, her face controlled, calculating. Only her eyes betray the sympathy, the sadness. I'm not sure how I feel about her pity, but I guess I have more important things to worry about right now.

She's going to send me home. Like I can even still call it that.

How can I go back? How can I walk down the halls I played in as a child? Sit at the table where my parents taught me to write my name?

I suppose I do have good memories there, but that almost makes it worse. It makes me look like even more of a screwup.

"I know there was probably a reason you left in the first place, Anna." She talks slowly, measuring each word. "Is there any reason for you to believe you might, in any way, be in danger if you go back home?"

I pause, considering the question. "I guess if someone followed me from New York."

"That's not what I mean," she says. She waits until I meet her eyes. "Your parents."

I shake my head quickly, finally understanding. No. My mom never hurt me. And my father? The only scars he left were emotional. But every disappointing look will dig deeper and deeper. If he decides to tell me this is all the proof he needs to believe I'm not worth anything, why I'll *never* be worth anything…

"I can help you, Anna. You just have to tell me."

Let's just say I've seen a lot worse than what my parents can deal out.

"I'm in no danger with them. They used to love me. They just didn't understand me."

She nods slowly.

I ask, "Will I ever see you?"

Her mouth opens a little. I guess she's surprised; I never let on that I might actually like her.

"We can talk anytime. I work out of New York, but West-chester isn't far, so I can come see you any time you need it. And if anything happens, you call me, okay?"

I nod, knowing that's not enough to get me through this... but at least it's something.

CHAPTER THREE

It hasn't really hit me what's happening until the van pulls up to my old house. It's big, white, with a full, manicured garden. The Japanese maple tree sitting there, right beside the stone steps that lead up to the wraparound porch, staring at me.

Everything is the same. Except me.

I stand there, looking at the house I fled three years ago.

I can't move. I can't make myself go in that house.

Sarah comes around the truck and stands beside me. "Ready?" she asks.

I shake my head. I will never be ready for this. Never.

She doesn't say anything, and she doesn't move. We stand there for at least five minutes. Five really, really, really long minutes. I'm still not ready to move, no matter how long those minutes seem. I'll stand here for eternity if I have to, if it can keep me from facing those memories. From facing my father. My mother.

But Sarah seems ready, so she begins to walk across the massive yard—through the grass. My mother won't like it— she hates anyone touching her perfectly sculpted lawn—but I suppose that's okay with me.

Sarah doesn't ask me to join her, doesn't plead with me to go inside. She leaves me behind, and that's what makes me go. Did she know that even the smallest of nudges would have kept me rooted even deeper in my spot?

I walk very, very slowly toward the house. I feel defiant for walking through the grass. One small thing at a time. My mother doesn't own me anymore.

Sarah reaches the top of the steps as I cross the garden. She knocks on the heavy door. I stop at the bottom of the steps, unwilling to go any farther.

Slowly, the door opens. I close my eyes and wait, but I hear nothing.

After a moment of silence, I can't take it. I open my eyes to see Sarah and the face I've been dreading—and hoping for. My mother's. Apparently she's gathered enough courage to see me face-to-face.

Her hair is done in a tight bun, and her makeup successfully covers whatever flaws she has developed over the last three years. It's obvious she spent a long time preparing herself to see her long-lost daughter up close, without a police station hallway between us. Because clearly looking put-together will make this easier.

I want to roll my eyes, shake my head, but in truth, I'm kind of glad to know she hasn't changed that much. I didn't ruin everything about her. Even if the thing that didn't change was something I never liked.

She doesn't move, just looks at me. But I cast my eyes to the ground, and she clears her throat.

"Why don't you both come in?"

I look to Sarah, who nods and walks through the open door first.

We walk down a very familiar hallway and into our huge, bright white kitchen. I'm a stranger in this house.

I'm not the little girl who used to see how far she could slide on the hardwood dining room floor and hid in the linen closet when she was in trouble. I'm definitely not the little girl who sang Christmas songs with her mother while doing the dishes, even in the summer. That girl is gone.

I left her in Grand Central Terminal three years ago.

My father is waiting in the kitchen, sitting at the table. I take in a deep breath, sit across from him, and run my hands through my hair. After a pause, Sarah takes a seat beside me. She gives me a reassuring smile that I don't return.

My mother jumps right into the role of perfect host, walking straight to the refrigerator. Her greatest skill was always ignoring the truth, pretending nothing bothered her, that everything was perfect. I don't know if she agreed with how my father disciplined me, how harsh he was with even the smallest of transgressions. I think sometimes I blamed her more than I did him. But she was too good at ignoring the truth. I supposed I shouldn't be surprised that she's doing the same thing now.

"Would you like some tea?" she asks Sarah without a single glance at me. I want her to look at me. I don't even know why. I should want to run and hide. I should want to hate her, want her to hate me.

But somehow, I don't. I want her to care.

Less than five minutes in this house and I already feel like a lost thirteen-year-old again. Maybe I'm not as different as I thought I was.

I'm still a stranger in this house, but that's not such a strange concept to Anna Rodriguez. I never belonged here.

I never understood my mother's Bible verse plaques that cover the walls of each hallway, or her obsession with being the trophy wife of the year. I never understood my father and his love of money and prestige. Both of them so good at hiding their imperfections.

And the times I didn't hide what they didn't want to see? My father reminded me of the price of failure. Why my disguise had to be perfect.

They were either proud or they weren't. You did what they wanted or you were a disgrace. Pretty sure I know which one I am now.

My mother sets two cups of tea onto the table with shaking hands. Sarah takes hers with thanks. I don't move.

The silence is thick. I can't even bring myself to look around the house. I don't want to remember this place. I stare at the wooden table, hoping to zone out, but a mark on the side grabs my attention. A simple "A" carved into the corner where my mother and father wouldn't notice it. I run my thumb over the carving and somehow feel like that girl again, desperate but still full of hope.

I take a deep breath and look up and my gaze crashes into my father's. I freeze beneath his stare.

Does he see his daughter? A girl he once loved?

Or does he see a stranger?

One look at the missing poster they gave to the New York City police tells you the kind of girl I was back then. And one look at my mug shot would tell you who I am now.

You can put all the fancy clothes you want on me, but the ripped stockings they replace will still itch my legs. I look around the room for the first time. The kitchen is exactly the same, down to the mugs that hang next to the coffeepot that was brand-new when I was eleven. The cups are even in the same order.

The refrigerator is bare. At least they don't have my report cards hanging there anymore. Not that my last year at school was worth hanging. Eighth grade wasn't my best year. By then I was already sneaking out at night to go to parties and sleep with high schoolers. Remember when I said my parents would have disowned me even then? Surprise! Anna was never a good girl, not really. She was just a good pretender.

One day you get tired of pretending, and the fear of all your lies being exposed becomes suffocating.

I knew I could never be who my parents wanted me to be. That's why I'm not sure what I'm doing here. Why would they want me back now?

"This is going to be hard on all of you," Sarah says, breaking the silence. "This situation, it's…difficult."

My father grunts indignantly. Mom says nothing. The perfect, obedient wife.

Sarah doesn't continue. She looks to my father.

"Difficult, that's what you call it?" he says.

"What would you call it?" I ask him, sounding braver than I feel. I know what he's getting at, and I'd much rather he say it out loud. He thinks I'm disgusting. A disgrace. He doesn't respond though, so I continue as if he had. "You're the one who brought me here. If you think I'm so horrible…"

"Anna, please," Sarah says, but she's too quiet. Too polite.

My father ignores her and stands. "I brought you back to save you from that evil place. An evil life."

"Mr. Rodriguez, please," Sarah says.

"It was my job as your father to…save you from the evil in your life. Even if it means bringing filth back into my home." He straightens his shoulders. "That's our burden to carry."

I laugh a little under my breath. It's bitter, even I can see that, but who can blame me? At least he said it. At least he was honest for the first time since I've known him.

"Mr. Rodriguez," Sarah says, louder.

He tears his hard, angry eyes from me to look at her. They soften slightly. Appearances, after all.

"I was saying that this is hard on everyone," Sarah says. "Including Anna. You must understand, this isn't her fault."

"Not her fault?" My father's hands shake on top of the table. "She…she…."

"I fucked men for money." Everything stops. The room is filled with a silence that's suffocating. But I'm not sorry. Not sorry at all. "There, are you happy?" I lean back in my seat and wait for his response. I'm not afraid of my father anymore, and honestly, that feels pretty good.

"Anna!" Sarah says, shocked at my bluntness, at my language.

I look at her and give an apologetic smile, but it's mixed with disdain. I guess I am a little sorry. Not for saying that to my father, but for saying it in front of Sarah. I have more respect for her than my whole family put together. Three years on the streets hasn't changed my lack of respect for parents who gave me more rules than love.

It's also the first time I admitted I am—was—a hooker out loud to Sarah. She knew, of course, but when I wouldn't talk about the years I spent in New York, she gave up and focused on the now. Why couldn't the lie have lasted a little longer?

My mother turns and then rests her head on the kitchen counter. To pray? To hide her tears? I don't know.

Truth is, she needed to hear it.

They *all* needed to hear it.

Sarah looks at me now. "Anna, you're back now. And your parents are going to do whatever they need to do to make this work for you. But they need to know why you came back. What is it that you want out of all of this?"

My life back.

"Freedom," I say lightly.

"What do you mean?" Sarah says.

"I…" I'm a little scared to say it, to tell them the full truth. I glance at my father. "I left, before, because of how controlling you were. I couldn't be who I wanted to be. I just want to have a little freedom."

"How? How can I let you do anything?" my father says. I've hurt him, angered him. "How can you expect us to trust you?"

"I don't need you to trust me. Just don't expect me to be your perfect daughter. I was never that girl. I'm not going to church, I'm not going to be a straight-A student, I'm not going to dress up and go to prom or be homecoming queen like you always expected. I don't know what I want to be, but I know I don't want to be that."

"So what is it? You want the freedom to 'be yourself'? 'Yourself' is a prostitute," my father says. He stands up. "I can't let you be that anymore. I won't!"

I stand up, too. "No! I didn't just wake up one day and say, 'Maybe I'll suck cock for a living.' That's all you think I am? Just a hooker? You don't realize I did it because of you. I left because of you!"

The words are out before I can take them back. God knows what my father would do if Sarah wasn't here. Something to make me take it back.

But Sarah is here, and however angry he is, he can't afford to let down his disguise in front of her.

Sarah stands and grabs me by the arm. Is she being tough? But her hand feels like a feather on my arm, so light it amazes me.

Still, I do what she wants and walk with her through the sliding glass door on the other side of the kitchen and out onto the back porch.

I know she brought me out here to talk, but I find myself looking at a doghouse at the back of the yard, a water bowl beside it. We never had a dog.

"Anna, I need you to calm down. It's hard for them to adjust to this, too."

"Well, at least they get to make their own choices," I say, still looking at the doghouse. There's no grass around it, just mud. "If they choose to have their hooker daughter back, they better be ready to face the truth."

"Listen," she says. "I agree that they'll have to accept the truth. They'll have to come to grips with it. But that doesn't mean you have to throw it in their faces."

I turn back to her. My only friend.

How pathetic.

What would Luis think of me now? At least he'd tell me to stand up for myself.

"Yeah, right," I say.

"Just stop for a moment and think. I want you to try to imagine how they feel."

I shake my head, not at her, at myself. Why does no one think about how *I'm* feeling?

"What if I don't want to think about what they're feeling?"

I don't know what she sees when she looks at me. Sometimes it's like she looks straight into my brain, or soul, or something.

"Why not?" she says in a near whisper.

"Why would I want to be okay with my parents thinking I'm trash? Disgusting? Whatever else they think?"

"You're thinking about this the wrong way. Yes, they think little of what you did while you were away, but that's not what I mean. You were their baby, their little girl, and you left them. Ran away. Don't you think that hurt them?"

I shrug. "Maybe."

"As a parent, all you want to do is take care of your children, protect them. And they couldn't." Her voice gets softer, and for the first time I wonder if she has—or had—a kid of her own. "Now, in some ways they feel like it's too late. It's hard for them. Not just about you being a prostitute, but about all of it. They feel like more of a failure at being parents than they think you're a failure of a daughter. I guarantee it."

I stare at her, unblinking. I don't know what to think about what she said. This is all so much. Now I'm supposed to feel sorry for my parents?

I turn away from her and cross my arms. "I didn't ask to be here. No one gave me a choice. It's not fair to put all of this on me." Tears well in my eyes, and I feel like a child. I hate feeling like a child.

Sarah sighs. "Why don't you hang out here for a while? Try to calm down a bit. Mentally prepare yourself. The truth is this will all go a lot smoother if you and your parents learn to respect each other."

Yeah, like I can just make myself respect them.

Sarah walks through the door and leaves me alone in the backyard.

I look back out to the doghouse, which stands almost one hundred feet away from where I am on the porch. But I haven't seen a dog yet, so I take a few slow steps toward it. I still see nothing; maybe it's not even out here right now. Maybe they don't even have a dog anymore. They might have killed it the way they killed me. Three years is a long time to live with people like them.

I see a large metal chain connected to a tree about ten feet away that leads directly to the house.

I take a few steps and see nothing. Another few steps and something moves, a small grunt of a lazy animal, and inside the dark hole of the large doghouse I see a bit of black fur.

A few more steps, even slower now.

Then I hear a deep growl. The kind of growl you don't want to mess with. Slow, confident. Scary.

I'm not scared of dogs, but I'm not stupid either. I've met my fair share of untrustworthy dogs in New York.

"Careful there." I whip my head toward the male voice and see a boy over the fence, standing in the yard next door.

He looks at me, and his smile seems so genuine, so confident, that it can't be real. He's probably about my age, freckles and thick-rimmed glasses. A bit nerdy, but cute in a way I've missed. The kind of guy I'd never have talked to in my old life because I'd have thought he was too good for me.

But he already made the first move, so…

"No?" I say.

He shakes his head, that small smile playing at his lips. He looks at the doghouse. "He doesn't have many friends, so he's not usually good with strangers."

A nose and a pair of eyes look out at me from the doghouse. Whatever's in there isn't growling anymore, it's watching.

I take a few steps away and look back to the boy, who's watching me, too.

Who is he? We never had a neighbor my age before. I'm not good at making friends, and I'm pretty sure this kid would hide under his bed if he knew just some of the things I've done over the last few years.

But somehow, the way he looks at me with those hazel eyes, bright and alive... It's like I'm not the girl from the streets, not the girl who sold her body to strangers and fell in love with the man who sold her. Not the girl with no future. Even Luis never looked at me like this. To this boy, I'm just...normal. Just a mysterious girl next door he's never met.

"You new?" he asks me.

I shake my head and open my mouth, but then I close it. How am I supposed to explain any of this? Nothing's changed. I'm still dirty, tarnished Anna. I can't throw that on some random guy.

He lifts up a Weedwacker I didn't notice before. "I'm Jackson. I mow the lawn here sometimes."

"Oh," I say stupidly.

"What's your—"

"Anna!"

I spin around to see my father standing on the porch.

"Get away from Czar. He's dangerous."

I see the dog's ears perk up, possibly at the sound of his

name. I shrug and walk away from the doghouse, but I don't like to turn my back to him. I don't like to turn my back to anyone. I listen intently and glance back, just a little, hopefully subtly enough. But the dog's in the shadows again. Hiding. Waiting for a safer moment?

You and me both.

"That's a guard dog," my father says. "You leave him alone."

I shrug and look back to Jackson. He waves to my father, who gives him a noncommittal nod in return. As soon as my father turns away and heads back inside, the boy pulls something out of his pocket and tosses it toward the doghouse, then winks at me before going back to trimming the grass of my neighbor's yard.

A massive black dog with a wagging stump of a tail rushes from the doghouse and gobbles up what looks like a Milk-Bone.

I take one more deep breath and then head back inside, feeling surprisingly less tense now. Something else to think about besides the way my parents look at me when I come back inside, something other than the odd tension between us. And more importantly, what kind of hell the next few days will bring.

Then I'm back in the kitchen and wondering why I didn't stay outside.

"We're sorry, Anna," my mom says.

I look up quickly, surprised to hear those words come from my mother's mouth, and I wonder if Sarah has magical powers. Five minutes alone with them and she's somehow given one of them a soul.

My father sits down, and his shoulders sag.

I look back at my mom. "Sorry for what?" I say. Knowing I'm pushing my luck to have already gotten this much, but I can't help it.

My father looks at her, as though daring her to say more.
My mom drops her head.

And suddenly I feel bad for pushing her.

Didn't Sarah say this was hard for all of us?

"I'm sorry, too," I say, and I decide that Sarah is definitely psychic.

CHAPTER FOUR

My heart pounds wildly as I stand in front of my bedroom door. I left my parents and Sarah in the kitchen so they could talk alone. They asked me to leave, as if I wanted to listen to them. As if escape wasn't the first thing on my mind.

But now I'm not so sure this is the escape I want.

It's amazing, all the horrors I faced on the streets of New York, other people's worst nightmares, but the thought of facing a thirteen-year-old girl's bedroom scares the freaking crap out of me.

How can I possibly be scared of my old bedroom?

Luis wouldn't let this go if he saw me now. I can almost hear his laugh. It always started light and rumbly, as if it bubbled up from somewhere deep and warm in his chest. I wish I could laugh with him. I wish I could go back to when I believed that laugh belonged to a safe space for just the two of us. Was any of that warmth real? Or was I just too blind to see the truth?

The fear of my childhood bedroom is laughable, but somehow this is different. Different from all the other horrors of my past. Like I'm not just facing physical pain or whatever, I'm facing my past. I'm facing myself.

And that is so much scarier.

I take a deep breath and decide I've wasted enough time being a wimp. That girl I left behind, she can't scare me anymore.

I twist the knob and try to ignore the pounding in my chest.

I take a step through the doorway and remind myself that this room means nothing. I'm not this girl, and it doesn't matter what she would think of me now. It doesn't matter what she hoped for when she ran away—naive dreams of stardom and freedom. I might have failed that girl, I might have failed myself even now, but there isn't anything I can do about it.

My heart still aches, no matter what my mind tries to convince me. My eyes still fill with tears, my mind with memories, images. A little girl with unruly curls and dreams too big for her own good.

That girl danced on the bed to all the stupid pop stars she hoped she'd become, stole from her mother's closet just to try on her high heels and earrings. Then hid under the bed when her father caught her. When the game turned serious.

That girl waited while her mother ran into the room to stop the girl's father. "She's just a child, Martin," she whispered.

"Hush," he said. Softly, but leaving no room to question him.

But then my memories won't let me pretend. It wasn't some other girl under the bed. It was me.

I squeezed my eyes shut and held my breath, hoping he wouldn't find me. That if I hid long enough, he'd forget.

But then a hand reached under the bed, grasped my upper arm, and ripped me out from my hiding place. My mother didn't try to plead with him again, and neither did I. I knew it wouldn't do any good.

His tight squeezes on my arms left yellow bruises, but those always faded after a few days. His belt was what did the most damage. Those swats left me stinging for days. But even those went away.

It was always the words that left me scarred.

"You run around here like a loose girl. Do you know what happens to loose girls?"

I didn't listen.

His stories were ridiculous. They'd never happen to me, I'd never be like that. But I guess he was more right than I ever realized.

That wasn't long before I started sneaking out the window to live my life in whatever way I could. When I started actually wearing high heels and earrings and short skirts, stolen from the mall and hidden from my parents—I got very good at hiding. All to attract whatever attention I could manage.

The purple walls of my room seem so close together now, pressing in on me and my memories. Rainbow-colored pillows cover the top of the pink bedspread and stuffed animals line the sides. My desk sits in the same exact place, and there's a purple grape juice stain next to the left leg.

Nothing's changed. Figured my parents would have made it into a workout room or something. I'm honestly not sure they've touched a thing.

The same pictures hang on the walls, my very last drawings before I ran away.

I suppose it makes sense that a sketch of the Empire State Building is pinned to the corkboard. I'd dreamed about going there for years before I decided to buy myself a train ticket. Before everything went to shit.

And the worst thing? I'm right back where I started.

I cross the room, grab the picture, and rip it from the board. I squeeze my hand closed and watch as the building—once the source of all my dreams—shrinks and wrinkles and disappears into my fist.

I toss it in the trash and walk out the door.

My parents are easier to face than this.

When I reenter the kitchen, my mother and father are talking quietly with Sarah.

"Welcome back," Sarah says lightly, like she's surprised I didn't get caught up being back in my old room or something.

I shrug and sit at the table. "I don't like it up there."

She cocks her eyebrow. "Well, it's good you came back when you did," she says. "There's something your parents want to talk to you about."

I look up, surprised. I have no idea what they'd want to say to me. I mean, I'm sure I can guess some of the things they'd *like* to say…

"Hi, Anna," my mother whispers.

My stomach squeezes, and my eyes water again. I really don't enjoy feeling like a child, but right now I'm not sure I've got a choice.

"Hi, Mom," I say.

This is so fucking weird.

My heart pounds. Thick, quiet awkwardness fills the air.

I turn to my mom and dad, who are both staring at the ground.

"Nora, why don't you start?" Sarah prompts. It's odd to hear my mother called by her first name. It's not something I'm used to hearing from even my father, who, if he ever speaks directly to her, calls her sweetie or sugar, or something equally cheesy. But I remind myself that I haven't been around in three years. Maybe that's changed, too.

"We want you to go back to school," Mom finally says.

"What?" I say, sincerely shocked by this. I've barely been back one day. I haven't been to school since I left here. What's the point in starting back now?

"We…" She pauses and plays with her hands some more. I wonder if she'll have blisters by the end of this conversation. "We think it's best that you go back…or try to go back…to your normal life." Now she turns to me. "We need you to try."

How could I possibly just go back? I'm not even the same person. But she said they *need* me to try, and my stomach aches a little. Why is it that after so long away from them, doing everything in my power and more to disappoint them, that I still want to please them?

"How?" I ask, so lightly I'm surprised they hear.

"You'll start in ninth grade. You were close enough to the end of eighth to finish. And you'll have a tutor, someone to help you catch up."

I shake my head. "No. I mean, how…how can I just go back?"

My mother meets my eyes for the first time. She's on the verge of crying. How can I love this woman despite everything?

"Can't I just get my GED, and then go to college or something?"

"No," my father says. "We can't let you go off to college, not for a very long time."

I want to argue with him that it would take me a long time to get my GED, I'm not smart enough for that to be easy, but I decide to keep my mouth shut.

It's only now that I realize part of me hoped things would be different. That if I ever came back, my father wouldn't be so cruel. And my mother might finally stand up for me.

I close my eyes and picture New York. I picture my old apartment, the streets, the subways. I hear the loud roar of the train as it passes overhead.

I open my eyes and look around. A weary mother and father who hate what I've become in a stuffy, too-formal room. I can't believe I'm back here, but what better choice do I have?

Luis doesn't want me, and even if I ran away again, I have nowhere to go.

A part of me just wants to see the city again. Why can't I be a normal teenager in New York? At least then I can pretend to be someone else. That was what got me through my time on the streets. It would help in this, too.

I just want to belong, I want to be wanted. But I belong nowhere, and no one wants me, no one but the johns, the nasty men who paid to have sex with me.

"We need you to be normal, Anna," my mom says. "We need it. We can't handle more…mistakes."

Mistakes.

"Is that what you think of me?" I say. "That I'm a mistake?"

My father says, "That's up to you—"

"No," my mother says, and I'm shocked when she continues, as though my father wasn't already speaking. "You're not a mistake. But we want you to get better. To have a chance at real happiness."

My father glares at her, and I know she'll hear about this later. She lowers her head, once again the good wife, but it's too late. I saw a glimmer of something in her that I haven't seen since I was a child.

"Okay," I say.

Her face lights up with surprise. "So you'll do it? Go to school, do your homework, join clubs—all of it?"

Wow, that's asking a little much. "I don't know about the clubs part."

"What about chorus?" my father says.

"Yes! You had a lovely singing voice," my mother adds.

I wince. Singing now would just remind me of more of my failures.

"Maybe give her some time to get used to it all before joining clubs or a choir," Sarah says. "The social aspect is what will make it hardest for her, I think. So give her time to adjust. "

"Fine," he says. "It's too late for her to join the Young Women's Chorus anyway, but they'll take new members around March or so. She has until then to 'get used to it.'"

That's my father. Why learn compassion now when he never needed it before?

We sit there in silence. After a minute, my mom speaks up.

"Anna, please," she says. "Please try."

I nod. For my mother, the mother I still hate in so many ways, I will try. Maybe I love my parents more than I'm willing to admit.

Besides, who the hell cares about what a bunch of teenagers think, right? I know I can do it; my skin is bulletproof.

Sticks and stones, fists and rope, can hurt me, but words won't get past first base. I hold back a laugh at my stupidity.

High school. I thought that was a torture I was going to be lucky enough to avoid altogether.

Yeah, this is going to be tons of fun.

CHAPTER FIVE

We eat a quiet dinner together, me, my parents, and Sarah. It's quiet and awkward and I hate it. Every second.

I spend my time thinking about anything except my reality. Anything but Luis and New York, my mother and father, my bedroom waiting to haunt me some more, or the whole new torture of high school waiting around the corner.

So instead I stare out the window between bites of roast beef and watch the too-still doghouse and the empty yard next door.

When my mother finally clears the table of our plates, the sun has barely gone down, but I should go to bed anyway. I need some time to process all of this.

Sarah pulls me to the side before I can head to my bedroom.

"Are you sure you're okay?" she asks me.

Not really, but I have to make a choice and stick to it.

I nod.

I know one thing. I'll find a way to be okay. I always do.

"All right," she says. "But I want you to let me know if that changes."

I nod and head back to my bedroom without waiting for her to leave.

My bedroom.

I don't know. Can I consider this my room now? Just because it still has my things in it? Just because it's where I'll be sleeping now?

That prison cell felt more like home.

At least there, nothing could remind me of what my life was like before. But in my room, there are the stuffed animals I used to talk to. These stupid pink pillows, my old sketches, and dreams. All reminding me of what it was like when I decided to leave. Why I had to go.

I made the right choice. I have to believe that.

But then what am I doing back here? Why am I not still with Luis?

It still hurts, knowing what he did to me.

I can't think about whether or not he ever cared. He had to care, at least at the start. I remember when I first went to New York. No one would help. No one would even look at me. But he took me off the streets. Saved me. Told me I was worth something. I don't think I knew how much I needed to hear those words until he said them. In a city of eight million people, he saw *me*. He picked *me*. That had to mean something.

I remember shivering on that lumpy old brown couch in his shoe-box apartment on that first night, and the way he whispered gently in my ear and told me everything would be okay. I hated that couch. And the peeling wallpaper. And the cockroaches. For a while, I hated everything about that apartment.

But Luis's warm, dark voice made me feel protected and safe, like I was cupped inside two enormous hands. Somewhere along the line, however, those hands had started tightening, squeezing…

On one of the bad nights, the kind where I felt sick and started to regret everything, a guy's filthy stare boring into me, the feeling of his hands rubbing on mine, of his body, and I want to throw up, I want to give up…

"It's going to be okay," Luis said to me afterward, when the tears rolled down my cheeks. "This is only temporary. The money is so good, it'll help us get where we need to go. We can be happy together forever. We just need that jump-start. You can give that to us."

"But the things I have to do…"

"It's nothing," Luis said. "It's just sex. Sex is a good thing. Do you know how many people would kill to make money on sex?"

I shook my head. I didn't understand it. But Luis's voice was so comforting and kind, everything made sense when he said it…

"Those guys pay for it," he said. "You get the money. That's not even fair to them. You are in one killer win-win situation."

I imagine his voice, the way I could almost feel it on my skin like a warm blanket. It wiped away every bad feeling.

Somewhere along the line, it all went wrong. I know that. But he had to have cared at the start. Because if he didn't, it means that it was all worthless. It means he stole everything. It means everything—everyone—I did was for nothing. All the men. All the johns.

I did all of it for Luis.

And if he was just using me…I can't even consider it.

I refuse to turn on the light. Instead I lie down on the twin-size bed. It used to be the perfect size, but now I feel the wall pressing in on my side.

I close my eyes, but sleep won't come.

Luis. Is he thinking of me? Does he regret what happened?

I picture his smile. I remember how easy it was to give in to what he wanted. How easy it was to trust him. Nothing mattered except Luis and how I'd do whatever it took to be with him. Forever.

What a load of shit.

CHAPTER SIX

It will officially be Monday in two hours and counting. Monday means school. Not exactly the most comforting of all thoughts.

I could run away again. But it's not just the thought of failure that makes me stay in bed. My mom finally spoke up for me. It was small and might not mean anything at all, but I can't get it out of my head.

I wish she had the courage to run away, too.

When I finally pull myself from bed, my eyes are heavy and dry. Great, I'm going to look like a crack whore on my first day of high school. Guess it's not far from the truth.

I try to dress according to my mother's fashion sense, not that I have anything to work with that she wouldn't approve of. In my family, like it or not, you always have what you need. I pick a pair of jeans, a blue top, and a scarf. I don't look like me, but I'm not supposed to, right?

I stop at the end of the hallway when I hear my parents around the corner, at the front door. My father must be on his way to work.

"I don't care what Sarah thinks is best," he says. "Taking it easy on Anna is what got us into this mess."

"I know," she murmurs. "But what she said last night. Maybe we could take it easy on her for a while."

"And then what? Break it to her that there are rules she has to abide by?"

Like I could ever forget. I knew there were conditions to coming back. But damn, does he have to lay into her so soon?

"I just think maybe we've…maybe we've been too hard on her," my mom says.

Dad's voice grows louder. "Don't think you're fooling me with this 'we' talk," he says. "I know you blame me. You always blame me. Well, it's not me who coddles her. It's not me who let her think she could get away with whatever she wanted. All I did was try to be a good father."

If it was anyone else, I'd think it was just him getting emotional, but he's always so calculated, I have to guess he's saying that so loudly because he wants me to hear all the way from my room.

"That's not what I mean," Mom says, and her voice gets so soft that I want to run back to my room, where I can try to forget how often this happened before I ran away.

He said she always blames him, but it's always the other way around. She can't complain about anything without him turning it around.

"Oh, here we go again," he says. "What you 'mean.' I know what you mean." There's a long pause, then he says, "One of us is ready to put our emotions aside to get Anna back in line. You better decide if you're going to help me. Because if I come back tonight and you're still giving me this nonsense, I swear to God, Nora…"

The door closes, and I rush back down the hallway as quietly as I can. I wait a few minutes, then come back down, stomping on the floor to let her know I'm coming.

When I come into the kitchen, she's at the sink, staring at the dishes but not actually touching them. Her eyes are red, but to her credit, she puts on a smile when she looks up at me. I want to say something, do something, but she'd say something if she wanted to talk about it, so the best I can think to do is be nice enough to play along with her like everything's okay.

I convince her to let me walk to the bus myself. I considered having her drive me, but I figure I'm better off pretending to be as normal as possible.

She even gives me a banana for breakfast before I leave. Then I head out the side door, because apparently my mother likes to have the dog chained to a pipe in the foyer at night. Makes her feel safer, she says. How does she expect the dog to protect her if she doesn't ever do anything to protect it in return?

The bus is pulling up as I approach the stop. Part of me hopes the driver will leave before I can board, but he waits for me.

Everyone gets quiet as I walk on. I speak to no one, just slink down into a seat by the window and watch as the stupid suburban houses, people, and cars fly by. It's nice, surprisingly enough. Almost like looking out the window on the subway in Brooklyn.

Then someone sits down beside me with a *thunk*, like he wants to be noticed. It's a boy. A strange, cool calm fills me when I recognize him. The boy from next door. Jackson.

He leans back in the seat, comfortable, his head high, his

shoulders back. The complete opposite of my sunken-down position, knees pressed to the back of the seat in front of me. I'm hiding; he's hoping to be seen.

I'm close enough to him now to see why he's so confident. Tall, skinny, wearing thick-rimmed glasses that look more chic geek than Clark Kent. His eyes are hazel and actually really pretty. He ought to be a typical nerd, but he's anything but. Smooth skin. Perfect teeth. The guys I met in New York, I was lucky if they'd bathed and brushed their teeth in the last few days.

But this guy… He smells clean. And he came and sat next to me, like he had nothing to lose. He nods to a young-looking kid—has to be a freshman—as he passes to find another seat, and the kid beams back at him. I'd call Jackson cocky, but his smile is quiet, so sincere that his confidence can't be anything but charming. It's almost like he chooses to wear glasses and a collared shirt just because he likes them.

"Anna, right?" His smile is big and bright, so sincere that I envy him for the perfect life he must have.

"Yeah," I say, but my smile doesn't come as easy as his.

He gives me that look again. The innocent, curious look that tells me he doesn't see the truth, he doesn't see the brokenness. To him, I'm a blank slate. A stranger. A mystery to be solved.

I don't know if anyone has ever looked at me like that. My parents certainly don't. Luis never did. Even Sarah doesn't. They see someone who needs to be rescued.

But this boy's eyes are so light and alive, and I realize that this is a fresh start. Not the tainted reboot my parents and Sarah are offering me. A *true* fresh start.

He doesn't have to know about my past. He doesn't have

to know that I'm more messed up than he'd ever be able to comprehend.

To him, I can be just Anna. Not ruined or broken or tarnished or pathetic.

Just Anna.

"I'm Jackson," he says, his fidget the only sign he might be a little nervous.

"I remember your name," I say.

He shifts his schoolbooks to his other hand and rubs his right hand on his knee. His face stays calm, though.

Maybe I can pass for a normal girl, after all. Better than that, maybe I can be someone new. Someone I want to be. Not the middle school slut, not a disappointment, not a whore, and not someone to pity. Maybe I can leave both of my old lives behind and find something new.

Sarah told me that the few friends I had in middle school either moved away or go to private school now, so most likely no one will know who I am. Most of my real friends were older, and they're already out of school.

This is a good thing, I try to convince myself.

It will at least take a while for the people at school to figure it out, figure me out.

I smile. I'll think of it like I'm walking through New York City, when I used to look at all the people and imagine their lives. I'd pretend I belonged with them.

This can be like that. Except this time, maybe it will work.

"Now that's the first real smile I think I've seen from you," Jackson says.

I want to cut the smile off. I can't be so transparent with a stranger, even if he is so cute and nice. But my smile won't seem to go away, so I just say, "Nice to meet you, Jackson."

"You're new, right? Where are you from?" he says, leaning in slightly.

I fidget in my seat and press my back against the cold glass of the bus window. As much as I like the way Jackson looks at me, I can't help but feel that if he looks too closely, he'll see right through me.

My smile? A hint at the past I'm happy to forget.

And being friendly with him? I've been friendly with nice guys before. In the end, I always found out opening up to them was a mistake.

"Yeah, I'm new," I say quietly, but I ignore the rest of his question. In part because I don't know how to answer it. I squeeze the ugly blue backpack Sarah bought me tighter, like it can protect me.

"You're living with Mr. and Mrs. Rodriguez, right? Are you related to them?"

I blink. How long can I maintain my cover if he keeps asking questions? It's not like anyone's going to figure it all out at once, but there can't be too many girls in town who disappeared for three years. I don't want him to know even that much.

He might not have any clue where I've been, but I didn't exactly have a pristine life before I ran away. I used to be the middle school slut, dated a college guy when I was just thirteen, and used to brag about how I wasn't sure if I was pregnant or not…

As much as I like pretending I'm a normal girl talking to a cute guy, I can't keep it up forever.

It's a double-edged sword. If I tell him the truth and he likes me for who I really am, I'll know there's something disturbingly wrong with him. And if I lie, pretend to be someone else, he'll just hate me even more when he finds out the truth.

So why do I feel tempted to keep sitting here with Jackson and see how much of his confidence can rub off on me?

Luckily for me the bus is already pulling up to the school, so I jump over him with a quick, "Sorry, gotta go," and make my way to the front as the doors open. Everyone stands up to exit the bus, and I see Jackson lost behind about a dozen kids. Just enough for me to escape into the crowd.

I'm comforted by the mass of bodies around me now. At least here I can blend in. But the glass doors stare down at me. I stop, my heart pounding. So much for stealing some confidence from Jackson.

I look at the crowd around me and step off to the side, behind a bush and an empty bike rack, and close my eyes.

My first day of school in three years and I've already blown my cover as a normal student.

Not that it would have taken everyone long to notice *something* was different. I'm a sixteen-year-old freshman. I didn't even complete my eighth-grade year. I skipped town a month before the end of the year.

My father wanted them to put me in the grade appropriate for my age, but apparently there are some things even he can't force people to do. The other freshman are thirteen and fourteen years old. I'm a total freak.

I take a deep breath and try to relax.

I don't expect to be Miss Popular here. I wasn't popular before I left, and it's not like I want that now, but I still have a little pride.

I can do this.

After a deep breath, I walk inside. Into the busy crowd of students. It reminds me of my first moments in New York City. Lost, alone, surrounded by hundreds of people who don't notice you, let alone ask if you're okay.

Like you're suffocating and there are hundreds of people who could stop and help you—but no one does. The same way no one stopped to help me.

Except Luis. He stopped. He helped me. Took me from Grand Central and showed me the city.

I press on. The girl at Grand Central is no longer me. I'm stronger. This time, I don't need help. This time, I'll do it all on my own.

I go into the front office and walk up to the counter. I stand there, content in watching the office drones fussing over a copy machine and filing paperwork, until finally a woman wearing an ugly turtleneck looks up and notices me.

"Oh! Why didn't you say something, sweetheart?"

"I, um... I'm new." It's close enough to the truth.

"My name's Mrs. Norberry. What's your name, sweetheart?" she says, rummaging around in a pile of paperwork.

"Anna," I say. "Anna Rodriguez."

"Right," she says. Grabbing a folder that was set off to the side.

She opens the folder and stares at it for a moment, too quiet. How much does she know? How much does anyone here know? I can't believe my parents would tell them much. Not the whole truth. But the way she's looking at whatever's in that folder, as though trying to make sense of what it tells her about me...

Finally she pulls out a piece of paper and hands it to me.

"This is your schedule," she says. "Let them know you're new. And the proper paperwork will be filled out later. Looks like you're meeting with Jennifer Thomas for tutoring? You have the same homeroom, the library. There's still a few minutes left before she goes to her next class. Would you like me to take you to the library to meet her?"

I force my lips into something resembling a smile. "That would be nice, thank you." I feel strange, like someone else is in my body. I don't belong here, and I can't help but feel like this lady knows it. What did it say in my file that made her get so quiet?

I pull the hem of my shirt down, like I'm trying to hide the ripped fishnets that expose who I really am. Even though I'm not wearing them, I can feel them.

The library is just down the hall, so it's a very short trip. The smell of dust and stagnant air fills me as we enter the room. Brown stained carpet lines the short entrance to the library.

I follow the office lady straight to a table at the back, where an awkward-looking girl sits. Her dark hair is pulled into a ponytail and is still long enough to reach the thick black belt on her jeans. She's very skinny, and even though she's sitting, she seems like she'd be a few inches taller than me.

"Jen, this is Anna. She's the new girl you'll be tutoring."

Her shoulders stay hunched over as she smiles. I sit in the chair next to the awkward girl, and she sends a quick smile to the office lady. "Thank you, Mrs. Norberry."

Just then the bell rings.

"Well then," Mrs. Norberry says. "I'll leave you two alone. But hurry on or you'll be late for class."

She leaves the room, and now Jen and I are alone.

I try to breathe deeply as we look at each other in silence.

"Want me to show you where your first class is?" Jen says.

I'm the city girl. It should have been me who was brave enough to make the first move.

"Sure," I say.

Jen leads me to my first class, history with Mr. Shelf.

"Thanks," I say. "I've got it from here."

And thankfully that's enough for her to leave me and go to her own class.

I stand there and stare at the room number and take deep breaths. I don't go inside.

I close my eyes and see Luis. I feel his breath on my ear as he says, "Everything is going to be okay." And I repeat that to myself.

I don't care what anyone thinks.

Everything is going to be okay.

CHAPTER SEVEN

I open the door, and a dozen heads turn toward me, curious. I stop and stare like a deer in headlights. They look at me, and I look back at them.

"Can I help you?" a young teacher in a button-up shirt and paisley tie asks. This must be Mr. Shelf.

"Yes, um, I'm new."

"Oh!" He grabs a few things off his desk and hands them to me. "Here, take these. This is your syllabus and your book… What's your name?" He's talking very fast, and I'm not sure I know what he's even talking about. What's a syllabus?

"Anna Rodriguez."

I sit down at the first empty seat, next to a redheaded girl with braces.

The young teacher begins talking about some group project. He tells me I can skip it and write an essay instead. He makes it sound so simple.

Group projects. Essays. Syllabuses.

Yeah, I am definitely in over my head.

But as much as an essay sounds like a trip to the dentist, I'd rather work alone than with these kids whose wide-eyed looks are starting to make me wonder if I have antennas poking out from under my curls. It's like I'm some kind of alien. Guess I kind of am.

The redheaded girl keeps glancing over at me. Easy enough to ignore. I'm just the new girl.

But then I hear someone whisper something to her that could be meaningless or could mean everything.

A boy leans over to the redhead and whispers, "She's that girl."

I raise my eyebrows.

That girl from L.A.? The punished heiress? The foreign exchange student?

"What girl?" the redhead says.

"The one that disappeared. For years."

My stomach twists. I'm pretty sure I might throw up. How in fuck's name would he know that?

My hands start to shake; my head pounds. Thanks, Mom, this was an awesome idea. I close my eyes and listen for any more whispers. Is this all they know? Is even this just a rumor? I need to know how much they've figured out.

"Mr. Thomas," Mr. Shelf says, louder than before. "Care to explain what the fuss is all about?"

The whole class turns to the now red-faced skinny boy behind us. "Anna Rodriguez is the girl they've been looking for since sixth grade. I remember seeing the posters."

"Do I look like that girl?" I ask. Blood is pounding in my ears now, but I know I don't look anything like that old Anna, and that might be my only way out of this now. "We could just have the same name," I say with a confidence I don't feel.

"Come now," Mr. Shelf says. "You'll have a chance to get to know our new student *after* class is over." The class quiets, and he leans down next to me. "Are you okay?"

I nod. The last thing I want to do is run out of the classroom. Then they'll *know* something is wrong.

Mr. Shelf resumes teaching, and I do my best to look normal, but I still see eyes darting toward me. I try to ignore them, but it's hard.

I cross my arms, feel my armor rising. They're just rumors right now.

They don't know the real truth. With a little luck, they never will.

I jump when the bell finally rings, much louder than I remember it being.

While everyone else leaves class—the only thing more interesting than the new girl is the chance to escape the room, I guess—I sit there and watch them exit. Desperate for a second alone.

"Do you need anything, Anna?" the teacher asks me. "Are you okay?"

Scratch that. There's really no chance to be alone, not here.

"Don't worry about them," he says. "They're just interested in the new girl. It happens every time."

I don't answer, just grab my things and head out into the packed hallway.

Strangely enough, things seem to slow down once I'm out there. It almost feels like I'm back in the city, surrounded by strangers. Almost invisible. No one says my name, no one calls me a hooker, and no one points in my face.

But when I start forward to my next class, the boy and the redhead point at me, and the people they're with, three other kids leaning against the lockers, they turn toward me all at the same time.

I want to wrap myself up in a sweater or something. Anything to keep myself away from their curious stares.

"Seriously?" the redhead says. "That's that girl from middle school?"

"I heard she had like three kids."

The redhead gasps. "What is she? Some kind of slut?"

So much for being someone new. I'll always be dirty Anna.

I duck my head and press my way through the crowd, and then I realize that I have no clue where I'm going. I just continue to walk. I keep my eyes mostly to the floor but glance up every once in a while to see if I can find something or someone to save me.

"I heard she was in rehab!"

They think it's funny to say those things about me. But all they have are rumors. If they knew the truth, the full truth, would they still be laughing? If they knew what I had to do to survive, would they hate me or pity me?

"I heard they found her shacked up with some rich sugar daddy…"

"No way!"

"Where's she been for three years, then?"

I shove myself past some big girl who's probably not used to being pushed around, but I don't care. She makes an indignant grunting noise, but I'm not scared of her, just like I'm not scared of anyone else here. Not the students. Not the teachers.

As horrible as this feels—the eyes, the name-calling, the thoughts in my head that tell me I don't have a future—none of it can be as bad as what I've already been through. I have the scars to prove it.

"Gross, I can smell the skank from here."

No one knows. No one will ever know what I've been through. No one but Luis.

Unfortunately, thinking about those bad things only opens the floodgates to memories I'd rather forget.

My breathing is quick and heavy, my heart pounding. I try to convince myself I'm okay, but the bodies pressing in on me are impossible to ignore.

A massive hand crashes into my chest. My back slams against a wall behind me. It's dark and I can barely see my attacker. But I can feel his hot breath on my face.

I shake my head. It's just a memory. The past. I'm not there now.

I close my eyes and hear Luis's voice telling me how strong I am. How amazing I was to live through everything and still come out fighting.

I was on the streets, ready to give up, crumple into a ball, and disappear. Anything to make it stop. Then he found me. Lifted me up—

A soft hand wraps around my wrist.

For a moment, I'm in shock, stuck between the memory and the present.

But the touch is gentle. Almost the way Sarah grabbed me the other day. Whoever it is doesn't want to force me somewhere. Whoever it is wants to help.

I look up to see hazel eyes surrounded by glasses and

freckles. I barely know him, but right now he's the most welcome face I've ever seen.

Jackson.

I follow him down the hall and through a set of double doors.

It's dark here, and my heart pounds for a second, unsure of where we might be, but then I see rows of seats, and down below, a stage with curtains. We're on the balcony of a theater.

The wooden doors close behind us and cut off the sounds of laughter.

Now I can breathe again.

CHAPTER EIGHT

"People can be really mean," Jackson says. "They're so bored that they have to make someone else feel bad to make themselves feel better. They're just rumors, but don't worry, they'll blow over."

"Oh?" I try to sound lighthearted instead of desperate.

Jackson ducks his head, blushing. Actually blushing. "Let's just say I have personal experience with the high school rumor mill. It never lasts."

If he only knew how much I want to believe that.

The bell rings, and I wonder if we'll be in trouble for being late.

"Want to see where I work?"

Now that catches my attention. "What do you mean?"

He grabs my hand and pulls me down the stairs to the left. Somehow I feel safe with him, this naive suburban boy who's nothing like the kind of guys I'd ever go for. Nothing like Luis. Guess I can't be too picky about the kinds of friends I make.

Is that what he is? A friend?

At the bottom of the staircase, there are even more chairs,

rows and rows that lead right up to the stage. It's old and dusty and in no way glamorous, but it's kind of beautiful.

It reminds me of my old dreams. I used to love Broadway, and I can sing well enough. I wanted to be a star. Ask me what plan A was when I ran away and you might already know. Back before I found out what New York was really like for someone with nowhere to go. Before Luis pulled me from the gutter and saved me. Before I needed to be saved from Luis.

Jackson and I run down the aisle toward the stage, and for a second I feel like the old Anna. Young, unscarred, innocent. Like dreams are still real, still attainable. We run all the way to the stage, then around it, and end up backstage.

Random things are strewn everywhere. A rack of costumes, cardboard boxes stacked in the corner, strange plywood structures. A big ladder with a curly blond wig sitting on top.

I almost laugh.

"Isn't it awesome?" he asks me, spinning around with his arms spread wide, like this is the most beautiful place on earth.

"This is where you work?"

He nods, smile still plastered on his face. "I don't get paid or anything, but I make the props after school and during my free period."

"You have a free period? Like no classes?"

He nods. "It's technically an independent study."

"And that's right now? You don't have a class to be in?"

"No, I do. My free period isn't until fifth. I'll probably have detention for skipping astronomy, but it was worth it." His smile slips for the first time. Maybe he's not so innocent after all. "I couldn't leave you alone like that. You looked like you needed a friend."

"Oh," I say. Unsure of what to say to that sort of kindness. He's willing to get into trouble just to help me? What's in it for him? "Um, thanks," I say.

He shrugs, then proceeds to show me some of the props he's made and acquired. He goes into crazy detail about some of them—a trunk with a false bottom, a wooden cane that detaches into three pieces that he found in a thrift store.

I sit quietly and listen to him, let his words drown out everything else. After a while he runs out of things to talk about, and we sit in silence for a couple of seconds.

"What class do you have next?" Jackson asks.

I pull out the wrinkled schedule and don't even bother unfolding it before handing it to him. He laughs as he pulls open the half ruined paper.

"Let's see. You missed math with Mr. Gomez. Good thing, he's rough. Next you have science with Mr. Schueller. Not too bad. Oh! You have art with me. I won't be there today because Mr. Charles needs my help setting up the risers for the chorus event tonight. But I'll totally be there most of the time."

"Cool," I say stupidly.

What will my life be like here? It's not what I want, not by a long shot. But I guess I just have to deal. Will the rumors fade or get worse? Will I find a way to fit in here, or be an outcast for the rest of the year? Who knows.

I lie back and look up at the stage lights. They're not on right now, only the regular ceiling lights, but I imagine what they look like, shining down on me. Jackson lies next to me and stares at the ceiling, like we're thinking the same thing. Maybe we are.

"Do you have any dreams, Anna?" Jackson asks me.

I blink but try to hide my surprise. "I used to."

He sits up. "Why not now?"

I shrug, still looking at the lights above me. "Dreams don't come true, not for people like me."

"What?" he says, like I'm a silly kid who said some random gibberish. "Dreams do come true, just sometimes not how you expect."

I let out one short laugh. I used to believe the same thing. As much as I want to tell him he's wrong, at least in this moment, part of me wants to believe his dreams could come true, even if it's too late for mine.

"What are your dreams?" I ask him in a whisper.

He lies back down beside me. "I want to go to college and be a doctor, or be a film director. Or travel the world helping all kinds of people. I dream of all sorts of things."

"Saving the world, one dewormed orphan at a time?" I ask him, amusement leaking into my voice. I'm not making fun of him. His dreams are all different, kind of beautiful, and impossible to fully accomplish. It's a luxury to imagine futures that contradict each other. I can't even come up with one that seems remotely plausible.

"Exactly. Simple vaccines can save lives in Africa and Haiti and places like that."

"Those are good dreams," I say.

"What about yours?"

"I don't have any." I want to laugh, but it's not funny.

He shifts to his side and looks at me. "Liar."

I turn to him, fake shock written on my face. "I am not."

"Fine. What were your old dreams?"

I take in a deep breath. "I wanted to be famous." He blinks, and I shrug. "It's a stupid dream."

He shakes his head and looks back up into the dull lights. "Not stupid, just overrated. You can do better than that."

I can? "Like what?"

"I don't know. You have to find your own dreams. If it's really to be famous, then don't do what all these other celebrities do."

"What's that?"

"Don't be fake. If you're going to be famous, be famous for who you really are. For something you love doing."

I say nothing. I don't tell him that I did go for it. And I didn't hide who I really was. That's what caused all my problems.

I ran away to New York thinking I'd find a glamorous life in NYC, the land of dreams, or at least my dreams. Not that I expected to get onto a Broadway show right away or anything. I just thought as soon as I was away from home, people would see who I really was. They'd know I was supposed to be famous. They'd love me.

That was my dream then, my real dream.

I didn't find it. I didn't find it because it doesn't exist. Someone's always there to show you what you're really worth. The second I left my parents, the man who tried to snatch me right off the train in Grand Central let me know what I was worth. Then Luis saved me, and he showed me what I was worth to him. And then the johns came, and they used their money to tell me how much I was worth, right down to the dollar.

We're silent for what feels like forever, until finally the bell sounds and I jump.

Jackson takes my hand in his. I don't like anyone touching me, not anymore. But it's like earlier, when he pulled me out of my memories. Just being around him makes me feel calm. Safe.

"You okay getting to class?" he says.

"Yeah." At least this time I know where I'm going, sort of.

I stand and take a deep breath. With any luck, the rumors are already over.

CHAPTER NINE

I take in a few deep breaths before I step into the one class I've actually been looking forward to—art. Drawing used to be one of my favorite things to do. Maybe it can be again.

There's a large gray-haired teacher sitting behind a desk at the front of the room, but he doesn't even look up from his papers, so I head to the back, sit quietly at an empty table, and pretend to be busy with something.

The teacher doesn't say anything, not even after the bell rings for the start of class. He's probably just in his own world. After a few minutes, he gives one quick intro, then sits at his desk and lets everyone work on some random project.

I spy on a few of the kids closest to me. Most of their artwork resembles fourth-grade drawings, but one catches my eyes. It's pretty spectacular. I wish I could draw like that.

I pull out a piece of paper and begin to doodle. Seems right since that's what everyone else is doing. Except that they're using pastels and charcoal and other random art supplies I've never used. And I'm using a pencil and notebook paper.

I draw my city—New York—though I'm pretty sure I'm

the only one who would know it's New York. Westchester isn't that far from the city, so I'm sure a few of the other students have been, but my rendition includes the people you only see if you're there all the time, because really, they're who make it spectacular.

Each line drawn on the stupid notebook paper gets me closer to that old dream, takes me deeper into my mind, where everything is fine. Good even.

Soon, I forget where I am. Forget the uncomfortable seat beneath me, the frumpy mom jeans and who bought them for me, the disappointment in my father's eyes.

I jump when someone speaks. "Interesting. New York, I'm guessing?"

I lift my head but don't turn to see who it is standing over me. Based on the age in his gravelly voice, I'd say it's the art teacher.

"Maybe," I say.

He doesn't speak for a moment, but I see eyes drifting toward us.

"Well, wherever it is, it's clear you love it," he says simply. I don't answer, but apparently he doesn't need me to. "But is it the city you love, or is it the drawing?"

Now I look at him, curious.

"What do you think?" I say.

"Both," he decides. "A beautiful city captured in beautiful art."

I'm not sure he's right, but I like that he believes it. It feels a little like he believes in me.

"Next time ask me for the proper supplies," he says. "A good artist deserves the right tools."

I actually smile as I nod at him. For the first time, I feel like a real student.

The bell rings, and I'm impressed with myself when I don't jump. I grab my things and follow the rest of the class into the hall.

"Miss Rodriguez," the teacher calls out. "I think you may have talent."

I'm surprised to find he knows my name, but it doesn't take much for me to realize oh, of course he knows my name. He has a list of the students in his class.

I give him a look that most people would take offense to. I hope he doesn't.

"I don't know if I have talent," I say.

He smiles. "Some people can draw effortlessly, others can't, but that's not the kind of talent I mean. It may take you more time to learn the technique, but you have the passion, and that is much more important."

I nod, because, well, I don't know what else to do.

I walk into the hallway and pause to find the right direction and walk through the crowd. The stares seem less obtrusive now somehow. Maybe it's just having someone actually on my side that helps. I used to like crowds in the city because I could blend in. No one noticed me. It could be the same here.

One kid shakes his head at me as I walk past. "How many?" he says.

"Huh?" I say, but I keep walking.

"How many guys?"

Now I stop. "What did you say?"

"I heard you like to sleep around."

Funny, really funny.

I flip him off, which only shows them it's getting to me.

"Maybe I could be your next date," he says.

I should keep walking, ignore him, but I'm still high on confidence from Jackson and art class.

"Go screw yourself."

The guy's face scrunches up. I've seen that look before, like he means business. I steel myself, but before anything can escalate, I hear someone behind me.

"Is there a problem here?" a deep voice says. No normal human's voice should be that deep. I freeze.

If I thought the other students maybe finding out about my past was scary, hearing this voice… My skin breaks out in a cold sweat, my entire body goes numb, my heart pounds in my ears, my head throbs.

I turn around, and the second my eyes rise high enough to see his face, my stomach twists and my head spins.

Calm down. Calm down.

I don't know him. He's just a middle-aged white man with a scraggly beard and bloodshot eyes.

But he looks so much like someone I'd give anything in the world to forget. That might be the only thing I'd turn Luis in for—to forget that man, that night.

Luis didn't care that the guy had paid for three sessions up front. He kept the money and made sure the guy knew to never come back.

You hurt my girl, I hurt you.

My hands start to shake as I fight to keep calm, to keep my head grounded in reality. The guy's wearing a blue jumpsuit and pushing a cleaning cart. He must be the janitor.

But he smells like cigarettes—*his* cigarettes—and suddenly

all I can feel are that old man's hands on me, forcing me onto the bed, undressing me, pushing me down, and I want to fight him, to call for help—

I close my eyes.

It's not him. This isn't real. I'm fine.

Everything is going to be okay.

I open my eyes and expect to see the real world again, but all is see is a large fisted hand coming right for my face.

I trip backward and fall hard onto the ground. I bring my arms up over my face, and one part of me knows it's not real, it can't be, but the other part can't escape the past.

A scarred fist crashing into my face.

A burst of pain.

The pressure of a huge body shoving me down onto a filthy, lumpy mattress.

Stinging. The horrible pressure of the man holding me down. Pinning me beneath his disgusting weight.

I scream, but the pressure only gets worse.

I push, but the weight only gets heavier. He takes and takes, and he doesn't stop.

I can't breathe. Can't see. Can't think.

Please. Make it stop.

CHAPTER TEN

I barely register the bustle around me as someone shoos away the gawking students and asks someone to call my parents.

I force my brain into the present, and by the time I have enough control over my body to open my eyes, it's not the janitor looking at me anymore. It's a young female teacher who leans over me and asks if I'm okay.

I nod, pull myself up, and walk with her down to the nurse's office without speaking a word. I don't look at anything around me, don't listen to the people. I don't let myself think. I'd rather be numb, kind of like when you're in the fuzzy almost-drunk place. I don't want to feel. Don't want to hurt.

After a while, Sarah and my mother come into the nurse's office. No sign of my father. Never have I been so glad how much he works.

They share a whispered conversation with the woman behind the desk, and I try my best to ignore it, to pretend I don't hear what they say about me, but really I wish they weren't saying anything at all, because my mother really doesn't need more reasons to think I'm completely insane.

It's Sarah who turns to me first, eyes full of sympathy and worry.

I don't like looks like that.

I mean, I get it. I'm a wreck, and that's how you look at people like me.

But I still don't like it. I want to be strong. Impressive.

If I want this to work, I have to be.

My mother turns, and at first she keeps her eyes cast to ground, but then she glances at me, and I see a hint of what I saw the other day when she spoke over my father, a woman who maybe cares but doesn't know what to say any more than I do.

"I'm going to talk with the office," Sarah says. "I'll be back in just a second." Her lips flicker up into a sad smile.

My mother shifts on her feet and rubs her hands together awkwardly. I don't say anything. Even if I knew what to say, I wouldn't have the energy to make the words.

I wonder if it'll stay like this. If they'll drop me off at home without asking me what happened. Maybe they already know.

My mother sits on the stupid plastic bed across from me and stares into her hands.

"Sarah…has some things she wants to talk with you about before she goes back to New York." She watches the clock, the computer in the corner, the cracked stone tile. "So she's going to take you to lunch and then home. I'll…see you there."

"Okay," I say.

Maybe she heard something in my voice, because she finally looks up. Her eyes are red, her cheeks flushed. She takes in a deep breath, and her voice shakes when she says, "I want to help you, Anna. I don't know how, but I'm going to try."

Then she stands, and before I can give in to the temptation

to ask her what that means—how she plans to help—she leaves the room.

When Sarah comes back and looks around, I don't say a word, I just stand and walk past her into the empty hall.

She leads me outside to her car and opens the passenger door for me. Once I'm inside, the door closes with a *thunk* that makes my head pound. Sarah gets behind the wheel and pulls out of the school parking lot before she finally speaks.

"Do you want to talk about it?"

I shake my head, and she nods like she already knew the answer.

"I think you should see someone."

I curl my legs up, wrap my arms around them, and lean my forehead against the cool window. I watch the streetlights, cars, trees, and buildings fly past.

"Anna?" she asks.

"What kind of someone? Like a therapist or something? Isn't that what you're for?"

She shakes her head. "No. I'm here to help how I can, but there's only so much I can do."

She's right about that. But I doubt a therapist is going to be much better.

"It was nothing," I say. "I didn't eat breakfast. You ever not eat breakfast?"

"Yeah." She's quiet for a few beats of my heart. "Anna, the teacher said you were crying out."

My eyes grow wide. "That's embarrassing," I whisper.

"From what I understand, this was after the hallway was cleared. Not that it changes what you said."

"What did I say?" I ask, my voice cracking on the last syllable.

"You called for Luis."

Ice-cold horror fills me. I don't know how much she knows. I haven't been brave enough to ask.

"What did he do to you, Anna? Did he rape you?"

"Who?" I ask, shocked. "Luis? No."

She doesn't say anything, I guess giving me space to say more if I want to. But I don't want to.

It's quiet again until Sarah asks me if I want something for lunch, much more upbeat than seems at all appropriate. I take this as a sign that she's done interrogating me, and I relax a little. Only a little.

My body sags against the car door, exhausted. I'd kind of rather just go to bed, but then my stomach rumbles. I really didn't eat breakfast. Some food actually would make me feel better.

We stop at a local diner and eat. I get a grilled cheese and fries and she gets a salad. Funny. She looks like a salad kind of person.

Which means she probably hates New York, land of hot dogs and pizza.

She doesn't press me any further with the thing at school, which is good, because I'm not talking any time soon. I wish I had as much control over my brain as I do my mouth. My mind keeps switching back to that night. My nightmare.

I wish I could be one of those people who blocks that kind of stuff out, you know? I've heard of people who experience something traumatic but forget the memory as a way of protecting themselves, or something.

Not me. Nope, my mind must think I'm strong as fuck, because I remember every damn detail. Every time I think I've pushed it deep down where it can't find me, it rises back up, more fresh than ever.

After the man finished—the man who paid for three sessions and then hit me, like he'd also paid for the pleasure of beating on me—he threw a ten-dollar bill on the ground and called it a "tip."

"There's more where that came from if you put that pretty little mouth to good use." Even his words tasted like cigarettes. "And I've got you for two more dates, so there'll be plenty of opportunities." He stood up and walked out, just like that. Like he was leaving a dentist's appointment.

Luis came in after him and ran up to me. He knelt next to the bed and pulled me into his lap. He wiped the blood off my mouth and pulled his sweatshirt over my naked body and started to sing.

"Everything's gonna be all right, be all right."

I started to cry, and he shushed me. Apparently that guy had paid extra, up front, for the privilege of being with someone as young as me. Like that was all that would do it for him.

But he wasn't supposed to get that rough. Or so Luis said.

The next day Luis bought a gun.

He said he wanted us to be ready in case that ever happened again.

He said he wanted me to be safe.

He said he loved me.

Maybe, in the end, he just loved the money more.

"Are you feeling better?" Sarah asks me when I clear my plate.

After thinking about how the one person I thought loved me betrayed me in the end, I should feel terrible. But with food in my belly and the hope that whatever comes next, at least the past is behind me, and I guess I do feel a little better, after all.

"I'm okay," I say.

"Good. Because I have something to talk to you about. Something I'm not sure you're going to take well."

"Like?"

"I have some things to ask you. Important things."

My eyebrows rise. "I thought we were done with the question part of our relationship. I already told you all I have to say."

She shakes her head, and her face turns serious, her hands folded all businesslike. She picks up a briefcase off the floor by her feet and pulls out a manila envelope that's thankfully not near big enough to hold all my secrets.

I stifle a laugh. *I'm* not big enough to hold all my secrets.

"When I questioned you before," she says, "I had enough to take you back home. I didn't need much, really, once we knew who your parents were."

I nod. I know this.

"That was always most important, but there are other things that are important, too. Like making sure what happened to you doesn't happen again."

My eyebrows pull down over my narrowed eyes. I have to admit, the thought of that kind of shit never happening again is appealing, but I've heard this kind of promise before.

"How can I do anything about that?" I ask.

"By telling me who did it to you."

I take a long sip of my soda, anything to avoid Sarah's eyes.

"Where did you live? Who did you live with? Who was your pimp? All of those things would help us greatly."

I close my eyes. I don't like those questions. Especially the last one. Those are the questions cops ask me. *Who is your pimp?* they'd scream at me.

She wants me to tell the truth. But I've seen what telling the truth gets you.

I was nothing to the cops. Worst of the worst of the street scum, and they always got away with doing whatever they wanted to get me to talk.

The more they hit, the more I shut down.

Some other girls gave in. They talked. But it didn't stop the police from hurting them. Or from hurting the people the truth identified.

I feel proud to say a cop never got one lick of information from me.

But I can't say they didn't fuck me up, inside and out.

"I don't have a pimp," I say.

Sarah must notice that I wince when I answer her question, because she presses her soft hands onto mine. I didn't even realize how tightly I was squeezing them together.

She was the first person to figure me out, but I don't feel ashamed of that. 1) She's not a cop, and believe me, that makes all the difference. 2) I'm already convinced she's psychic or has some kind of superpowers, and how am I supposed to contend with Superwoman?

"You don't have one now, you're right about that," she whispers so soft and slow that tears form in my eyes. "But I know you did have one. And if we find him, if you help us find him, we can stop him from hurting other girls like you."

I shake my head. Was he my pimp? Was he my boyfriend? I don't want to think about it. I don't want to face it. And I certainly don't want to tell anyone about it. Besides, who am I to decide Luis's fate?

She opens up the file, spreads it over the table. "Honestly, Anna, we've already found some things about your time in New York, but we still need your help to fill in the holes."

I look into her eyes, more scared than I've ever been. Not terrified, not like when I was raped or when I was attacked in Grand Central or when Luis and I were jumped that one time and he had to pull a gun to get away. Not that kind of fear.

This is bone deep. The kind that stings your eyes with a deep pain in your heart. The kind that you know you'll never heal from because it's not physical.

Doesn't she get it? Doesn't she understand that I want to forget about everything that happened in New York? Good. Bad. It's over.

At least I want it to be.

"We know about Luis," she says. "He's going on trial and we need your help."

I press my eyes closed and one small tear escapes, trickling down my cheek, exposing me. I wipe it away quickly, but the damage is done. If she was bluffing, she got the answer she was looking for.

She pulls out a mug shot of Luis. He's not smiling.

This isn't a picture of the Luis I knew, the man I gave everything for, and my world crashes in a way it hadn't before. Even when he abandoned me, he still seemed alive. He still seemed like he had hope for the future.

The Luis in this picture is vacant, his eyes dead.

Is this because of me? Is he empty because I'm not there? Does he regret giving me away?

I shake my head and push away the picture, holding back the panic in the back of my throat. "I don't know who that is. I don't know him." It's a desperate tactic that I'm sure won't work, but I have to try. I have to.

"Anna," she whispers.

I shake my head.

"You don't have to protect him."

I keep shaking my head, back and forth, back and forth. My heart breaks, cracks slowly, splinters. Shatters.

"He's already been arrested," she says. "There will be a court case in a few months. We're rounding up witnesses now. He'll go to trial for quite a few things. Child prostitution, statutory rape—"

"Rape?"

"It means he's too old to be sleeping with a sixteen-year-old girl. They consider you too young to choose for yourself. Especially since you've been with him since you were thirteen. The question is, how long were you sleeping with him?"

She acts like she knows so much.

"Look Anna, we need your help to put him away. We don't need much, we just need you to testify…tell us what happened. Tell us the truth so we can give him justice."

"What?"

"We want you to testify."

"Against Luis?"

She nods.

Maybe Jackson was right. We're nothing without hope, and as angry as I should be at Luis, as happy as I should be to see him suffer without me there, my very last hope was that he would be okay.

Now she wants me to talk. To help put him in jail.

I don't know what he deserves, but I know I don't want that power.

I stand. "That's the reason you asked if he raped me. You just want to charge him with more things!"

I can't believe she would do this to me. Or that she'd ask me to do this to Luis. She's supposed to be a friend.

"I'm not looking to get him in more trouble," she says. "But if he raped you—"

"No! He saved me. You don't get it. He saved me!"

Sarah just looks at me. She still doesn't get it and she never will. No one ever will.

Usually she knows everything, can see the things no one else does, but she's missing the point here. I was a hooker, yes. I did have a pimp...sort of.

But the only reason he became my pimp—if you could even call him that—is because we didn't have a better option. I had a dream, and he wanted to help me go after it. We needed money.

In the end, he abandoned me. He sold me to someone else, like I was property. I guess that shows what he was willing to do for money.

But he also helped me. If it weren't for Luis, I'd have been in the gutter before the sunset on my first day in New York. Was he perfect? No. Especially not toward the end. But if Sarah thinks that just because I left that life I'll throw him into the gutter he pulled me out of?

She's not nearly as smart as I thought she was.

I walk out to the parking lot and sit on the hood of her car until she finally comes out. I ignore her until she says my name.

"Anna." She points to the passenger side door. "I should get you home."

I give her a look that says she better not say another word, and she doesn't the whole way home.

Sarah pulls the car up to my parents' driveway. I pop open the car door, intent on getting as far away from her as possible.

"Anna," she says lightly.

I stop but don't look at her.

"I have to go back to New York," she says. "I'm sorry you're mad at me, and I wish I didn't have to leave now, but I do. There are more girls who need my help."

Why do I feel like she's accusing me? Like I'm refusing to help those girls with her? And that's why she's leaving.

"This isn't good-bye," she says. "I just won't be around for a little while. You can call me anytime."

"Fine. Bye," I say and hop out of the car and practically run into the house.

I barge through the door and slam it shut behind me, and for a full second I don't notice the dog crouching in the hall in front of me.

His bark shakes the mirror next to me. I jump back to get away from the dog and his snapping jaws. Shit.

I can't handle this. No one wants me. No one likes me. Not even this stupid-ass dog.

"Just *shut up*," I yell at him, tears welling in my eyes.

He stops barking.

I blink again, then slump to the ground. Right there, in the middle of my parents' home with a damn guard dog staring at me, I lose it. Completely. Sobbing in a way I don't know that I ever have.

It has to be a full five minutes before I calm down enough

to breathe and open my eyes. The dog just sits there, watching me curiously. He doesn't understand, but I wouldn't expect him to.

He sits with his head so high, his chest sticking out, like he's so proud to be him. It looks like confidence, but I think it's the way he is. He's beautiful, in an odd, sorta scary way.

And as I wipe my tears from my eyes, he inches close to me. I watch closely, unsure if I should move away from him. He doesn't seem to be the most friendly or trustworthy dog I've met.

I drop my hand to my bent knee, and he leans in closer, slowly. His wet nose touches my hand, but his eyes never leave me. I wonder if he wants me to pet him, but then he starts to lick my hand. I'm not really sure what it means, but it feels like he's being nice to me. Like instead of expecting me to pet him, he's doing something for me. A slimy something, but it's the thought that counts.

I wait a moment, then pull my hand away and try to sneakily wipe it on my pants as I stand up. He lies back down like nothing happened, and I sneak past him and hide in my bedroom. I lay there, staring at the ceiling, thinking about everything.

I should know better. I know I'm not supposed to think about the present. I guess the problem is that the past and the future are just as painful.

I didn't belong here the first time around, so why do they think it would work now? Now that I've been raped and beaten.

Beaten and sold by the man I loved.

Now I'm supposed to be normal.

I can physically feel the breath—the life—seeping out of me. Each and every moment pulls the things I thought I had further away and gives me nothing new to replace them. What do I have now? A naive boy who's nice to me but if he knew the truth he'd be disgusted. Parents who are disgusted, a dog who doesn't bark in my face when I cry, and a woman who pretends to be my friend just so she can put Luis in prison.

Yeah, that's a life worth living, right there.

I'm becoming emptier and emptier. Soon there will be nothing left.

High school isn't where I belong. Hell, I don't have any clue where I belong. Maybe prison—maybe I should be in prison with Luis. That's the only place that makes sense.

I don't come out for dinner, and after a few knocks my mother stops pressing. I cry myself to sleep before the sun even sets.

CHAPTER ELEVEN

Today isn't just another day of school. That's bad enough. This is the day after my ridiculous episode in the hall. They'll call me crazy now.

Maybe that makes it better. If they've already judged me crazy, maybe they'll forget the other rumors. The ones too close to the truth.

"You coming or what?"

I blink and realize I've been standing in front of this stupid brick building for too long again. Jackson's waiting, eyebrow raised.

I'm not really in the mood to be angry or nice, or to even decide which I should be. So instead I pretend that finally entering the school was my own idea.

I'm pretty good at maneuvering through a crowd, so I squeeze through the small gaps of people. Jackson follows right behind me. I don't care when I hear more whispers from the other students.

"That's the crazy girl."

"She had, like, eight kids. That's why she was gone."

"Ew, the crazy slut just touched me."

That last one hits a little too close to home, but it's one truth among a bunch of rumors, and as long as I'm careful, no one will know which is which.

The crowd slows to watch me passing through, the geeky boy still following behind me, almost like he doesn't notice the difference. But he also doesn't call for me to slow down or wait up.

Once we reach the lobby, I pause. He catches up and stops beside me.

Now that I'm here, I realize this was the worst possible place to stop. It's where most of the people congregate. I see groups of kids standing around, some looking at me, some not paying any attention to anything but themselves.

A group of guys, a few of them in football jerseys, talk animatedly and glance over at me.

"I dunno, dude. She's pretty hot. I wouldn't mind tapping a little of that."

Yeah, I'd say it's definitely time to go.

"I know a place we can hang out," Jackson says. "Follow me."

I follow him, because I'd rather be anywhere but in the watering hole of high school, especially when I'm obviously the prey.

"Look, the virgin and the slut! How cute."

I spin to see a pretty dark-haired girl, freckles sprinkled on her cheeks, with her arms crossed and a grin that tells me she thinks she's very clever. I pause for a second and feel Jackson's grip on my hand tighten. He always seems so calm, but a hint of anger crosses his face.

The girl leans in. "You won't get anything from him, sweetie. Might as well give up now."

Jackson pulls me away from the girl before I can respond. I don't really know what she means, but now I'm curious. Not about what mean things she decides to say about Jackson, but about whether Jackson's life might not be as perfect as I think it is.

I guess he's a geeky kind of kid, but in an almost cool way. He's nice and confident, and it's hard for me to imagine him being bullied and made fun of.

Maybe that's the real reason he helped me the other day, because he knows what it's like.

Jackson guides me down the hall, past the main office and nurse, and into another lobby by the cafeteria. Even though this is my second day back, I still haven't been into the cafeteria. But he doesn't take me there; he turns into a stairwell that I didn't notice before, past a few vending machines and glass cases full of trophies and plaques. At the bottom of the stairwell are a whole bunch of lockers.

There are a couple of kids sitting at the bottom of the steps. Jackson goes to the opposite side and sits. It's a wide staircase, making us still about five to ten feet away from the other kids.

I just stand there, looking around. There are still kids walking around, slamming lockers, and talking, but it's much more quiet down here.

"Have you been down here yet?" he asks.

I shake my head.

"The gyms are that way." He points to the left. "The locker rooms are this way." He points to the right. Then he smiles at me.

I can't forget that flash of anger or my question about why he defended me yesterday. He's not perfect. I get that. But no one does something for someone else for no reason. What does he want out of this?

"Why are you trying to be my friend?" I ask.

"Someone has to."

"That's a good reason." I roll my eyes.

"I want a friend. Isn't that a good enough reason?"

I sit down but don't look at him. "I'm not really good at the whole 'friends' thing." Least of all when it's with a guy who, if I were anyone but me, I'd definitely want to be more than friends with.

He pulls out a bag of fruit snacks and pops one into his mouth. "I don't expect much."

Well, that's good, because he isn't going to get much.

He offers me a fresh bag of fruit snacks. Bad idea. I shouldn't take one. But it's been years since I had one of these…

He smiles as I take the bag. "So, I heard about what happened yesterday," he says as he pops another fruit snack into his mouth.

I don't want to talk about it, but I'm not really a fan of silence, so I answer. "Had a freak-out, I guess."

"They're saying you're going to murder us all." He smirks. Awesome, more great rumors. At least he's not looking at me like I'm crazy. "I don't put stock in rumors," he says. "But sometimes the truth is the best ammo."

I have no idea how to explain this, not without giving up my secrets, but he wants an explanation, so I try being vague.

"Something, a memory, came back that I wasn't ready to deal with." I don't know if this made sense at all, but it's all I can think to say.

"What's the big deal? Everyone's been through something."

I shake my head. "Not like I have."

He stops and looks me right in the eyes. "Okay, you've been vague about a lot, but that one got my attention."

"Jackson, I'm not…normal."

He raises his eyebrows. "So?" he says. "I mean, what's normal, anyway?"

I shrug. "A suburban brat who's got nothing to worry about but homework and who'll take them to homecoming. Kids with friends, dreams of college and settling down…mostly people whose nightmares don't come back to haunt them at the worst possible moments."

He smirks. "Whose idea of normal is *that*?"

"That's what my parents want from me. I just don't know how to do it."

He rolls his eyes. "Don't tell me you do everything your parents want."

I raise an eyebrow. "Oh, and I'm sure you're a total rebel."

That gets a laugh from him so big that I can't help but join in. "Don't let the nice guy look fool you," he says. "My dad *wishes* I did everything he tells me to do."

I can't help but notice he only mentioned his dad. "Your mom doesn't care?"

A burst of pain flashes across his face. It's quick but strong enough that I know I hit a nerve.

"Sorry," I say. I should know more than anyone that you can't expect people to be an open book.

"My mom passed away," he says.

"Oh." I play with my bag of fruit snacks. Only now do I

realize that in the midst of us talking, I ate all of them.

Jackson reaches over and puts his hand over mine. My heart speeds up. My instinct is to pull my hand away. No one's touched me like that in a long time without expecting something else. Something more. But he's not demanding. Just letting me know things are okay.

"We're all messed up in some way," he says. "You're not so different from the rest of us."

His sparkling, kind eyes look at me like I'm special. He knows I've got something dark in my past I don't want to talk about, something that made me pass out in the middle of school and cry out to someone, but he still looks at me like I'm normal.

It's nice, but I know better than to push my luck. I can't tell him the truth. I can't stand the look he'd give me if he knew that for the last three years I'd been sleeping with men for money. That's too much for anyone to take, let alone a boy like Jackson.

I jump when the bell rings, and I realize I've got to go to class and be a normal student again. Awesome. I pick up my backpack and try to figure out how to get from this part of the school to my first class.

Jackson eyes my backpack. "You have a locker?"

I shrug, and he grins. I pull out my folded-up schedule and hand it to him.

Jackson looks down, then stands. "Come on Miss Normal, I'll show you where your locker is so you don't break your back carrying that thing around."

We walk down the hall and to my locker, and Jackson attempts to show me how to unlock it. We had lockers in middle school, so the concept isn't completely foreign to me, but I'm not exactly a natural.

I finally get my locker open without help, and I drop my bag off. My locker's completely empty except for a small slip of paper on the top shelf.

I unfold the note. In sloppy letters it reads:

> i KNOW WHO YOU REALLY ARE
> OR SHOULD i SAY "WHAT"

I stare at the writing for a second and then crumple it up, ignoring the pounding in my chest. It's just someone playing another stupid trick one me. That's it. No one knows what I was in New York.

"You okay?" Jackson asks.

I jump, despite myself. "Yeah, no problem."

I won't let this get to me. I crumple the paper in my fist and throw it back into my locker. Whoever left it can move on to someone who cares.

CHAPTER TWELVE

Jackson sits beside me in art class, and Mr. Harkins gives me a book of canvas paper and some pastels and tells me to draw anything I want. I take in a deep breath.

I'm not sure what to draw, so for a minute I just sit there, staring at the blank canvas, wondering what in the world it's going to become. This is another fresh start, I realize. It can be anything.

The class is quiet. Only the sounds of pencils, charcoal, and pastels scraping and scratching against paper. I pick up a yellow pastel stick and begin with one long line.

Within seconds, all of my tension is gone. There is only me and the paper. Me and the picture in my head.

This. This is perfect. No talking, just drawing.

I feel so completely free, thinking about the colors and the lines and what I'll do next, planning and preparing and doing.

It's freaking magical.

The outside world falls away. The classroom. The students. Even Jackson. All I need is the pencil and paper. Art.

I draw a carousel and a little brown-haired girl with pigtails and pearls around her neck. She laughs wildly as she rides the plastic tiger around and around.

The little girl is free, and for a moment, so am I.

I leave that class with a soaring feeling in my chest. My picture isn't finished yet, but I feel so very accomplished. I've finally found something that matters. Who cares if the picture sucks? If the people around me don't even know what it is? I know what it is. It's my world. And that's all that matters.

I walk to the bathroom, and this time I set my books down on the windowsill and look out the window that leads to the courtyard. It's been so long since I felt like this. Real hope. Real happiness.

I stand there for so long the bell rings, and I realize I'm late for lunch. At least I can't get detention for that. I know if the hallways are bad, the cafeteria will be ten times worse. Maybe I should skip lunch? But damn if I'm not hungry, so I suck it up and rush down the stairs.

I manage to blend into a small crowd of freshman as they enter the cafeteria. Just because I don't care about the whispers and the stares doesn't mean I have to invite them. But everyone's preoccupied with whatever drama their own lives hold for now.

Good, keep your mind on your own business.

I wait in line for some food. There are three different lines, and they seem to be pretty identical. Same food at each one. I end up just getting a soft pretzel, a cookie, and a Gatorade.

"Two fifty," the lunch lady says.

That's it?

I hand her three dollars, wait for my change, and then head out. I stand there for a moment, holding my tray, unsure of where to go now. As I look out into the sea of high school students, all I can think is: how the hell did I end up here?

Then a voice comes from beside me.

"What's up?" Jackson says with a goofy smile. "Need a place to sit?"

I shrug, hiding my immense relief. He motions for me to follow him, so I do. I guess I'm not interesting enough on my own anymore, but seeing me with Jackson, people twist their heads so far they look like they may break their necks to watch me walk by.

Jackson leads me toward the back, at a table next to the window. I look to a small outside patio with picnic tables and see some stoner-looking people and a group of younger boys playing hacky sack.

Jackson sets his tray down with a *clink*. A few heads look up quickly, all boys. Two of them are white and skinny like Jackson, but they look a little less chic geek. In fact one of them is in a school football jersey, and the other in an Abercrombie T-shirt.

I try to smile, but I'm not good at making friends. They surprise me by smiling back anyway.

"Hey guys," Jackson says. "This is Anna." He points at each of them. "This is Doug, Garry, Kurt, and Jason." I haven't the slightest clue who is who, but that doesn't really matter, because I won't remember their names in about thirty seconds.

Jackson pats the chair next to him. I blink, realizing I was staring. I sit down and stare at my food. I want to eat it, but it feels weird to do something so natural in such an odd situation.

Is it really this easy? Say hello, sit down, make instant friends?

I look up and realize none of them are looking at me anyway; they're all looking at Jackson and seem to be having some kind of silent conversation. That's more like it. Smiles one minute, weird looks the next.

They exchange a few nods and mouthed words. The Asian boy notices me looking now, and he stops, wide-eyed. He clears his throat.

I raise my eyebrows as the other guys look to him, then to me. One of the white boys begins to blush. I still have no idea what's going on, but I'm sure it's about me.

This moment takes the awkward up about ten notches, and it was pretty high to begin with.

I sit there in silence for a few seconds, pretending not to notice their silent conversation. The dragon shirt kid's eyes are big, and he looks across the lunchroom like there's someone watching us or something.

One kids shrugs like he doesn't care one way or the other and just shoves a huge piece of pizza into his mouth, and the last boy shakes his head.

"I can leave," I say.

Jackson cocks his eyebrow. "Come on. They're just being weird."

I have no idea what's going on, but I do know that I'm not very comfortable.

I'll have to take his word for it. "Okay. But I need to get some mustard for my pretzel."

Eyes follow me as I cross the room, and I have an urge to jump up on a table and scream "food fight!" or something stupid so I'll actually deserve the looks.

When I make my way back to Jackson's table, I stop when I hear the hushed voices.

"Dude, seriously," the boy with the jersey says. "I get you like the charity shit and all, but you don't need to drag us into it."

I stop around two feet short, unsure of what to do. No one

looks at me.

Jackson stands, leans forward, and puts his hands on the table. "When I say she's cool, I'm not just blowing smoke. She hasn't even spoken a word and you want nothing to do with her. What does that say about you?"

"That I'm human, dude," the football player says, sending a glance across the room.

I follow his gaze and see a group of kids watching us. The cool kids, maybe? Is there really such a thing?

Then the football player sees me. His eyes flicker to mine and grow larger, but he doesn't say anything.

"Guys," Jackson says. He hasn't seen me behind him, and that fills me with a warmth that takes me by surprise. He's not saying these things for my sake. He means every word. "You can't listen to these rumors. She's just the new girl. What does it matter?"

"How do you know they're just rumors? Maybe she really is a drug addict or just got out of juvie," the dragon T-shirt kid says.

"Yeah, and maybe she was abducted by aliens, or the Soviets. Maybe she's really a Russian spy." He straightens his shoulders. "Besides, didn't you go to juvie last year?"

"Well, yeah, but—"

"Yeah. So worst case, she's just like you." He looks around the table. "Like all of us."

His friends are silent at that. What would they say if they knew those "rumors" are just watered-down versions of the truth? If they knew that the things they've done pale in comparison to my past? If they knew I was really a hooker…well, let's just say his friends might have every right to look at me like I'm Bigfoot.

I make up my mind then. I turn and walk away. I'll see

Jackson later. I'm not sure what he wants out of this, what he expects to get for being so nice to me, but I need to get out of there before things get worse.

When I look back, Jackson's watching me go, a look on his face that I hate. Sadness. So I wave and smile to let him know it's okay. He cocks his head, confused, but nods, seems to get that the world hasn't ended just because his friends were jerks.

I find a table in the middle of the cafeteria that's empty. I sit and pick at my pretzel and sip on my Gatorade and pretend I'm fine being alone. But then a tray clinks down in front of me, and I see a girl sitting across from me.

She smirks. "Do you mind?"

I shake my head. She sits and dips an odd-looking crinkly french fry into a cup of ketchup. She's pretty, but the kind of pretty that tries to hide it. Choppy short hair, dark eyeliner, and an eyebrow piercing.

"What's your name?" I ask.

"Alex."

"Oh, hi Alex," I say.

She waves goofily.

She looks too old to be a freshman. Maybe even my age. "What grade are you?" I ask. I'll be jealous if she's a senior. That should be me. Except, you know, I'm technically stuck in the ninth grade.

"That's up for debate." She smirks.

I blink. "What's that supposed to mean?"

"I'm sort of a junior, but most likely I won't graduate with that class."

"Why's that?"

She shrugs and bites off a piece of one of her odd-looking

fries. "Failed a few important classes."

"Like what?"

"Like gym," she says and laughs.

I'm oblivious. I have no clue if she's joking or not. "Gym? Isn't that a ninth-grade class?" I'm surprised I haven't seen her in gym with me.

"No. I mean yes, I'm in a freshman gym class because I've skipped a few too many times the last two years. But no, it's not one of those important classes. You only need two of them to graduate."

"Oh." Guess I just don't know how this all works.

"I failed English freshman year. I want to just leave, but my parents won't let me drop out. I figure if I fail enough classes, they'll just give up and let me get my GED."

That never even occurred to me. All I have to do is give up on good grades and I'll get out of here for good?

"Maybe I should go that route, too," I say.

She nods.

I see a girl walking slowly down the side aisle close to us with a tray in her hand. I recognize her. She's Jen, the girl who's supposed to tutor me. She looks even shier out here in the wild than she did in the library—which is saying something.

"That's Jen," Alex says, head lowered like it's a secret or something. "She slept with Marissa Larson's boyfriend a couple of weeks ago, so now everyone hates her."

That sounds familiar. But looking at this lanky shy girl, shuffling her feet, I can't imagine she's very much like me.

"Everyone?" I ask.

"Well, almost everyone. Marissa is Miss Popular and thinks she owns the school. Unfortunately, she kind of does. If anyone even thinks about being Jen's friend, Marissa and her friends make their life hell. Which apparently scares everyone enough that they won't talk to her. Losers."

"Who's Marissa?" I ask quickly.

Alex stands and looks around for a moment, then points to a table toward the front of the cafeteria. "Curly brown locks," she says.

I stand to see. There's a group of girls and boys about my age, the same ones Jackson's friends seemed nervous about. Yeah, definitely the cool kids. How lame is that?

I recognize Marissa from the "curly brown locks" Alex described her by. She's sitting next to the girl who said that nasty thing about Jackson this morning.

"So what, they're like the popular kids?"

Alex snorts. "Hell no. They're just mean to everyone and it makes them think they're cool."

Jen's slow steps bring her past our table. Her head's down. I guess she doesn't expect to find help any time soon. Is it like this every day? I notice a hint of red in her eyes as she finally passes us.

Screw this. I stand. "Hey, Jen!"

The shy girl whips around so fast her apple falls off her lunch tray.

I smile and look down at the empty chair beside me. "You can sit here," I say.

Alex's eyes grow wide, but I see a hint of a smile.

Jen pauses. She looks at me, then at Alex. Then her eyes dart to the "popular" table and she says, "Are you sure?"

"Can't get much worse for me."

"I'm not sure about that," she says, but she sits anyway.

Alex no longer hides her smile.

The lanky girl looks down at her plate. She doesn't eat any of it. "You're coming to my house after school, right?" I ask her. She's supposed to come every day after school, but yesterday I wouldn't leave my room, so my parents canceled the appointment. Good times.

"I didn't realize you knew each other," Alex says.

Jen takes in a deep breath and drinks a small sip of her milk. "I'm her tutor."

Alex raises her eyebrows, and I just shrug. Is it embarrassing that I need a tutor? I think I've got bigger problems than that.

After a few moments of silence, Alex asks Jen, "Was it good at least?"

"What?" I ask, but Jen's wide eyes give me a pretty good clue. Alex just raises one thin eyebrow.

"I was drunk, he wasn't."

Apparently this wasn't what Alex expected to hear. She doesn't speak.

Of course, it wasn't what I expected to hear either, but I guess you don't have to go to New York for a guy to take advantage of you.

I find myself looking over at Jackson's table. He glances at me, just long enough to catch my eyes and smile, like he's checking up on me.

The popular kids are watching us with hate in their eyes, Marissa especially. I have a feeling I made the wrong kind of enemy here. But it kind of feels good, to be honest. I'm not a victim anymore. I chose this. I'm in control here.

Besides, it's a hell of a lot better for them to hate me for their random high school drama than for them to find out the truth.

CHAPTER THIRTEEN

I open my front door to see Czar, the dog, staring at me. His tail twitches slightly, but mostly I'm just impressed that he's not barking or growling at me. Guess he knows I'm not a threat now. I mean, I did sort of lose it right in front of him.

My mother stands behind the kitchen counter reading a magazine. Not sure why she's not sitting down or something. I hear the oven counter go off and realize she must be baking.

"Hey, Mom."

She looks to the oven first, then to me. "Hey, sweetie. How was your day?"

I take a long breath. Exhausting, but… "I lived."

She places a baking sheet into the oven and looks up. "Oh! I should have told you. You aren't supposed to go through the front door. I'm surprised that dog didn't eat you alive."

"Yeah, I keep forgetting. He didn't do anything today though, guess he's used to me now."

She looks skeptical. "He doesn't 'get used' to people, sweetie. He's ferocious. Goodness, he almost bit off my hand just for trying to fill his water yesterday."

If the dog's been here for three years, I kind of can't blame him for being easily agitated. I at least had the chance to run away. Imagine if I'd been chained up in the backyard. A prisoner.

Mom smiles. I've seen that look before, but after that glimpse of concern I saw from her the other day, I have to wonder if she's as naive as I always thought. Maybe she knows something's wrong but is just trying to make the best of it.

Maybe she's a prisoner, too.

"Just use the back door, okay?" she says. "I don't want you to get hurt."

I'm not sure that avoiding the dog in general is going to make it any better, but there's no point in arguing. Besides, I don't know if I'm willing to push things with my dad just yet.

"I'll have brownies ready in a few minutes. If you want some."

I attempt a smile. "Maybe in a little while. I need to get ready for my tutor."

I head to my room and hide for a few minutes before Jen comes over. I'm kind of eager for the distraction, but she won't be here for at least a half hour.

I look through my drawers and come across my old diary. It looks untouched, but I have a hard time believing they didn't read it when I went missing. Did they read about how I had sex for the first time at thirteen? Did they read about how I sneaked out and spent the night with my older boyfriend when they told me I couldn't go to the movies?

If they'd let me have a life, even just a little bit, maybe I'd never have left. I'd be a completely different person. Looking at colleges, doing my homework, going to choir practice (really, I was pretty good).

But the more I fought for freedom, the more my father came down on me. Sometimes with more than words. I rub my arm, like I can still feel the bruises. And my mom just let it happen. The more I pulled away, the more disappointment I saw on their faces.

Until I couldn't take it anymore.

I flip to the last diary entry I wrote before I ran away.

> Mrs. Brown made me eat lunch in her room today, which I guess is better than eating in the cafeteria when you have no friends, but still, it sucked. She told me she was going to talk to my parents if I didn't start doing my homework again. Said she'd tell them about the rumors going around school. Like that I was pregnant, and had herpes and slept with the gym teacher. None of them are true, or even close to it, but that won't stop my dad from freaking out.
>
> He'll call me a "loose girl" and tell me I'm going to hell. I don't think I can handle that, even one more time. How he looks at me, talks to me. The way my mom ignores my tears. Pretends she doesn't see me at all anymore. She doesn't care so why should I care about them? I swear, the next time he tells me how disgusting and horrible I am, the next bruise... I'm leaving. I'm going to do it. I'm going to hop on a train and go to New York where no one will tell me what to do again.

Pretty clear map to where I was going. They had to have read it. Probably why my poster was all over NYC. Doubt they put it up that many other places; they knew I loved it. I always wanted to go, but it was just another thing that my father thought was "evil."

One day I should ask him to define it, "evil." How is everything in the world evil? That doesn't even make sense. Although I'm not in much of a position to defend my stance anymore. I'm sure New York is even more evil to him now. It corrupted his sweet baby girl.

Yeah, right. I sit down at my desk. I used to have a computer here. That was the one thing I did have—they didn't really realize how much a computer could do. I remember the moment I opened it up, took out the Visa gift card they gave me for my birthday, and bought a one-way ticket to the city of my dreams.

I left a week later and never looked back. Even after I was raped, even after Luis had me sleeping with his friends for money, I never considered returning home, mostly because I knew that I'd only made myself worse in their eyes. More broken. A worse fit for this family than ever.

But here I am again.

I hear the dog bark, deep and loud—that dog is seriously scary shit. Then I hear a scream.

I run out into the hall and see Jen pinned up against the wall. The dog is crouched down, growling at her. It's that scary growl again, not the kind you hear from a friendly dog just defending itself. This dog is terrified. Why wouldn't it be? You can only get hit so often before you think any raised hand is headed your direction. I would know. It's a fear I'm no stranger to.

I see my mom frozen in shock, big eyes and a hand over her mouth.

"Martin isn't home yet…" she says, as if this means anything.

She reaches out her hand, like she wants to help but isn't sure what to do. I step forward. I'm not sure what I can do, but I figure this dog likes me better than my mom.

My mother's frightened eyes flicker toward me.

"Czar," I say calmly. The dog doesn't react. He probably doesn't even know his own name.

I take another step forward, and this time I see his eyes flicker to me. I plan on stepping between the girl and the dog. It's less likely he'll attack me.

I slowly walk around and take a big side step so that I'm between Jen and the growling dog. I keep my hands up in surrender and pray that this isn't a huge mistake. But it's the least I'd want, someone to take a chance and be patient while I figured out they weren't out to hurt me.

I keep my voice and gaze steady. "It's okay. It's all right."

Czar's eyes dart around the room, but his stance relaxes enough for me be confident he's not going to pounce on me. I tell Jen to inch past me, and I wait until she's past the reach of the chain before following her.

Czar just watches us go.

When I'm about to take another step, my father walks through the front door.

"Martin!" my mother calls.

The dog's head whips toward him.

My father takes one look, and in a single quick motion he pushes the dog to the ground and hits him with an open hand across his head. My guess is that this isn't the first time he's treated the dog this way. Czar doesn't fight back at all. That beautiful dog falls to the ground and takes the hit with only a wince.

"Dad!" I say as he raises his hand to swing again. "Hitting him isn't going to help."

"He needs to know who's boss!" His hand lands on the dog's

head with a loud *smack*. I wince and turn away, only listening to the sounds as he drags the dog out the door, nails scratching the hardwood floor on the way, as I take deep breaths to keep calm.

I'm just lucky Jen's here, or else he might be dragging me down the hall, too.

Once I reach the kitchen, my mother is in the corner, rubbing Jen's shoulder. I only have a moment of jealousy before my mom sees me and gestures to come closer. When I'm close enough, she takes my hand.

"I'm sorry," she says.

"For what?" I ask, taking a page out of her book and pretending nothing is wrong at all.

"Everything."

I blink and consider asking her again. Does that mean what I think it means? Is she sorry for letting my father get away with hurting me for so long? Even when he didn't hit me, it hurt. I'm not sure which pain was worse.

My mother's calm facade is back in an instant, and I know my moment has passed. She's covering up her emotions again. "Anything to drink, Jen?" she asks.

I take in a breath and look out the window as my father chains the dog in the backyard.

Can I blame my mother for not doing anything to help the dog? I'm just sitting here, too. Because to stand up to my father would mean asking for him to turn his anger on me.

After an orange soda and a few minutes of small talk, Jen is calmed down and ready to work. I tear my eyes away from the dog in the backyard and focus on the books Jen pulls out.

We work on math first because that's my biggest problem area. Math seems to come back pretty quickly though, at least the basics. Once I get a chance to work out some of the kinks, I remember the multiplication and even the division just fine. Then it's a matter of following the equations and doing it right.

My mom is nowhere to be seen now, which kind of surprises me. Usually she'd be standing over my shoulder, making sure I didn't do something wrong.

I used to think she didn't want me to embarrass her. But after seeing her with Czar, her attempt to protect the dog by keeping it on the straight and narrow, I wonder if she was really trying to protect me, too.

"That was a good session," Jen says. "I guess I'll go now."

I take my opportunity and ask something I've been wondering about.

"You know Jackson well?" She seemed to know him yesterday morning, so I'm hoping she'll be able to answer my question.

"Sort of. Why?"

I shrug. "Just something someone said this morning. What's his deal?"

"What did they say? I don't know what his 'deal' is. He's a nice guy, that's about it. He's cute but doesn't really date much. Not anymore."

He's definitely nice. And hot.

And he doesn't date much? There's got to be a reason for that.

"Some girl said something about him being a virgin and that I should just give up on him now or something."

Jen's eyebrows shoot up. "Pretty brunette with freckles?"

I nod.

"Well, that's kind of old news. Her name's Liz. Jackson and

her…used to date."

"What!?" Okay, not what I was expecting.

"A while back, freshman year I think. It was for a long time though. Once they broke up, Liz got all popular and started dating seniors and stuff, and Jackson, well, didn't. He never really moved on."

"Why did they break up?"

"She cheated on him. The rumor is that he was too scared to have sex with her, so she dumped him for a more experienced guy."

"That's ridiculous." And kind of weird. Shouldn't that go the other way around? Isn't the guy supposed to be the one to push sex and get mad when the girl holds out on him?

She shrugs. "It was a long time ago."

"Why wouldn't he have sex with her?"

Jen blinks. "What?"

"It's weird, isn't it? Don't guys want it all the time?"

Jen doesn't speak for a second. "Not all of them. I don't know. I guess he's being careful."

I hold back a bitter laugh. This kid just gets better and better. The celibate hot guy who has no idea he's befriending the whore.

I'm probably going to be the worst thing that ever happened to Jackson Griffin.

"Like I said, it was a long time ago. Jackson's usually left alone now. I'm surprised she even said something. They don't talk about it much anymore. I usually try not to give them anything to say. But I guess if you don't give them something, they'll make the drama themselves."

Jen doesn't look at me now. She's kinda hard to figure out.

She seems so crazy shy on the outside, but she doesn't seem like it when she talks. And the way she spoke about the "incident" with Marissa's boyfriend, I wonder if she had as much of a choice as people say. I know all about doing things you don't want to do just because you can't see a way out.

Guess the suburbs have some darkness, too. They're just better at hiding it.

CHAPTER FOURTEEN

The worst times are the in-between times. Between classes, when I have to deal with the stares. Between tutoring sessions, the quiet time after Jen leaves and dinner is done and I'm all alone in my bedroom. The silence, the stillness.

Like now. I try reading the book Jen gave me for English—I'm desperate—but give up ten pages in. How do I read about someone else's messed-up life when mine's even worse? So tonight I sit on my bed and watch as the shadows shift and change in my room with the setting sun.

I stand and walk over to my desk. There's a pile of old sketches in the corner, almost all of them of New York, and for a moment I actually miss it. I stepped off the train at Grand Central with a brain full of postcard-perfect images of New York. The Empire State Building. The Statue of Liberty.

It was Luis who showed me the real city—the spice and excitement beyond the tourist-friendly lights. He knew where to score the most realistic knockoff bags, the tastiest cannoli, and the party spots. He knew the city, and he taught me how to know it, too.

When things got hard, I'd close my eyes and pretend I was riding the aboveground train in Brooklyn. Cold brown seats beneath me, but a whole new world around me, flying by. The buildings, the people, the cars.

It feels good to think about that now. That's one thing that hasn't changed. New York hasn't betrayed me. Not the way Luis betrayed me, or the way I'm being pushed to betray him. It wasn't always Luis that was my escape, it was my city.

How do I feel about him now? I've loved him since I was thirteen, and I'm sure that he loved me. He must have. But one day it just changed.

Three years of us, together, perfect, and then all of a sudden…

I don't know why he gave up on me.

I wonder if this is how my mother felt when I left.

That I just abandoned them suddenly. They didn't see the signs. I was good at hiding the drinking, the smoking, the boyfriends. Even though they found plenty else to be disappointed about.

I suppose it's easier to blame all of your problems on someone else instead of owning up to them yourself.

So what were the problems with Luis that I was blind to? Can I really picture him as a monster, after everything he taught me? After he saved me and protected me?

Was Luis ever in love with me? Was I too young to hold his attention long enough? Did he only do it for the money?

All I know is that I loved him.

But he sold me. Not just all those times he sold me to other men for slivers of my life I'll never get back. He sold me that final time, when he gave me away to someone else for good.

I close my eyes. I don't want to think about my old life.

My head spins. *Old life.*

It's so strange knowing that life is gone forever. Yes, there are things that I want to leave behind forever. But now that it's gone, now that New York and Luis and my freedom are all gone, I don't know what to think about it.

I want to be happy. If you'd asked me a week ago, I wouldn't have thought I could be.

A week ago my life was full of johns and forced sexual favors.

Now that hole's filled with controlling parents, sure. But it's also a nice boy, new friends, a mother who just might care more than I expected her to, and just a tiny little bit of hope that I can finally start over.

I want to think this new life can be something better. Maybe if I can keep my past as far away as possible—so far away no one can ever see it—I can figure out how to make this work.

The sound of slow, careful footsteps outside my window catches my attention, and I freeze. I must have fallen asleep, because I don't remember it being this dark.

I sit up on my bed and listen for anything out of the ordinary. The muffled sounds of the TV in the living room float through my bedroom wall, but other than that? Nothing. Silence.

That's what bothers me. In my experience, the only time it gets this quiet is before something terrible happens.

There's probably nothing out there, but my heart pounds wildly. Like my body knows something is wrong, something's not right. Sometimes instincts are the only thing between you and death in the city, so I've learned to listen to them, and right now they're blaring like a foghorn.

Someone is outside my window.

I inch off the bed. As carefully and quietly as I can manage, I tiptoe to the window and pull back the blinds just slightly. My bedroom light is still off, so while I can see outside, no one can see in. But the bit of moonlight isn't enough to see much. I let the blind fall back down and then retreat to the hallway.

I sneak a look down the hall and see my mother rocking in the recliner. My father must have gone back to work. It's the only reason Mom would be alone in the living room this late.

I want to check out the backyard, but I probably won't be able to get past the kitchen entrance without being seen. Lucky for me, I grew up in this house. I know there's another back door out of my parents' room that leads right to the back deck. I sneak down, the opposite way of the kitchen, walk into their too-perfect bedroom with quilted sheets and satin blinds, and unlock their sneaky little back door as quietly as possible.

The door opens an inch, enough for me to listen.

Nothing.

My body has calmed down a bit now, so I wonder if the danger is over.

I looked to the doghouse and see Czar's head sticking out just a little. If there were something wrong, someone here, he'd be freaking out, I'm sure of it.

I take a step onto the back deck—

Czar's head whips up.

Yeah, he's paying pretty good attention. And the fact that he's not barking means nothing's out here.

Poor dog. I hate that they leave him out here all night. I

hate how they treat him in general.

I take slow steps into the dewy backyard and then stop and look around.

My parents had such a pretty and perfect backyard before I left. Now all you notice is the black hole of mud that's the dog's area.

Honestly, though, I like it better this way. I don't feel like I'm expected to be as perfect. Maybe they've lowered their expectations now that they have a dirty guard dog and a prostitute for a daughter.

"Czar," I say in a loud whisper. He crawls out of his barely-big-enough doghouse. "Hey, buddy," I say as calmly as possible. I want him to know I'm a friend.

His ears perk up, but then his head lowers and a scary growl rumbles out of him.

I stop dead in my place and hope I'm far enough that his chain won't reach me.

Czar steps forward, and I don't dare move, my heart pounding wildly. Maybe this was a bad idea. He's only a few feet from me now, enough that he could take one big lunge and have my arm for a snack. The hair on the back of his neck stands up.

"Czar?" I reach out my hand—

He takes that lunge I was dreading, and I close my eyes… but when I don't feel inch-long teeth sink into my skin, I open them. Czar is next to me, barking into the darkness.

Shit. There really is someone out here, isn't there?

Another step puts me behind the dog. A few seconds later, he stops barking and starts sniffing around. He walks all around, anywhere his chain will let him, and every few seconds he stops to watch the darkness.

I let him do his weird freak-out dance, avoiding the chain whenever I have to.

I'll follow his lead. When he thinks the coast is clear, I'll rush back inside, and not a second sooner. Finally, he returns to the spot where he first barked into the darkness and just stares. I listen and look with him.

Nothing.

Finally, he lifts his head to me, and then he sniffs my feet.

Very slowly, I let my fingers drift across the top of his head. He closes his eyes, and I squat near him.

His house doesn't look very comfortable, probably barely even fits him inside it. He's so damn big. That hardly seems fair, even if he did almost bite my kind-of sort-of friend/tutor.

He was just doing his job, right? It's not his fault they didn't teach him to learn the difference between good people and bad. It's not his fault they taught him he can't trust anyone at all.

I look back to the door leading to my parents' room, and I look through the glass door leading to the kitchen. The light is still off, but there's no telling if my mom is still watching TV. If I do this, I guess I'll have to take a gamble.

I unclip his chain and let it fall to the ground. "Wanna have a sleepover?" I ask him.

He follows me up the steps of the deck, into the house, and through my parents' room.

I tiptoe, still holding on to the collar of the big guard dog who could probably pull me down the street if he wanted, enter my room, and close the door behind me with just a soft *click*.

He stands there, watching me curiously as I take a few steps away from him and sit on the bed.

Now what?

I wish I had a bone or something for him to chew.

Please don't pee.

He starts sniffing around the room and throws glances my way every few seconds, as if to make sure I'm not doing anything sneaky. He must like me more than some other people, but he still doesn't trust me. Poor dog, I don't blame him.

I pat on the bed, and immediately he jumps up next to me. Now his head is higher than mine. Yikes. If something sets him off, I could end up without a face.

He gets close, but he just looks at me with those big brown eyes, then he lies down and lays his head on my arm. I gently stroke behind his ear. The hair is so soft, I find myself rubbing my hand against it absently. Not only for the dog, but also for me. It feels comforting.

When I look back down at him, I realize his eyes are closed.

Why can't a dog be both a friend and a guard dog? I don't understand why my parents treat him the way they do. He means nothing to them, just a little extra security. Imagine if they were actually nice to him.

I lie there and close my eyes, but I open them quickly when I hear a knock on my door.

I open the door a sliver and see my mother standing there with a plate of food and a can of soda.

For a moment, I don't move. The last time I was at home, she'd have never been so bold as to bring me something to eat. Father's rules. No food after dinner. And if you missed dinner? You'd better show up for breakfast.

But here she is.

What else has changed since I've been gone?

"Hey, sweetie," she says. "Hope I'm not bothering you."

Why would she think she was bothering me? Part of me wants to rush forward and hug her, but I manage to restrain myself. I'd have to be crazy to let down my guard just because she brought me some food. Still, I feel a small smile spread across my face. I guess I'm not as good at hiding my feelings as my mother.

She must see my smile, because she pauses, tilts her head to the side, and after a moment, she smiles, too.

"Anyway, I brought you some leftover dinner."

"Thanks," I say, taking the plate from her.

She starts away from me, but then turns back around and says, "I'll have apple pie a little later if you want to come out and get some."

Those feelings I want to keep hidden are about to burst out of me, and I can't let her see me when they do. I want her to love me, but can I ever give that love back after everything?

"Probably not," I say. "But thanks."

She drops her gaze to the ground, and her smile looks like it's fading.

"Mom," I say.

She lifts her head back up. "Yes, sweetie?"

"Rain check?"

Her smile comes back. She nods and leaves me to be by myself, and I don't feel quite so bad about turning her down anymore.

I close the door and sit on the bed with the plate in my hand. It's pork chops and mashed potatoes. I take one bite of the chop and a few of the mashed potatoes and look behind me to see a salivating dog.

I put the plate onto the floor. He jumps down and scarfs the whole dinner down in a few seconds. And I thought *I* was hungry.

I sip my soda and sit back on the bed. Czar licks the plate clean, and then he walks over and sets his head on my knee and looks up into my eyes. He's so weird. I pet him for a moment, but my mind is off in other places.

What just happened with my mom? Not that I don't want her to be kind to me. To show me she loves me. But it doesn't make sense why she would do this. Why now? Why not years ago?

And why does it matter so much to me? Luis came for me at the station and suddenly I was ready to do anything to make him love me. And now my mom brings me a little food and I'm ready to go eat apple pie?

I guess the difference, though, is that she never sold me. She never left me.

I left her.

I crawl into bed and get under the covers like a little kid. Czar jumps up and lies next to me, his back just barely resting against my leg. I close my eyes and try to stop myself from crying.

I rub Czar's side absently. After a moment, he rolls onto his back so I'll rub his stomach. He must be getting more comfortable with me.

It was probably the food. They say a way to a man's heart is his stomach. Must be the same for dogs.

I scratch his tummy, and his paws go up in the air goofily. I mostly stay up toward his chest, 'cause it's a little creepy to go any lower, but that doesn't stop me from noticing something.

Czar, supposedly a boy, doesn't have…well, boy parts.

My parents named a girl dog Czar. I can't help but laugh. As if the name wasn't bad enough. Her paws are pushing in on me now, but I just shift a little and it's fine.

"I think you need a new name." I pause and think. "How about…Zara?"

Her ears perk up a little, and I take this as a yes. It's pretty and close enough to her old name that she'll know we're talking to her.

My stomach growls. Even if I don't really want to face my mom, I probably need to eat something else. And apple pie sounds amazing. Czar—excuse me, Zara—watches as I move across the room and sneak a peek out the door.

I listen and hear only some clinking dishes in the kitchen. I'm not sure I really want to expose myself just for apple pie, but I take a deep breath and venture out into the hall.

I see my mother alone, doing the dishes.

"Is that offer still up for the apple pie?"

She looks up. I almost gasp. Her face is red, like she's exhausted from crying, but she smiles when she sees me.

I walk up and sit at the counter. It's a small one, with two stools that barely ever get used. But it allows to me to watch as my mom pulls out the half-eaten pie from the fridge. She cuts a slice and puts it in the microwave. She looks at me, as though considering something, then pulls out the vanilla ice cream.

If I were in New York, ice cream on top would cost extra. I don't know what this gesture costs her, but I can't help but be grateful for anything I can get.

She cuts out a piece of pie, carves out two perfect circles of ice cream, and places them all on the plate.

She hands me the plate, then goes back to her dishes. She scrubs and rinses each dish by hand. They have an expensive dishwasher; I don't know why she doesn't use it. Guess she likes the work or something.

She doesn't say anything, and she's doing the same thing I did when she brought dinner to my bedroom. She's hiding her face. Is it just me or is that a smirk I see on her face?

I take one bite—

And the taste hits me hard. It's so good there are no words. I haven't had real apple pie in so long.

It's perfect, exactly what I need. So satisfying that the question's out of me before I can stop it.

"Why did you bring me back here, really?"

She drops whatever dish she was working on into the murky water, but she doesn't look up. Maybe now's a bad time. She really does seem exhausted.

"A lot of reasons, Anna." She still doesn't look up. She's staring down into the water like she'll find something she's been looking for there. Or maybe so she doesn't find what she dreads, something she'll see if she looks at me.

Will she see the daughter she lost? Or worse, will she see a whore where the daughter she always wanted is supposed to stand?

I could leave the room before she answers. But I hesitate, and that gives her enough time to respond.

"Because you're our baby," she says. "You're supposed to be here." Now she looks me in the eyes. Only a moment, but long enough for me to see that her eyes are full with tears. Then she turns around and leans on the counter. "Because we want to help you."

"Don't you mean fix me?"

Now she turns back. "Not fix you. Just help you be better."

Those are the words I was afraid of. "Because I'm not good enough like I am?"

Her eyes go wide. "No. No, that's not…" She takes a deep breath. "I just want to help. That's all."

I shrug. Maybe I do need help. I'm just not sure yet what that means.

"Good night, Mom."

I stand up to leave but pause and actually consider reaching out to touch her. My hand twitches, but I pull it back. I'm not sure what I want, or what to do. I don't know how to be a good daughter.

Finally, I give up and turn away from my mom, hoping she can see that I don't hate her. Hoping that maybe things might be getting better, after all.

When I open my bedroom door, the dog lifts her head, on alert. Then she sees me and her tail twitches, almost a wag. Does she like me?

I sit beside her and stare at the door. She stretches over, almost taking up the whole bed now, and licks my hand.

Maybe she does like me.

Or maybe she tastes the apple pie and ice cream.

I pet her again, then get undressed, flick off the light, and slip under the covers. She curls up next to me, and before long I'm almost hanging off the bed. I need a bigger one with her here. But at least I'm not alone.

CHAPTER FIFTEEN

I put Zara back outside at the ass crack of dawn, before my parents even get out of bed. They'd be pissed if they knew she'd slept with me, but it felt good to have her there. It's so simple with her. No confusion about what she wants, what she has to give. She wants to be petted and fed. She wants me. When I let her go outside, I'm already thinking about tonight and if I'll be able to get her back into my room again.

I get dressed quickly and head out the door to school, a little less scared than I was yesterday—but not by much.

If you asked me a few days ago what I thought about school, I'd have given you a clear answer. I hated it. But now? In some ways, it's everything I was afraid it would be. The cool kids punishing everyone else. People like Jen and Jackson have every right to enjoy their suburban life, but people like Marissa and her stupid boyfriend have to make it horrible for them.

Jackson deserves better. He stood up for me in front of his friends, even if they were more right than he knows.

I've never met someone like him. He has some pain in his past. Being cheated on and made fun of for it, losing his mom, that all had to be terrifying. But he doesn't show it. Ever.

So when he sits next to me on the ride to school, I give him a smile. I don't look at him, and he doesn't speak, but I'm glad he's sitting next to me.

When we stop in front of the school, he waits to make sure I'm not zoned out again. I nod at him to let him know I'm okay.

He files out into the crowd. I follow him inside and go to my locker instead of joining him at the staircase where he likes to sit before classes.

It's not that I don't want to sit with him. Eventually something will go wrong. It always does. I'll just try to enjoy this while it lasts. And the longer I space out how often I see him, the longer I can keep this warm feeling.

There's one thing I know for sure: Jackson is way too good for me.

Once I finally get my locker open, I take out my history book and drop off my backpack. I'm about to shut it when I notice a piece of paper sitting on the shelf…the same place as the last time.

I pick it up and I close my eyes for a moment before unfolding the wrinkly paper. My stomach sinks as I read the same sloppy writing as the last note. A note I was sure was some kind of joke. Except this time, it can't be a joke. It hits way too close to home.

> DEAR EXQUISITE,
> i KNOW WHO YOU REALLY ARE AND i'm GOING
> TO TELL EVERYONE.

My stomach drops. Exquisite. My street name. No one should know that name, not here. Is this a coincidence? My hands shake as I study the writing, trying to find some kind of logical explanation.

The only thing I come up with is an image. No, not just one image, a thousand. Faces. Men. Too many men.

I squeeze my hands into fists and try to push down the urge to throw up.

Someone walks up to the locker next to mine and I jump. My stomach roils again. I fling the note back into the locker and run to the nearest bathroom until classes start.

I hide in one of the stalls like the biggest geek who ever lived. After a few minutes, the bell rings, letting me know I'm late for class, but I don't move. I stay in the stall for several minutes. At first I worry someone will realize I'm hiding out in here instead of going to history, but after ten minutes, then fifteen, no one is slamming on the bathroom door and I figure I'm safe. Alone and safe.

Still, memories I'd rather forget plague me.

"Hey there, Exquisite," a man who smelled like cigarettes would ask. All johns are gross, all johns are nasty… This one was the worst of them all.

He never left me alone, always following me around when I was on the street. It got to the point that I had to change my usual tracks to avoid him. He was the violent one, the one…the one I want to forget forever.

Yet it's his memory that follows me the most.

Even here, he won't leave me alone.

I force myself back to reality. I'm in school, not in New York. He can't find me here.

Instead I think of the possible explanations for the note. It's filled to the brim with possibilities. Whoever left it, if they do know more, why would they tell me first? Why not just shout it out to everyone who would listen?

Maybe they don't have proof. And without proof, no one would believe them, right?

So instead, they want me to freak out about it and expose myself.

I won't let that happen. If I could keep myself together while strangers climbed on top of me, a note in my locker won't get anything out of me.

Eventually the bell rings again, and I realize I was in here for the entire first class. I'm just about ready to pull myself together and get to my next class when a group of girls enter, talking in hushed, panicked tones. The room is filled with the sound of a girl sniffling and huffing. Guess I'm not the only one having a bad day already. I quiet my breathing and hold myself as still as possible. I'll wait this out.

"Seriously," one girl says. "Why is Brandon such a jerk all the time?"

I lean forward to look through the crack of my stall, thankful for the distraction, even one as lame as high school girl drama.

"He's just..." the sniffing girl says between a sob. "He's horrible!" she says much more adamantly, like it's the first time she'd admitted it out loud.

"Why don't you dump him?" I see a redhead rubbing the back of the crying girl.

"I can't," she whispers.

No kidding. I've been there. Really, who would listen?

The bell rings then, and I realize I'm late again. I can't hide out in here anymore. Missing one class was dangerous enough, but I can't have anyone come looking for me.

The girls continue their conversation in whispers, clearly not worried about being late themselves.

I unclick the lock to my stall and take a slow, awkward step toward the sink, hoping they don't notice my own red eyes and blotchy cheeks. There are three girls surrounding the crying girl, whom I recognize much too quickly.

Marissa. The girl whose boyfriend slept with Jen even though Jen didn't want to. The popular girl who makes the "uncool" kids' lives miserable. For one second I think she deserves whatever happened that brought her crying in the bathroom. But then I figure I don't know her, and I really have no right to judge.

No one deserves to be treated like trash. Boy cheats on her and she's still with him? Treats her like trash and she's still with him?

She "can't" dump him…

There's definitely more to the story here.

If I were the kind of person to talk to strangers, I'd tell her to hang in there. Eventually, it won't hurt as much.

It's none of my business, though, and based on the way the girls stare at me, some shocked I overheard them, one girl horrified, and Marissa…oh, Marissa looks like she's ready to set my hair on fire.

Yeah, guessing she's not exactly my biggest fan. I'm probably not in a good position to help her, even if I knew how.

I walk past them without a word and head down the empty hall toward art class, knowing that somehow the note isn't the only thing that's going to bite me in the ass.

CHAPTER SIXTEEN

interrupt Mr. Harkins's lecture and apologize, then find a seat at my empty table in the back. Jackson sits at the front with another group of kids. He watches as I pass him. I'd like to give him that smile that lets him know I'm okay. But I'm not sure I actually am okay, and I don't want him to see my face like this.

Mr. Harkins gives me a look and waits until I sit before continuing.

"I expect you've all turned in your first-quarter projects," he says. "If you haven't, you're late. See me after class." He searches the class until his eyes meet mine. "You, Anna, are excused, of course. We have a new project starting today. If you need extra help, just see me any time before or after class."

He has a few people present their projects, but not everyone. I thought at first it was just the projects with the best technique, but it only takes a few for me to see what's really going on. Even the ones that aren't as good are interesting. Different.

Out of the box, as Mr. Harkins often says.

Wow. So they just put some creativity into it and it's good enough? What must that be like for the students presenting, knowing what they do doesn't have to be perfect?

Then Mr. Harkins flips on a slide show and teaches a more typical lesson. As the clock ticks closer and closer to the end of the day, I'm disappointed to realize that I won't get to draw today. I'll just learn about art history or something. Lame.

He shows us some famous artists who painted some depressing paintings in all blue. Some of them are kind of neat, some just plain old ridiculous. I zone out a few times, but I figure out he wants us to do a project using our emotions. Sad, angry, scared, happy. Pssh, who's actually happy? And who would want to see it plastered on a canvas?

I bet that's what everyone in here does to express their emotions and their lives. Pink flowers and clouds and butterflies. I'll draw a ditch in the inner city, full of trash and used needles. Yeah, that sounds fitting.

Then he starts calling on people and writing down pairs of names.

"Anna, who would you like to work with?"

"With?" I ask, and I can feel my eyes growing wide and my face getting red.

"Yes, this is a group project."

"I don't know anyone," I say quickly.

"I'll work with her," I hear someone say. I don't know who; my mind is kind of fuzzy. As stupid as this is, it's freaking me out.

Mr. Harkins nods and writes down two names. "Anna" and "Jackson."

Oh boy.

What the hell am I going to do with Jackson? Not that I don't want to work with him, but I don't see how we're supposed to make something that shows how both of us feel. I'm dark, he's happy. We have nothing in common.

The bell rings, and I start out of the room before Jackson can talk to me. Maybe I can buy some time.

But he calls to me before I get out of the room.

"It's you and me, partner," he says.

I smile. Maybe it'll show him I'm okay. But really, I'm so nervous I'm shaking.

"I'll see you later," I tell him, and then I go into the hallway and escape into the crowd.

I'm running down the steps when someone reaches out their foot, and I trip and crash into three kids in front of me. I roll, not so gracefully, onto the landing between floors.

I wipe the hair from my face and look up to see Marissa, smiling at me with a glare in her eye. Yeah, she totally did that on purpose.

"It's okay, you're better off down there. Bitch."

I blink. What?

I open my mouth to say something, adrenaline pumping. Girlfriend doesn't know how pissed she just made me.

Someone runs past her and leans down to me. "You okay?" Jackson asks.

I tear my eyes from the nastiest girl I've ever seen (which is saying something) to look at the sincere worry in Jackson's eyes. "I'm fine," I say.

He stands. "Get a life," he says to Marissa, and I smile. I don't need his help, but it's kind of nice to have it.

"I'd say he was just trying to get in your pants," Marissa says. "But we all know that's not true. He wouldn't know what to do when he got there."

Jackson's face gets blood red, which makes me even more furious. It's one thing to trash-talk me. But him?

I stand, having no idea what I'd say to the girl, but I'm pretty damn close to pulling out my earrings and taking the bitch down with me.

Except she's already backing away, a smirk on her face, like she knows she's gotten away with it.

"Coward," I whisper.

I start after her, but Jackson touches my arm.

"Not worth it," he says.

I watch as the girl disappears into the crowd, disappointed I'm not following. If it were anyone else, I wouldn't care, wouldn't listen. But I guess respecting what Jackson wants is more important than making a point.

The crowd disperses, leaving just Jackson and me alone.

"You okay?" he asks me again.

"Fine," I say. On top of what happened earlier, now what happened with Marissa, my face feels like it's on fire. I can't let him see me like this.

"Please talk to me," he says.

"How can you let her get away with that?"

"Marissa?" He shakes his head. "Waste of time."

I cross my arms and say nothing. Why do I care? Why do I want to go after her? It's not like I haven't been in his exact spot before and done nothing to defend myself. But maybe that's why I have to be there for him. No one ever stood up for me, and I won't just stand here and do nothing.

He's actually proven a damn good friend. I'm just not sure I can handle having a friend like him. A *real* friend.

"I don't know if I can do this," I say.

"Oh." He pauses. "Does that mean you don't want to do the art project with me?"

"No, it's not—"

"Because we can go back and tell Mr. Harkins. I'm sure he'd reassign you."

My stomach drops, but I don't want him to see my disappointment. He's taking this the wrong way. It's not him, it's me. "Then who would I work with? I don't know anyone."

"So then can you forget about Marissa and friends and whatever else is bothering you, and work with me on this? I think it might be fun." He looks me in the eyes, a hopeful gleam in his.

"Fun?" I roll my eyes, but my stomach gives a new kind of twist, one I kind of like. "Fine, I'll give it a shot. What do we do?"

"Come to my house after school," he says. Just like that. As though he's a normal boy and I'm a normal girl, and there's nothing more to this.

I try to imagine this boy in New York City. Confident. Self-assured. But too willing to take a chance on people he barely knows. He wouldn't last a minute.

"We can talk about how we want to do the project," he says. "We're so different, so we'll need to makes some decisions."

He's right about that.

"I can't," I say, and I think about Marissa saying that about her boyfriend.

"Oh," he says, and I'm afraid he thinks I'm just blowing him off.

"It's just… Jen tutors me after school. My last few years… haven't left me very well off in the school area."

"Oh," he says. "Well, what about after that?"

I shrug. "She leaves at four."

He smiles, big and bright, and I almost—almost—smile back.

"'Kay," he says. "I'll come to your house, then."

I nod and do everything in my power to hide that I'm actually excited about it.

CHAPTER SEVENTEEN

I sit with Alex and Jen at lunch again, and this time, I invite Jackson to join us.

Alex and Jackson make up basically all the conversation. Jen and I just listen and laugh as they argue over some of the strangest things.

"Luigi is so much better than Mario," Jackson says.

"Are you kidding me?" Alex says, a look so full of shock I have to hold back a laugh.

I shake my head as Jackson gives his way-too-thought-out explanation as to why Luigi is better than Mario. "Seriously, Mario is just typical. And boring!" he says, leaning in, his face red like this is one serious debate.

"But Luigi is a *wuss*!"

"No! I mean, okay, a little," Jackson says, and I laugh, awarding Alex a debate point. "But that's part of what makes him awesome. He has so much more to overcome. He's insecure, but he's always there for his brother. Besides…" He holds his hands out and moves them up and down like a scale. "Green"—he lifts one hand high—"versus red." The other hand dips below the table.

Alex shakes her head, and I can't help but agree with her. Jackson's weirder than I ever thought, but I'd be lying if I said I didn't kind of like it. He's the cutest geek I've ever met.

"You're impossible," Alex says.

I don't even notice the stink-eye the "cool" kids are giving us the whole time until I notice Jen staring absently at them.

What can I do about it? Not like I expected to be beloved here. I'm just happy to actually have some friends.

Jackson turns to me. "Star Crunch or Fudge Round?"

I blink. "What?"

"Which do you like better?"

"I don't know what either of those things are."

He opens his mouth in exaggerated shock. "Wait a second."

He runs, seriously runs, up to the lunch line and then comes back with two chocolate treats. One looks like a Rice Krispies Treat covered in chocolate, and the other is a thin sandwich kind of thing with frosting in the middle.

I try both and find that the crispy treat has caramel on the inside, and it definitely earns my vote. "That one," I say, then lick my fingers.

"Ha!" Alex says, pointing at Jackson, who puts his head in his hands.

I guess he lost the bet on which one I'd choose, but he doesn't seem too broken up about it. In fact, he shares a laugh with Alex as I take another bite of the Star Crunch.

Never in my life have I felt so completely normal.

Today, I don't feel like a hooker.

walk through my front door to see Zara wagging her tail at me. I look in the kitchen. No sign of my mother.

I figure I should move Zara to the backyard before Jen comes over this time. Don't need to freak the poor girl out again.

I unclip Zara and call her to the back door.

She follows me out. I don't really want to just clip her in and go, so I look around for a second. She sits, her chest puffed out all proud, and watches me. I find a stick, pick it up, and wave it in front of her. She wags her tail and follows the stick with her eyes. Then she jumps at it, but I pull it away at the last second.

She barks at me, not mean, more like she's saying, "Throw it already!"

So I do. I throw it and she runs after it, but she gets surprised when I run after it, too. She's a lot faster, so she gets to it first and then runs around me, taunting.

I laugh and chase after her. She runs around the tree and then stops. I wait, then she sneaks her head over a little to look at me. I run at her suddenly, stomping my feet. She drops the stick and runs away, then stops and crouches. Her mouth's open, her tongue's out. If a dog can look happy, this one does.

"Haha!" I say as I lean over to pick up the stick.

She crouches lower, but I throw it before she jumps on me to get it.

I hear the sliding glass door open. "What are you doing?" my mother asks.

Both Zara and I stop and look up.

"Playing," I say.

She puts her hands on her hips.

"Come inside, please."

I give Zara a look and a shrug. I clip her back onto her chain, and then I slowly walk up to my mother, leaving Zara standing there watching us.

My mom closes the door behind us slowly.

"That dog is not safe."

"She's only not safe because you treat her like she's not." She doesn't get it. She never has.

But now she's looking at me with what seems genuine curiosity. "What does that mean?"

Fine. If she wants to know, I'll tell her. "It means she's lonely. If her only interaction with people is hitting and yelling, what do you expect her to do?"

"So running around in the backyard with a dangerous dog is going to make the dog not dangerous?"

"How else is she supposed to learn to trust people?"

She glances at the dog, then back at me. "What if it's too late for her to learn how to trust people? What if she needs a…"

"A what?" I can feel my voice shaking, but there's no stopping it. "A firm hand?"

Her eyes go wide, and something flickers across her face. I'm not sure what it was, but I think it's fear.

"No," she says. "But after everything that's happened, I need to know you won't do anything that could get you hurt. I want you to be safe." Her eyes seem to get sad. "I want to be able to trust that you'll make the right decisions."

I turn away from her, my mind flashing through all the wrong decisions I've made. I hate that she's actually right. But more, I hate that she still just doesn't get it. My heart pounds wildly as I turn back to her, slowly.

"You sure as hell never trusted me, that's for sure. I was just a kid, but you treated me like I was evil," I say, my face burning red, my voice getting high and louder than I mean it to. I wonder how much of that was my father, but I can't excuse her. I can't. She never said a word to refute my father's words. "Automatically, everything I did was wrong, and you never, not once, stopped to listen to my story! It's always my fault. I'm always wrong. Well, I can't live like that, and neither can that dog. It's not fair!"

I squeeze my eyes closed, unsure why I even bother. I knew she wouldn't understand. She never does.

"Anna," she says softly. "I didn't know." I catch a glimpse of that thing that might be fear crossing her face again. "I didn't know you felt that way."

They're the words I always wanted her to say, but they feel wrong. Utterly and completely wrong.

"I'm sorry," I say before she can say anything else. My eyes sting with tears. "I'm sorry I'm the horrible daughter who could never do anything right. Who ruined everything when I ran away. I wish I could be the perfect daughter you both need me to be. But I can't. And I'm sick of trying."

I sit down at the table with a flop, like I'm too exhausted to stand anymore. I cover my mouth with my hand for a moment, trying to stop myself from crying.

She shakes her head. "I only ever wanted the best for you," she whispers.

I don't respond. I can't. There's nothing more to say.

"I just…want you to leave that dog alone," she says.

"Yeah, good luck with that." I stand suddenly. Why does she have to do this? It's so stupid.

When I was younger, I let my father tell me whom I could

be friends with. I let him steal my childhood from me because I didn't know what else to do. And my mom never stopped him. She was like his silent partner. He took whatever he wanted, and she let him get away with it.

I won't let them take anything else.

If I have to sneak around to be nice to a dog, then I will. But if I have to fight head-on, I'll do that too.

walk to my room without another word. When I slam the door behind me, I feel like a child again, like I'm eleven years old.

Jen comes over a few minutes later. Both my mother and I pretend like nothing happened. Like we didn't fight at all. It's a skill, one I clearly inherited.

Jen helps me with math and all my homework. She gives me an easy book to write my English paper on and says I should read it this weekend. Um, she seriously expects me to read it in two days?

About that.

It is small, though, so I guess I can at least start it and see how far I get.

I find myself watching the clock, eager for four o'clock to come. Not because I don't like Jen, but because I'm…well, shit, I'm kind of excited to hang out with Jackson.

Jen leaves, and I head to my room to pretend I'm not waiting for something. Someone. Finally the doorbell rings and I fling open my bedroom door, but my mother answers the front door first.

I stand at the end of the hallway, watching awkwardly.

"Hi, Jackson. Is something wrong with that dog again?" she asks.

"No, ma'am. I'm actually here for Anna. We have a project to work on together."

"Oh," she says, her shoulders stiff. She turns to see me smiling innocently.

I run past her and out the door before she says anything else. "See ya, Mom."

"Wait, Anna!" my mother calls.

I almost don't stop. I don't want another argument with her, and I'm afraid that's all our relationship will ever be. But there's something in her voice that stops me. It's quiet, almost scared.

So I stop. I don't turn around, but she doesn't need me to.

"I just…" Her voice is quiet. "Want to make sure…you're okay." She pauses, and now I turn around to urge her to finish. "I mean, you're coming home tonight, right?"

My mouth falls open. "You think I'm going partying or something?"

"No!" she says, her face suddenly turning red. "No, I just…" She swallows. "The last time you left…you didn't come back." She shifts her feet. "I never saw that coming, and after our argument today…"

I blink, all anger gone. "Oh," I say, looking to the ground.

I want to say that I wouldn't make that mistake again, but that would be admitting it was a mistake. I mean, it was, but that's not something I want to admit to her, or to anyone. But I have to say something.

I step forward and do something I don't remember ever doing before. I wrap my arms around her. For a moment she stiffens, like she's in shock, but then she relaxes and hugs me back.

It's a weird moment. I'm not sure when to let go, or what to say.

"I'm sorry," I finally get out.

I hear her sniffle and wonder if she's crying. When I finally let go, feeling a little embarrassed, I turn away before I can see her tears.

I turn back just as I'm walking out the door and say, "Sooner or later, you have to start trusting me."

She nods and smiles sadly. After a moment, she says, "Be home before dark."

I turn and leave the house, and for the first time, I feel sorry for my mother.

CHAPTER EIGHTEEN

We walk down the clean streets of our neighborhood, house after house that all look the same. Some have brick on the outside, some have white siding, some have blue. But they all seem to have the same setup. The same windows, a paved path leading up to the small patio, and the same thick door. Even the same doorknobs.

The only difference is in the gardens. One has a big tree in the front yard with a cheesy tire swing. I can only imagine a girl in a white cotton dress swinging from it—although I have no idea where that image comes from.

Another house has an overload of flowers. They're everywhere. Nearly half the yard is covered.

Another looks like it's trying really hard to be different. A fake well sits on one part, an angel statue on another, and a big gnome across from it. It looks completely ridiculous.

Then there are a few that were obviously professionally landscaped, with their perfectly mown grass and pretty brick ponds with waterfalls cascading down.

"I hate this neighborhood," I mutter.

At first Jackson doesn't respond. We keep walking slow steps down the concrete sidewalk, but when I glance over to him, his eyebrows are pressed down like he's thinking really hard about something.

"Why?" he asks eventually.

"It's trying too hard. Too perfect." I miss my stupid apartment in New York that smelled like a bizarre combination of piss, fried chicken, pot, and cats. I don't want this pretend-perfect shit.

Then again, what I probably miss most about my apartment was that Luis lived in it. And I can't pretend he's perfect anymore, either.

Jackson looks around. "I don't think it's so bad."

I sigh. He would. Just more proof we're too different for this project. This friendship. Or whatever this is.

He stops walking, a stress line appearing down his forehead. "Sometimes I don't know what to think about you."

That's more like it. He shouldn't know what to think. "Me either," I say.

He surprises me with a light chuckle. "Touché," he says. A smile spreads across his face. "You really don't like it here?"

I shake my head. "Not really."

He nods. "Then let's go somewhere else."

"What about our project?"

"We'll do that later. I want to show you something." He must see the hesitation on my face, because then he says, "Besides, we can't really do that project without knowing anything about each other, right? Maybe we'll find inspiration."

I narrow my eyes for a second. I hate that my mind wanders to those dark places even with Jackson. He's been nothing but good to me so far, and that's why I don't trust him. At least when people treat me like trash, I know I'm getting what I deserve.

"Where do you want to take me?"

His smile is sweet enough to make me forget, just for a second, everything bad that's ever happened to me. And when he takes my hand, my heart races, and I know I'm in trouble.

I like him. Really like him.

The way he looks at me. The way his hand feels on mine.

I glance at his lips, but then I look away. No one's kissed me in years. Not in a way that didn't leave my mouth full of the taste of cigarettes. But his lips look so inviting. And I already know what they'll taste like. I've seen the fruit snacks he loves to eat.

There's no way he wants to kiss me, too. And I guess that's for the best. One kiss and he'd see right through me. Taste the garbage that I can't get rid of.

With way too much pep, Jackson spins around and gently grabs my wrist to pull me along. His hand holds on to mine as I follow him, and I can feel the warmth of his fingers seep into my cold skin.

He turns and smiles, a glint in his eyes that's different from before. So this isn't just an innocent suburban boy. He has a mischievous side, too.

"Come on," he says. "Let's be bad."

My stomach flips and my lips curl into a smile, even though his version of bad can't possibly match mine. Somehow, I like the sound of that.

We walk down one of the streets, and just when I think we're about to walk to someone's house, one I'm sure isn't Jackson's, we walk right past it. There's a big gap between two of the houses that's nothing but grass. It's almost like a suburban alleyway.

Behind the houses is a big field, and I mean *big*. For a neighborhood, anyway.

It's smaller than a football field, I'd guess, but still big enough to play a game of touch football or something. This is probably the kind of place teenagers play all the time, the kind of place I should have come to play tag and Frisbee or whatever else kids play. Watch the boys tackle each other playing football. Ya know, if my mother had ever let me out of the house without her.

I went straight from reading books and playing puzzles to drinking and getting in cars with boys. One day I'd given up on my mother's rules and decided to live however I could. I did anything I could have to have a life, experience things.

I wonder how long Jackson has lived here, if I would have played with him as kids. Assuming my parents would have let me out of the house. Mud fights, sledding, and stolen secret kisses in the dark. A whole life I could have had as a kid, a life I'll never have now.

But maybe tonight's a chance to taste the impossible.

Jackson walks over to a patch of yellow flowers that grow like weeds at the edge of the field. There's a small batch of trees there, and as we get closer I can see a little stream flowing behind them.

He picks one of the little yellow flowers and hands it to me. I put it to my nose and smell. It's fantastic! It smells so good, like spring. I smile ear to ear. For a moment we're not just students working on a project, not even just friends. For a moment he's a boy giving me flowers. A boy looking at me with bright shining eyes.

It's cheesy, but I've never had cheesy before.

For a moment, I feel beautiful.

"We're lucky they're still here. It's getting cold pretty quick. They'll probably be gone soon."

"What is it?" I ask, mesmerized by the little flower.

"Honeysuckle. You've never had one?"

"Had one?"

His eyes grow wide. "Seriously, who are you?"

I shrug.

He pulls another flower to show me. "Watch," he says.

At the bottom of the flower is a little white end. He pinches it and pulls slowly. A little white string-looking thing comes out, and at the end is a drop of liquid. He holds it up, like I'm going to let him feed it to me.

First of all, I don't know if this thing is even edible. Will it make me sick?

Second of all, even if it is edible, no way am I letting him put it in my mouth.

"What is it?" I say, wrinkling my nose.

"Don't you trust me?" he asks.

"No offense, I don't trust anyone."

"Just try it. It's mostly water, but it's good. That's why they call them honeysuckles. 'Cause of the honey."

"Honey?"

"Sort of, but it's not that thick. It's good, trust me."

I narrow my eyes, looking at him, then at the little flower. I pull the white nub and watch the string pull through the back of the bud. A little drop of liquid sits on the end.

I hang it over my tongue, and it drops before I get a chance to change my mind. It tastes a lot like it smells—like springtime. Being reborn. I don't know what that means exactly, but I like it.

"Is this what you wanted to show me?"

He smirks, so cocky, but he wrings his hands together. "No, that's not what I want to show you."

He motions for me to follow him, then he starts running.

He runs along the tree line, then darts inside and disappears. I can't see where he went.

I should feel afraid. A boy I barely know leading me who knows where. But my own words come back to me. Eventually, you have to trust someone.

In my world, trusting someone can get you killed.

But I don't feel afraid.

With Jackson, I feel safe.

I jog a little more and see a break in the small tree line. There's a little path with a bridge over the tiny stream, but I still don't see Jackson. I walk slowly now, looking around. The little batch of trees is only about ten feet wide. It seems to split two rows of houses; their backyards aren't visible to each other only because of this little forest.

A dog barks, but I pay no attention. Right now I'm not in the burbs. I'm in my own mini Central Park.

Inside the batch of trees, there's a tiny clearing with two chairs and a log on its side. Sprinkled around the area are cans of soda and beer, an empty bottle that looks to have once been filled with Jack, and a couple of cigarette butts.

Did Jackson take me to his secret party spot?

Does Jackson really have a party spot?

I walk over the little wooden bridge, and then I see him

standing next to a tree, waiting for me, a playful smile on his face.

"What did you want to show me?"

He smiles. "My favorite spot."

I turn back to the clearing full of beer bottles. Not as glamorous as I'd imagine Jackson would be into, but…

"Oh, not there," he says, following my gaze. "Some of the kids in the neighborhood meet up here sometimes, but my spot is a bit farther down."

"Your spot, huh?"

He straightens his shoulders. "Yeah. It's mine. I claimed it when I was seven."

He climbs back down into the stream by stepping on some big rocks. It's almost like he has the path memorized.

"So you did grow up here?"

"Yeah, why?"

"I was just wondering, you know, if we would have played together as kids if…"

He blinks. "I didn't know you grew up here."

I nod. "My parents didn't let me out much."

I was only ever allowed in my backyard. They didn't even trust my friends' parents to watch me. Sometimes me and Lo, my only friend my age, played back there, climbing the one big tree and swinging from the play set. But as we got older, that just wasn't enough. We both wanted more, except I wasn't allowed any more.

So I had to find new ways to live.

Ways they couldn't keep me from trying.

I follow Jackson down into the little stream, slowly and carefully stepping on the stones. One of them wobbles beneath me, and I almost fall in, but Jackson takes my hand and keeps me steady. He won't let me fall.

When we come off the stream, Jackson takes me to a big rock on the bank. Above us is a particularly big tree with branches that hang down just a little. It looks almost like a weeping willow, but the leaves don't hang down that far.

"Is this your tree?" I ask.

He nods. "You can get to it through the trees, but I figured it was better to take the scenic route with you."

"Yeah, thanks, I could use a bath." I lean down and touch the cold water with my fingertips, then flick it at him. He tries to cover his face with his arms. He looks at me like he's ready to throw a slew of curse words at me, then laughs. "I'll remember that."

I smile and join him on the rock. I look around at the trees and the gently flowing water.

I stand and walk back to the tree with saggy branches. I grab on to one of the limbs, like I'm going to climb.

"Want to go up?" he asks me.

I look through the branches and notice a few pieces of wood nailed to the bark leading to a tiny little makeshift tree house.

When I say makeshift, I mean it looks like a death trap. Boards haphazardly joined together, none of them lined up, everything askew. I mean, it looks like I made it. Old, uneven wood and rusted nails.

"Is that thing even safe?"

Jackson smiles. "It's nicer than it looks. You'll see." He hops over the bank of the stream and joins me by the tree. "But you have to get onto that first branch to make it to the ladder. Think you can handle it?"

I shake my head in disbelief. I can't believe I'm going to do this, but I can't say no to a challenge.

I take a jump and hang on to the branch. I swing my feet up to it, impressively ungraceful, and cling to it however I can. I pull my up body up and awkwardly am able to twist so I'm sitting on top of the branch. It shakes beneath me.

"You need practice," Jackson says.

I look at my scraped-up arms. "I'm not bleeding. I call that a success."

I stand on the branch and test out the ladder. This isn't going to be fun, but I don't let myself second-guess it. I'm already this far.

While I'm climbing the boards, trying to keep myself from shaking, reminding myself not to look down, Jackson easily pulls himself into the tree with just one quick jump and makes it all the way up to the tree house without using the ladder at all.

I pause to watch him. He makes it look so easy it's crazy.

"Cheater," I say when I finally reach the bottom of the tree house and pull myself up.

"How am I cheating?"

"You've climbed this tree too many times."

He laughs, and I roll my eyes.

The tree house is like four feet wide. Just enough for a little bookshelf full of junk and a couple of beanbag chairs. Technically, you'd be hard-pressed to call it a house. It doesn't even have walls. There are wood beams for a floor and a small plastic sheet he can pull out as a canopy, I guess in case it rains.

"See? Not everything is as it seems."

I smile. "Yeah, this tree house definitely isn't trying too

hard."

"Hey!" he says. "This is my house. I built it with my own two hands. You think you can do better?"

I shrug. He's joking, but I can tell he's also serious. "Jackson."

"Yeah?"

"I think it looks great."

He rocks his head back and forth, like he's deciding whether to accept my sort of apology, but the smile on his face tells me he's just giving me a hard time. "Okay," he finally says.

He flops down on the beanbag chair and pats the spot next to him.

I pause for a beat, then sit next to him, my arm brushing his as I do.

Thanks to the lack of walls and all, there's actually a pretty good view. You can see a baseball field not too far out and the big blue sky.

For a while we sit there, watching the clouds roll by, a slight breeze trickling in and blowing my hair back just slightly.

"Anna?" Jackson asks lightly.

I blink, his seriousness taking me by surprise.

I look into his kind hazel eyes, which are a bit closer than I'm used to in this tiny space. I wish I knew more about him and what those eyes have seen.

But that would mean him knowing more about me and what I've seen… I don't even want to know the things I've seen. I definitely don't want him to.

Now he's looking at me. At my mouth. And suddenly I find it very hard to do anything but feel an excited anticipation.

For a second, I think he might kiss me.

For a second, I want him to.

I lean toward him, hoping he'll meet me, ready for it to happen, when he instead asks me something I didn't expect.

"What happened to you?" he says lightly, looking down at his hands like he's afraid of my reaction.

My stomach drops, and I look away. I was kind of hoping to avoid this conversation…like forever. "What do you mean?"

"Well, we said we needed to get to know each other…for the project, I mean."

My eyebrows pull up, and I look away, unsure of how I should be feeling about this right now.

"I don't mean to pry. It's your business, it's just… I'm curious about you."

I nod but won't look him in the eyes anymore. "What do you want to know?" I force myself to say.

"Everything," he whispers, and a blush inches across his cheeks. "Like was it really you in the missing posters?"

I nod, knowing there's no way of getting around that.

"So what happened? You don't have to tell me," he says. Contradicting himself.

I take in a deep breath. Here goes nothing.

"I grew up here, but I had some problems with my parents. Or they had problems with me…" My stomach twists even thinking about my past. Somehow, here in this tree with Jackson, I'm not that girl.

I'm not the lost and lonely but pretending to be okay thirteen-year-old, and I'm not Exquisite the hooker. I'm… just Anna. And talking about my past, any of it, would be like marring this moment.

"…so I moved in with my cousin in New York City." I wince, calling Luis my cousin, but how else can I explain this? Not like

I haven't lied to the police about who Luis is before, anyway. I once had to pretend he was my brother so he could bail me out of jail. Talk about embarrassing.

"What about the posters? Your parents were looking for you."

I nod, hating how easily the lies come. "I didn't tell them where I went. Took them a long time to figure it out."

"That's not so bad. The way people talk about you, and sometimes the way you react to things, I thought…" He looks down at his hands, his feet no longer swinging.

"I know. I get it. Just because it's easy to explain like that doesn't mean it's simple. Life in New York…wasn't the easiest thing in the world."

My eyes sting, tears threatening to expose me, but I keep it under control. He can't see what's really underneath.

What would he think if he saw the real me? The disgusting bits that I won't let see the light of day?

Would he still like me? Still be my friend?

If I never stop hiding, can my wounds ever really heal?

Because as much as I like to think about my nightmares as scars…I know that's not true. Scars are healed wounds. Mine are still festering.

Jackson's hand brushes against my cheek, right there in that stupid little tree house in our own mini Central Park, and my stomach flutters. I take a deep breath, holding on to that feeling, and then it spreads from my head to my toes.

I want him to pull me closer. I lick my lips, wondering what he'll do.

He leans in and kisses my cheek, then pulls away and points to the way we came. "We should head back."

I take a long look out of the tree house, at the world around me, and let myself cool down. I don't want him to see how much I enjoyed his lips on my cheek. How much I wanted him to kiss me on my mouth.

Finally, I let him lead the way out of the tree house.

My cheek's still on fire from where he touched me.

Would he still look at me like this if he knew who I really was?

I can't tell him the truth. It's not worth the risk. I can't do it. I won't.

But maybe he doesn't need to know the truth.

That part of my life is gone.

I have a chance for something new now.

I have a chance for something good.

CHAPTER NINETEEN

He walks me all the way home, and things are real quiet between us. Now that we're so far from the tree house, I can't help but wonder why he didn't kiss me. I mean really kiss me. On the lips. Did he see something in me he doesn't want?

"Hey, I was wondering," he says. "Homecoming is next weekend. Would you, I mean, do you want to go?"

Oh.

"Homecoming?"

Seriously? That's another high school thing I thought was long behind me.

And absolutely something I never thought he'd ask.

"Yeah," he says. "I was just going to go with some friends, but if you wanted to go with me…"

"Oh… I don't know if that's a good idea." His face falls for an instant so I quickly say, "Not you, I mean. The dance. I get enough looks at school."

"Yeah, I know. I get enough looks at school, too." He smirks. "But I still want to go with you."

"Maybe."

"Just think about it."

"Okay," I say. Smooth. "Thanks, you know, for showing me around the neighborhood and stuff." Wow, that sounds stupid.

"Sure," he says, then waves good-bye and walks back toward his house.

I wait for a moment, unsure what to do, what to say. What to think.

Homecoming. Pretty sure that's something Luis and I used to laugh about, how stupid those things were. How we were so far beyond that.

But maybe I'm not as far beyond it as I thought.

I walk inside to see the dog chained in the entryway again. She's sitting up, her ears perked, when I walk in. She takes a step forward and nudges my hand with her nose. I give her a quick rub behind the ears.

I look up and my gaze crashes into my surprised mom standing in the hallway, holding a towel and a coffee mug. Her eyes narrow as she looks from the dog to me, but then she smiles and says, "Hey, honey."

I wait for her to say something about Zara. She told me once already to keep my distance.

But I guess she's going to take a chance, because instead she goes back to drying the dishes and says, "I almost didn't hear you come in. We got a huge vicious dog, and he doesn't even bark when people walk in the house."

Did my mom seriously just make a joke?

Maybe I should laugh, but it's so weird.

"It's not a he," I finally say.

"What?"

I raise my eyebrow. "Mom. It's a girl dog."

She looks at the dog, at me, back at the dog. "How do you know?"

"How do you not know? She doesn't have boy parts, pretty simple."

"Are you sure?" She puts her towel down. "Well," she says and clears her throat. "They told us he was neutered when we got him. We just assumed."

I stand at the edge of the kitchen, able to see both my mother and the dog. "You know a dog is supposed to be more than just protection. They have feelings."

"I know they do." She pauses. "Is there something else you think we should be doing?"

After a moment, I say, "We should call her Zara."

My mom takes a deep breath. "Okay, honey. Dinner will be ready in an hour."

I pause to look at Zara, who's watching me with those big brown eyes, her tail twitching. I'd like to take her with me now, but I think I'd still rather keep our relationship secret if I can. I don't need one more thing to fight about with the parents who clearly still don't know what to think about me.

I play a little music and lie on my bed and try to pretend I am someone else.

I listen down the hall as my mother huffs and puffs, trying to coax Zara outside. By the sounds of it, she's not having an easy time.

About a half hour later I know my father is home because Zara is barking like crazy. I hear the door open, my father yell at her to shut up, then footsteps to the back door. He must be putting her outside.

I sigh. I wish he'd treat her better. I pick up my math book and decide to make an attempt at homework, honestly just for something to do. I should have stayed in the woods, if you can call that little batch of trees that. It was much better than sitting here doing nothing.

Finally I hear a knock on my door. "Dinner's ready."

I head to the dining room to a nice big dinner. Grilled chicken, mashed potatoes, green beans, carrots, and fresh dinner rolls. My stomach growls just looking at it.

This time I'll try to finish the full meal before starting a fight. Yes, that sounds like a good plan.

"How was your day, sweetheart?"

I look up, unsure if my father was talking to me or my mom. They're both looking at me. I grab a big scoop of mashed potatoes.

"Fine," I say.

"Anything interesting going on?"

"A boy asked me to homecoming." The words are out before I realize what I said. That's what I get for letting my guard down.

I have absolutely no idea how they'll react to me saying someone invited me to a dance, and I'm honestly a little scared.

My father sits up straighter. "What guy?"

Oh God, here we go.

"Jackson. He lives nearby. It's not a big deal."

My mother and father stare at me, but I continue to eat. My mom knows about the Jackson thing, but I know she'll hop onto whatever my father says about the matter. It all comes down to if he's okay with it, and I'm getting the feeling he's not.

I shove a piece of grilled chicken smothered in garlicky mashed potatoes into my mouth. My God, this stuff is good. I can feel a meltdown coming, and I want as much of this food as I can get.

"I won't have it," my father eventually says.

And now I'm starting to get angry. I want to yell at him, tell him that I'm sixteen, he can't stop me from talking to boys. But I don't. What did fighting back ever get me?

I take a big bite of my dinner roll and try to enjoy it.

"Well, we did say we wanted her to be normal," my mother says.

That's new. I'm not sure my mother has ever been on my side for anything. Or maybe it's just because she doesn't know what side I'm on since I refuse to stop shoving food into my mouth.

"Nora," my father says in a low tone. "This will not turn out well."

Now I can't help myself. "It's just a dance. It's not like—"

"The boy is the cop's son," my father says. "He's probably watching you."

"He's *what*?"

He's the son of a cop? And he might just be watching me? For what?

Whatever. Who cares? I take a big deep breath and continue to eat. I'm not a fan of cops, like at all, but I don't do anything wrong, not anymore. So I shouldn't have anything to worry about. He's making a big deal over nothing.

"Sweetie," my mom says. After a moment, I realize she's waiting for me to look at her. When I do, she says, "Do you want to go to homecoming with this boy?"

That's a question even I hadn't really thought of an answer for.

What do I want?

My father grips his knife and fork. "It's not a question of what she wants. I forbid her from—"

"But Sarah said we should give her a little freedom." She's holding it together, but when I look at her lap, I can see her folded hands shaking.

Sarah. My father's narrowed eyes say it all. To him, her very name is a threat.

"Sarah said?" He shakes his head. "I won't let anyone—not her, not you—tell me how to fix this. At least in New York, it was just Anna's reputation on the line. But now it's us. Our family. You know what'll happen if we let her do this, don't you?"

My mom takes a deep breath and looks at me. "We have to start trusting her sooner or later, don't we?"

My words coming from her mouth.

My father says nothing, just stares at both of us, dumb-founded, his rage festering.

I can't believe what Mom said.

I could be wrong, but...I think she just stood up for me.

I rise to my feet. "Jackson asked me to go," I say, wiping my hands on my pants. "You want me to be normal, right? Home-coming is normal, and I'm going."

I drop my plate in the sink and walk out of the kitchen. Now they're looking at each other, but my father hasn't said anything else. I think that means I win.

Or at least that my father lost.

Just before I reach my room, I call out, "And I'll need money for a dress."

CHAPTER TWENTY

I wait until my parents go to sleep, then I sneak Zara into my room again. I set my alarm for early. *Early* early, since I already have to get up around six for school. Why do they do that? We're teenagers, we need our sleep.

Zara curls up next to me and licks my hand. It's gross, but it's a worthy sacrifice to have her here.

I feel better, safer, with her next to me. Not because I expect her to bite an intruder—that's just ignorant to me—but because I'm not alone. Feeling her warmth next to me is comforting.

Zara and I are in this together now.

I wake up not to my alarm but to the harsh sound of my father's voice echoing down the hallway.

What time is it? The clock says 1:14, and the lack of sunlight tells me it's most definitely not the afternoon. What in the world is my father doing up—and yelling—in the middle of the night?

Zara lets out a little huff and rolls onto her side, and within a few seconds she's snoring. Even she thinks it's crazy to be up right now.

I close my eyes and wonder if I'll make it back to sleep so easily, but now I'm awake enough to make out what my father says next.

"This is not our fault!" he yells.

My mom says something, but it's too distant—the volume too indoor-appropriate—for me to make out her words.

Zara lifts her head when I get out of bed, but I lift my index finger to my lips, then point at the bed, and she seems to understand what I want, because when I back up to the door, she doesn't move, just watches me tiptoe out the room. I shut the door behind me.

The carpet in the hallway tickles my feet, a soft reminder of how many times years ago I crept down this path in the middle of the night, sometimes to sneak out, sometimes to get a snack, but always to avoid my parents.

It feels eerily similar now. Except while I don't want them to notice me, I do want to hear what they're saying.

The glow of the living room light reaches the end of the hallway, and I stop at the corner and peek around the edge enough to see them.

My mom's on the couch, her arms crossed over her chest. My dad's pacing in front of her.

"You want to say it," he says. "I know you want to say it. So go ahead."

She holds her arms tighter around herself. "I talked to Sarah, and she said that maybe we were right to be concerned about Anna—"

"Sarah said? *Sarah* said?"

She pauses, and it's like I can smell her fear, pungent and powerful.

"Nora, if I have to ask you one more time to just spit it out…"

She nods, and after another second continues. "She said we were right to be concerned, but that maybe, well, we should take it easy on her because…well, she ran away for a reason, Martin."

"So Sarah thinks this is my fault, too?"

"No. Not your fault. It's mine, too…"

"This is *Anna*'s fault, Nora. No one else's."

"But Sarah says…"

He puts his hand over his eyes and rubs them. "You think *Sarah* knows a thing about how this family works? Or how it needs to work?"

"I just think she has more experience with this kind of thing than we—"

"You think Sarah knows better than me?"

Mom hunches her shoulders forward and bows her head. "I didn't say that. But she cares about—"

"We didn't push Anna to run away. And if that's the kind of insight her 'experience' has given her, she's got a lot further to go if she wants to be any good at her job."

"Martin, you're being ridiculous," my mother whispers.

My father paces in front of her like he didn't even hear. Maybe he didn't. "Everyone thinks I'm a bad father. That I did this." His voice is lighter, softer than I think I've ever heard. He always tried to be so tough in front of me, never letting me see anything but the disciplinarian. "I'm just doing what needs to be done. It's the way I was raised. If anything, we were too soft on her. *You* were too soft. If we let her get away with…"

"Then maybe she would have never run away."

He pauses. The whole room seems to freeze, and even my heart stops. Not the right thing to say, Mom.

The shadows shift over his face as his jaw clenches. My mother's eyes grow wide as she realizes her mistake.

She quickly says, "I'm just trying to imagine what it was like for Anna." I might be imagining things, but I think I see her lower lip tremble. "I want to know why she left."

He throws up his hands in mock defeat. "For God's sake, Nora, I did everything I could to teach her, and for her to know those lessons, however hard, were because we loved her. It's not my fault she took things the wrong way."

"I know you tried. You did your best."

"My absolute best," he says. "But you keep acting like that's not good enough. That's what you think, right?"

"No. Of course not. But if that's how she felt…"

He paces away from her, then with his back to her, he says, "Then what? Just say it."

"Then maybe we had something to do with her feeling that way."

He turns around, a look in his eye that I know well. He means business. Any softness he had is gone now, back to the father I always knew. My mother shrinks into the couch, and that must be enough to satisfy him, because he turns away.

He takes his coat off the rack by the front door. "I'm going for a drive." He opens the door. "I'm giving you some time to think about this. If you haven't dropped this nonsense by the time I get back it, just don't say anything at all."

An annoying buzzing sound fills my room, but I just throw a pillow over my head. No, I do not want to wake up. It took me another hour to get back to sleep, and even then I woke up at least three or four times.

A cold wet nose nudges my arm, and she's so strong she actually starts pushing me toward the edge of the bed.

"Fine!" I say in a hiss.

I sit up and press the stupid button to turn off the alarm. This is ridiculous. Zara tilts her head at me.

I am not in the mood this morning.

I grab a hoodie and throw on my tennis shoes. She runs out the door the second I open it. For a moment I think she's making a break for it, but when I walk into the kitchen, I see her waiting at the back door. She's pretty damn smart.

I open the door, and she runs out. This time though, she doesn't run right to her doghouse, she starts running around the yard. I realize after a moment of watching blankly—it's too early in the morning for me to think clearly—that she's playing. Now it's my turn to tilt my head.

She runs one way, stops suddenly, then runs the other way. It looks, strangely, like she's smiling as she does it.

"Girlfriend, you have to pick a decent hour to play next time."

Still, I walk to a stick a few feet away and throw it for her. She runs, stops to sniff the stick before picking it up, then brings it to me. I think she wants me to throw it again, but when I reach for it, she jerks her head away. Then she starts jumping around again.

I make a sudden move, like I'm going to try to take it, and she runs joyfully around. My lips curl into a smile. She's so goofy. Goofy like Jackson.

I run toward her, and she runs the opposite way, but already my toes are going numb. Shoes would have been a good idea.

Giving up, I walk to the doghouse and hold up the chain. She brings the stick to me, and I click the latch onto her collar. She barely notices. When I walk away, she just stands there looking at me.

I look back once I reach the door, and she's chewing on her stick.

I feel really good that I can make her life a little bit better. Like my life has a small amount of meaning.

I go inside and take a quick shower. By the time I dress and walk into the kitchen, my mother is awake and sitting at the table with a cup of coffee.

"Morning," she says.

Once, I'd have hated her for being so nice. Why pretend? But after last night, maybe I can try taking her seriously.

"Morning," I say, I say, then glance toward their bedroom. "Is he…?"

"Still asleep. He was up pretty late."

"Oh."

Of course I know that she was up late, too. Her cup of coffee. The fresh pot on the counter. This isn't just her morning ritual. She looks…exhausted. At least I made it back to bed. She looks like she didn't sleep at all.

She sips from her cup. "What are your plans after school?"

"Going to Jackson's to work on the art project, I guess."

"What about tomorrow?"

I shrug.

I guess she takes that as an opening, because she gives me a surprisingly bright smile and says, "Okay, we can go shopping."

"Shopping…?"

"You'll need a dress. You said so last night."

Oh God. Shopping with my mother. That's not what I meant when I said I'd need a dress.

I sigh. I guess there are a lot of things I need anyway. I'm still wearing the expensive but much too conservative clothes my parents had waiting for me when I came back home.

I want to ask her whether it's worth the fuss knowing how Dad's probably going to react. Oh, who am I kidding? Probably? I *know* he's going to be pissed. He's already about to blow.

But I can't take it if she says I'm right. If she says we shouldn't go shopping.

I want to get the dress. I want to go to the dance with Jackson. If that's a problem for my father, I'll deal with it later.

"Okay," I say. I grab my bag and head for the door.

"Have a good day," she calls sweetly.

Well, that was interesting. I always wondered where I got my rebel streak when my mom's such a pushover, but the way she's acting now?

I'm not sure what she's up to. I sense some kind of diabolical plan.

I sit next to Jackson on the bus, and even though nothing seems any different between us, it's impossible to ignore the whispers around us that say we're a couple. Original.

I don't really care what they have to say. I wonder if Jackson does, but he doesn't seem to notice at all.

We walk into school together and sit at his spot at the bottom of the secret staircase. I mean, it's not really a secret, but not many people go there, so that's what I like to call it.

Jackson talks about his friends calling him last night, how he told them he was going to homecoming with me.

"How'd they take it?" I ask.

"They're worried."

"Because of me?"

He raises his eyebrow, like he's confused by my question. "No. Because of what happened with my last girlfriend. They'd be like this no matter who I was going with."

I nod, because I get it. "I kind of did the same thing."

"What do you mean?"

"I told my parents I was going with you."

"Really? How'd they take it?"

"Like your friends." I shrug and leave it at that. It's way too complicated to get into. "Guess that makes it official."

His eyes light up in a way that makes my stomach flip. I like seeing him happy. Happy about me.

He really does make me feel like a normal girl. Happy. Innocent.

Special.

Then the bell rings. I drop by my locker first, then head to class. I feel almost like a real high school student. I know my schedule, I have friends (plural!), and I'm going to homecoming. I even did my homework.

Nasty looks and whispers aren't something you ever really get used to, but you can certainly pretend. I have perfected my "fuck you" look, and people steer away from me for the most part.

The school day goes fast for me. Or at least, it doesn't feel like a full year, which is an accomplishment. My new misfit group of friends sit together at lunch and discuss more random things like what country would we most like to travel to and who's funnier, Tina Fey or Stephen Colbert.

Jen tells me she had something come up with her family, so she's ditching my tutor session for the day. That's okay. I figure I can do my homework alone for one night.

Or I could not do homework at all...

I nudge Jackson with my elbow. "We still on for later?"

His eyes light up. "You know it. Why?"

"I might be available a little earlier than expected." I nod to Jen. "She's ditching me today."

"Hey!" she says. "I'm not ditching anyone." I give her a quick wink, and she blushes.

"But now I'm free right after school."

"Awesome!" he says, smiling bigger than I've ever seen.

Today I feel very far from the girl living with Luis in New York.

After lunch I have health, which is basically just a class about sex. We learn all about STDs and pregnancy and all the things they try to teach us to keep us from having sex. I figure I'm pretty well past that, so it's not a class I take very seriously.

When the last bell finally rings, I rush from the room and out to the courtyard to call my mom and let her know I'm going to Jackson's after school.

She sounds worried, but I don't give her a chance to argue. As soon as I click the phone shut, I rush back inside to find Jackson. I keep my head low as I pass a group of boys crowded in the corner. One of them is Marissa's nasty boyfriend Brandon.

"Dude, that's hot," one boy says low, like it's a secret. I take a peek at what they're doing. They're crowded around Brandon, who's holding his cell phone. I can hear the muffled sounds of a video playing, too indistinct to make out.

Then I hear the moans.

Are they seriously watching porn in the middle of school?

Perverts.

Please welcome the future johns of America, everyone.

I shake my head and turn to keep walking, but then Brandon calls out, "Eric says you've got one of these floating around, don't you?"

I stop. Two boys walk right up next to me on either side, Brandon and a redheaded jock who must be Eric.

The jock leans in. "I'd love to see it one day." He puts his arms around me and I don't move. I know better than to struggle; it only makes it worse. Besides, I'm no stranger to sticky breath in my face.

"Like I'd be that stupid," I say, keeping my eyes forward, my expression calm.

Brandon laughs. "You know how much power there is in sex, then."

The redhead drops his arm from my shoulder and adds, "Marissa's learning that lesson, too." Then walks away laughing. Brandon joins him without another word.

I still don't move, my mind totally blown by what they just said. I don't think he realizes that he just told me Marissa's secret. He thinks I'll be scratching my head, wondering what that could have meant. Except that I already know more than he realizes.

That's what Brandon has over Marissa. Why she "can't" dump him. She's had to put up with him because if she doesn't, he's going to show everyone a video of them having sex. How much power would that give him? He could show her parents, colleges, jobs. He could put it on the internet and she'd never get it back.

She'd be marked, like me.

I walk toward the bus slowly, still thinking about Marissa and Brandon. He's more of a dick than I realized. But as much as I know Marissa doesn't deserve what she's getting, I know there's nothing I can do to help her.

It's none of my business.

Except that now I can't get it out of my head.

CHAPTER TWENTY-ONE

I'm quiet on the bus ride home. That's nothing unusual for me, but by the time we get off the bus at Jackson's stop, my thoughts are a mess. I know there's nothing I can do to help Marissa. I have to let it go. I've got my own problems to worry about.

Like the fact that Jackson's the son of a cop.

Yeah, I forgot about that.

A hundred horrible memories of the police flood my mind. I stop.

Shit.

"What's wrong?"

"Will your dad be home?"

"Yeah. Why, you don't trust me or something?"

My eyes refocus. His face is a little red. "No," I say. "I mean, yes. Of course I trust you, I'm just… Parents don't usually like me."

His face is still a little red. "My dad's not like most."

No kidding, your dad is a cop. Cops hate everyone.

I try really hard not to drag my feet as we walk up the path to his house.

Jackson laughs, still as lighthearted as ever. "It's going to be fine."

Yeah, I've heard that before.

We walk through the door, and I find myself looking around like I'm in a spaceship or something. It's warm and smells like vanilla. The floor is mahogany, the walls a pretty burgundy. It feels warm and inviting. I kinda wish my house were more like this.

He closes the door behind us. I rub my hands together and then cross my arms.

"I'm home," Jackson calls out.

A large man peeks around a corner. "There you are!"

I take a stumbling step back.

I can't breathe. Everything stops.

Just Anna. I'm just Anna. He won't hate me. He doesn't know I'm a hooker.

He's wearing a black police uniform. Funny how cops all look the same.

Same uniform. Same badge. Same smile.

"Hi there, this must be your friend. Anna, right?" he says, holding out one of his huge hands.

My eyes shoot to the floor, and I can't, no matter how hard I try, make them look the man in the eyes. He's a cop, and the only person I know to be with cops isn't Anna. It's Exquisite.

I squeeze my eyes closed.

That's not me. Not anymore. I'm Anna.

Just Anna.

My body doesn't listen to my head and my heart beats faster, my head pounds.

Cops don't shake hookers' hands. They cuff them, they hit

them, they scar them.

But he wants to shake my hand.

How can I trust him?

A terrifying thought occurs to me.

How closely do police departments communicate? Is it possible he knows about Exquisite? Is it possible he knows who I really am?

Is it possible he'll tell Jackson?

I chance a glimpse at his face—to test his reaction to me—but he doesn't seem to recognize me. He just seems confused that he's still holding his hand out and I haven't shaken it.

"Yes," Jackson says for me. "This is Anna, I guess she's shy." Confusion is laced in his voice.

"Well," the man says awkwardly. "It's nice to meet you."

He drops his hand and slowly walks away from us.

Jackson doesn't move or say anything. What's he thinking? Does he regret having me over? Being my friend?

"Come on," he says, and I follow him up a set of stairs. We walk into a room, and he shuts the door behind us. "What the hell was that?" he asks.

I've never heard him talk like this. He's so innocent that the almost-sort-of cuss sounds strange coming from his mouth.

"I…" But I'm not sure what to say. Should I apologize? "I'm not a fan of cops. They kind of freak me out."

I'm still feeling flustered, so it takes a little effort for me to meet his gaze, but I want to watch his face. I want to know what he's thinking, or at least be able to formulate a guess.

He'll be angry now. That's okay. I deserve it.

But his face is much softer than I expected.

He sits down on a bed. I'm guessing we're in his room…and

that would make this his bed.

My cheeks grow hot.

What's wrong with me?

"Police are supposed to be the good guys," he says, but it's almost like he's trying to convince himself as much as me.

Maybe he knows more about how cops can be than I realized.

"A uniform doesn't make them good."

He looks me straight in the eye. "But it doesn't make them bad, either."

I nod. He's right. It's just a job, it's not who he is. But God, if my own father can be so harsh, I can't imagine how bad Jackson's father must be. A cop.

"So what happened?" he says. "What made you hate police...if you don't mind me asking."

I take a deep breath and sit down beside him. I breathe in and out slowly. I don't want to get too worked up about this.

I can't tell him everything. But words don't mean much anyway. He'll want proof.

I push back the hair around my temple, exposing a small scar. Jackson reaches out and touches it with gentle fingers. That's the only time they left a permanent mark, but I've had plenty more injuries that eventually healed, leaving no evidence.

I don't explain what happened, and he doesn't ask. I'm not sure I'd have a good explanation for this one.

He stares at the ground, his eyebrows pulled tightly over his eyes. It's like he's deep in thought, like I've stolen a beloved belief. Kind of like I told him that Santa Claus didn't exist.

"I'll be honest. I don't think I've ever met a good cop."

He looks up and smiles sadly. "You just did."

"I'll take your word for it."

To his credit, his arms don't have any bruises, and he didn't seem afraid of his father. It's weird. Is Jackson really so perfect that his dad never has to correct him?

Or is he just so good at hiding it that his dad never finds out? My mind flashes back to us at his hidden tree house, his hand caressing my cheek.

And then I remember I'm on his bed. In his room. And my face gets red all over again. I look down to hide it, but it's too late.

He smiles, and the tension in his face fades. "Maybe that's what we do our project on."

"Cops?"

"Perception. We draw one man. Half of him is an evil-looking guy, a shadow over him or something. And the other half is kind with a smile."

"Actually, that's a good idea."

Jackson stands suddenly and grabs a big piece of sketching paper.

"Horizontal or vertical?" he asks.

I ignore the opening for a dirty joke and just say, "Vertical."

CHAPTER TWENTY-TWO

Friday night my mom takes me to the mall. Not once since that night has she mentioned what she said to my dad, the reason we're here shopping together at all. But it's hanging over us, and it feels even heavier knowing what he said to her later that night.

The mall is different than I remember. In the food court, the carousel I used to want to ride is gone. Even most of the shops have changed.

No one looks at me strangely here, which is quite refreshing, and I think helps my mother to relax. She can be a normal mom with a normal daughter.

We take our time going through the shops. I'm not sure how much my mom is willing to spend on me today, so I don't pick out much.

"What about these?" My mother holds a pair of dark-wash jeans.

"I don't really need jeans," I say.

"You always need jeans."

I take them and keep looking through a rack of sweaters.

No point in arguing if she's going to buy me more clothes than I planned on.

I find a sparkly cream sweater and hold it up to her.

"Your tastes haven't changed," she says with a pinch of her lips.

I shrug.

She follows me to the fitting room, and I show her the clothes I have picked out. Despite how normal she's trying to pretend we are, things still feel really tense. Like she can't even trust my choice in clothes or something.

I come out wearing a black lace top.

"You sure that's not too…" she says, but she doesn't finish her sentence. I think I can guess where she's going with it, though. It's not like I'm trying to get knee-high stripper boots or fishnets.

I roll my eyes and take a few steps farther into the store and point out two other girls in similar tops. Neither of them looks slutty in the slightest. "It's cute, Mom."

I can see her weighing her options here. "What about if you get it in another color?" she asks.

A compromise. I supposed I can handle that. "Okay, can you go grab me the tan one?"

She smiles and hops up to grab the top. She comes back with a black jacket and a T-shirt. Both of which are actually really cute. And best of all, they *feel* like my style. Okay, one point in Mom's favor. At least she's trying.

Next is the dress shop. Super.

I have absolutely no idea what to look for here. I've never been to a dance, and it's not like I have friends I can take cues from. Jen and Alex aren't really the dance types.

My mom grabs a hideous high-collared dress that looks like something *her* mother wore in high school. Not cute. I can't help but laugh.

"What?" she asks.

"How about no."

Her mouth opens in surprise. But then she seems to get that I'm just giving her a hard time, so she smiles, shakes her head, and puts the dress back. "Fine, what then?"

I pick out a cute blue cocktail dress that's probably a little too short for my uptight mother, but it would look good on her. Fantastic, even.

"Really?" she says.

I smile and shrug. "I don't know any more than you do," I admit.

She looks around for a second and then comes back with a lady who works at the shop. The lady pulls five dresses for me to try on.

At least we're getting somewhere now.

One dress is floor length and red with a low neckline. Surprisingly, my mother likes this one. Unsurprisingly, she suggests the purple one instead of the red.

Another dress is puffy and hideous. We both laugh when I come out in it. I spin around like I'm a stupid fairy-tale princess.

"Stop, stop! Take it off." She points behind me. "How about that black one with the pink lines?"

I close the fitting room door behind me to try it out.

I come out really hoping she likes this one. It's more casual than the rest of them, but I kind of like that. I'd rather look like I just picked something out of my closet than look like I'm trying too hard.

"Ooooh," my mother says.

"Do you like it?" I look at myself in the mirror. The dress is on the shorter side but still reaches my knee, with a black skirt that's just a little flowy, and it has a cool pink zigzag pattern at the top.

"Do you like it?"

I smile. "Yes. I do. Now tell me if you do."

The smile she gives me is the biggest I've seen on her in years. "I'd say we have a winner."

We stop at the new food court for dinner, and it's the first time things actually seem good with her. Not pretend-normal. Not trying too hard. It's just me with my mom.

Maybe she finally feels like I really am her teenage daughter. Maybe she's okay with whatever that means.

I figured we'd be done after dinner. I have my dress and some other clothes. But my mom seems energized now. She isn't finished.

We go into a department store and end up getting me jeans, two pairs of shoes, five more tops, and a necklace. I'm feeling a little spoiled.

With a tug, I fall back into a memory. Me and Luis in a tiny New York boutique with an unpronounceable name. Tucked away from the sounds of shouting and traffic. He held out a necklace—a pendant of a golden swallow with tiny diamond eyes. I turned my back on him so he could put it on. His heavy hands circled my neck.

"Gotta make sure my girl looks good."

It's like every line is blurred with Luis. When we were together, I was his. When did that change from being his to cherish to being his to trade away as he pleased?

I drag myself back into the present. This is different.

My mom is doing this for me.

She doesn't have to. I can live in the shitty clothes I already have. She's just being nice. She's being my mother.

And it feels really good.

Jackson and I spend the entire weekend working on our art project together, which is pretty incredible. He's the only person to put me completely at ease, and when we're working on art, my only real mental escape…it's perfect.

Our project is pretty amazing, if I do say so myself.

Together we draw a man, nothing special or different about him at all, except a hat that says "police" on it. He wears a goofy blue-collared shirt. Then we draw a line down the center with pencil and each use our half of the canvas to make him into what we see.

I draw storm clouds at the top, rain pouring down, and a gray background. I put shadows under his eye and across his cheek on my side. He holds out a nightstick, something I'm more than familiar with, in his tense fist.

There's something still missing about him, though. He doesn't look real. The surroundings make it pretty clear what I think he is, but he doesn't quite show the heart of my fear.

I close my eyes and think about the first cop who hit me. Officer Rodrick. How do I remember his name? The same way

I won't ever forget my first john. Maybe the better question is: how do I forget?

I erase the cartoonish man's face and picture Officer Rodrick. He had hooded eyes with bushy eyebrows. Thin lips that made a weird squiggly line when he smirked at me. The kind of smile that makes your gut twist because you know he's enjoying the pain he's doling out.

I draw this man, concentrating so hard my head starts to pound.

This wasn't the man who gave me the scar, but I know Jackson assumes it is. Truthfully, there were a dozen men I could have pictured here, and that's only the cops.

Jackson draws a man with blue eyes and a smile, holding out his hand like he wants to help you up or something. He puts a badge on the cop's chest that says "hero." He takes my lead and colors the background blue, like the sky, but leaves it completely cloudless, and then colors in a slight yellow-white haze around the man's body, like he has light behind him. Like he's glowing.

When we erase the penciled-in line down the middle, you can't see the exact place where each of our own visions start, and it almost blends together.

We actually finish the project a week early and decide to turn it in on Monday at the risk of looking like total geeks. Actually, that was my idea. I'm too eager to show Mr. Harkins to wait.

Mr. Harkins takes about thirty seconds to look over the canvas, then smiles. "This is fantastic."

"Really?" I ask, even though I already know. Or at least, I already know what I think, and really, anyone else liking it is just icing.

Really thick, delicious icing.

His approval feels better than I imagined.

We explain the concept to him even though he seemed to get it without any explanations. Then he asks to talk to Jackson alone for a few minutes. I walk back to my seat, glowing with pride and happiness that I helped create something like that. Something beautiful.

CHAPTER TWENTY-THREE

Jackson is smiling too when he comes back to sit with me.

"Good news," he whispers. I raise my eyebrows, wondering what he means. "I'm in charge of helping decorate for homecoming, and Mr. Harkins wants me to invite you to join the decorating committee."

I blink. "Really? He wants me to help?"

He nods. "And since we both finished our projects early, Mr. Harkins said we can go to the theater and work on the decorations during class. And after school, if you want."

"That sounds awesome!"

"Then come on."

I grab my books and follow him out of the class and down the hall. We go through the double doors that were once my escape from the rumors and prying eyes, down the stairs, and all the way behind the stage.

"So who's in this committee?"

"Me and you."

I stop. "What?"

He laughs. "Homecoming is in the gym, so there's only so

much you can do to make it look good with our budget and, well, people kind of give up on it. The prom committee is like the entire senior class."

"I thought homecoming week was like huge here."

"It is, but the dance isn't a real priority. The pep rally, which I'm not really into, will have more people helping."

"So…me and you are going to decorate the room for the homecoming dance all by ourselves?"

"Pretty much."

"Oookay."

"So first, we need to come up with a theme," he says.

"Are you serious? I…wouldn't even know where to start."

He pulls something out from behind a big plywood set. It's a folder labeled HOMECOMING. "Earlier this year we asked students to put in ideas for the theme, and we got a few answers. So we at least have a starting point. I took out the ridiculous ones, and here are some I think we could probably do. Las Vegas. Secret Garden. Under the Sea. City of Light. Wild Wild West."

"What's 'City Of Light'?"

"Paris is known as the city of light, so it would be Paris themed."

I take a few moments to think. We're under a small budget; that's the biggest problem. We can't make a gym look that great without a huge makeover, which we can't do.

"I like City Of Light," I say. Paris is okay, whatever. It's the light part that I'm into.

"Okay, what are you thinking?"

"White Christmas lights. We can get them cheap, even borrow them. I bet my family has enough to cover the gym. My dad freaks out about decorating for Christmas."

"Covering the gym with strings of light?" He stares at me for a second, then he beams with excitement. "We could actually make it look good this year."

"That's what I'm thinking."

"I like it. So if we're doing that theme, we should have a sign or something with the Eiffel Tower, too. Think we can draw or make a big Eiffel Tower or something?"

I shrug.

"We'll need two big signs, I think, one a welcome sign for when you walk into the school that says WELCOME TO THE CITY OF LIGHT, and the other a poster of the Eiffel Tower. With the lights, the gym won't really need anything else."

"Sure," I say. I'm glad I was able to suggest the lights, because I feel a bit oblivious about everything else.

"I'll talk to Mr. Harkins after school to get his okay on it all, then we can figure out exactly how to do it."

"One more thing," I say. "We'll need more help, don't you think?"

He blinks. "Who?"

"Think Jen and Alex will be down?"

CHAPTER TWENTY-FOUR

Jen agrees eagerly when we ask her to help us decorate for homecoming. Alex is harder to convince.

"That's seriously lame," she says.

"It'll be fun!"

Alex shakes her head. "No way."

"You know, we'll probably need to work during school," Jackson says, wiggling his eyebrows.

"Meaning?"

"Meaning I can get you out of some of your classes."

She pauses, her hot dog midway to her open mouth. "Even French?"

Jackson smiles. "It's Paris themed. I might be able to get you extra credit for skipping French."

Alex sighs. "Fine." Then she smirks and I smile. How could she say no to *that*?

"Yes!" I say.

But after lunch, apparently word is already out about who's decorating for homecoming, and someone isn't happy about it. I hear her voice before we even clear our trays.

"Oh my God, you've got to be kidding. Homecoming is going to be horrible this year."

Marissa and Liz are staring straight at us, arms crossed

"The freaks are decorating. What's the theme? Sexual dysfunction?" Marissa says.

I actually laugh at that and turn to Jackson. "That's a good idea. What do you think?"

"Yeah. We can put cardboard cutouts of Freud and Viagra bottles everywhere. Serve hot dogs and doughnuts."

"Ugh, I'm so not going," Marissa says. Her friends roll their eyes, which I kind of find amusing. Then a boy walks up from behind her and wraps an arm around her shoulder.

"Oh, you're going," he says.

I narrow my eyes.

"Brandon, it's going to suck," Marissa whines.

He whispers something into her ear, and she looks to the ground, defeated. Is it normal that I feel sorry for her? Even a nasty girl like her deserves a choice. Still, I turn and walk away with Jackson, Alex, and Jen.

"Come back here, bitch," Marissa calls to me, but I don't stop, and neither does Jackson.

We walk down the hall, ignoring the jeers they send our way. Halfway down, Alex and Jen go right while we turn left. I think we've avoided more jabs from Marissa and Brandon—

Until a hand grabs my upper arm and pulls me toward them.

I pull back. "Don't touch me."

Marissa crosses her arms, and her boyfriend grins beside her.

What's their deal?

Two more girls stand there with worried looks on their faces.

Her friends from the bathroom. I remember the blank looks.

"I wasn't done talking to you," Marissa says to me with a sneer.

"Marissa, just drop it," the dark-skinned girl says. "It's not worth it."

"Yeah," the brunette next to her says. She leans in and starts to whisper, "She—"

But Marissa whips a hand up and swats her away. "This is my business. Cool it."

Her business? What business could she possibly have with me? She just wants to make someone else feel worse than she does.

I can't do it. I can't stop myself from saying *something*.

"Just because your boyfriend treats you like shit doesn't give you the right—"

"Excuse me?" Marissa says much too loudly. Her eyes grow wide, and her boyfriend takes a step forward. "You don't know anything."

"I know more than you think."

Like that your boyfriend is blackmailing you with a sex video, I want to say. Yeah, I know plenty enough. I don't say anything, though. I let my eyes tell her what I know.

Brandon gives me the kind of sadistic smirk I've only ever seen in johns. Maybe my joke was closer to the truth than I thought.

"You're a whore, Anna Rodriguez. We know it. Everyone knows it." He spits my name like it's disgusting.

It *is* disgusting.

But my advantage is that he's lying to get under my skin. He doesn't know how close to the truth he is.

Does he?

I think of the note in my locker.

Did he somehow find out what happened to me in New York?

A soft hand grabs my arm and pulls me back, and Jackson puts himself between me and them.

"Shut the hell up," he says. "You know nothing about her."

I get that sick feeling again. Jackson's standing up for me again. Only...I don't know if Brandon is only calling me a whore to get under my skin or if he really knows. But it doesn't matter, because he's right.

I am a whore.

Or was.

Or...I don't know. Can you ever stop being a whore? Somehow, it becomes part of you.

Brandon grins. "And you do?"

"Yes. I do."

"Keep telling yourself that, buddy."

At this I turn and push my way through the crowd of bodies. They part for me like they're afraid to touch me, but I'm glad, because I need to get away as fast as I can. Tears sting my eyes, but I blink to keep them back.

"Anna!" Jackson calls, and he runs after me, but I don't stop.

I keep pushing, keep running from the horrible past I won't ever be able to escape. But hell if I'll stop trying.

Finally I reach the end of the hall and I stop. I'm far away from the crowd of gossipers, and the bell is going to ring soon, so the halls are clearing out.

I press a hand over my mouth and cry. I want to stop when I see Jackson coming closer, but it's too late now.

"Anna," he whispers from behind me. When I don't turn to him, he walks around and stands in front of me. "You can't let them get to you."

I shake my head, fighting the tears. The more I react, the more he'll suspect I'm not what he thinks I am. I'm not that good girl with a slightly troubled past. No, I'm royally fucked up.

I'm not the damsel in distress.

I'm the villain.

It's only a matter of time before he realizes this.

"I don't understand why you let it get to you so much, Anna. What they say…it's stupid. It's *not* true, so it doesn't matter."

I choke on another sob. Only it *is* true. I wish I could tell him this. Maybe I should. Maybe I should just rip the Band-Aid off. Take off my mask and let him see the scars beneath. Then I could stop being so scared he'll figure it out on his own.

Except I can't bring myself to do it. I don't want him to see.

I don't want him to change the way he looks at me, the way he feels about me. I need his faith in me. It's the only thing keeping me going right now.

The bells rings, leaving only Jackson and me in the hall. He wraps his arms around me, and I press my wet eyes onto his shoulder. He doesn't say anything else and only pulls away when I do.

"Ready for class?" he asks me.

I nod and wipe the tears away. I feel so stupid for crying. So what if some idiot teenager called me a whore? I've been called a whore a million times, hooker a million more. I've called myself those words. They've been true for years now, and I've never been afraid of that truth. Until now.

Until Jackson.

CHAPTER TWENTY-FIVE

After school, Jackson, Jen, Alex, and I stay to work on the decorations. We only have two weeks to get everything together, but today isn't the most productive day. Jackson starts off just showing us some of his old props and some pictures of last year's homecoming decorations. They're pretty lame, I won't lie. Ugly red ribbons tied in bows all over the place, one big sign that just says HOMECOMING. They didn't put much effort into it, that's for sure.

If Jen and Alex saw or heard about what happened in the hall after we left the cafeteria, they don't say. No one speaks about it at all.

This is both good and bad. Mostly, I'm just not in the mood to be happy. Not anymore.

Then, as Alex lies back to take a nap and Jen and I flip through the book of old decorations and sets, Jackson disappears behind the curtains of the stage.

It's quiet on the old stage, only the sounds of Alex's fake snoring and the plastic of the photo album crinkling. Then Jackson emerges from backstage with an armful of beanbags and an enormous grin.

"They left the prop box unlocked," he announced.

"Uh-oh," Alex says.

Before the rest of us can react, Jackson gives a blood-curdling yell and starts throwing little beanbags at all three of us.

Jen screams. I cover my head, the beanbag hitting the wall right behind me with a *thump*. Alex jumps up, does this weird roll thing, and grabs some of the discarded beanbags to throw back at Jackson.

I crawl to hide behind a mural of a sunset, feeling pretty numb. I'm not mad, or scared or happy. I'm nothing. I want to be happy. I want to be able to play with my new friends, but my heart still hurts.

I pick up one of the beanbags that hit the wall next to me. It's softer than it looks. I take a deep breath and allow some of the pain, the heaviness to fall away. I let my lips form a small smile and I step out from behind the mural and throw the beanbag back at Jackson. It hits him in the side of the head.

Everything stops.

Jackson turns slowly to me, his face unreadable.

Then he yells "Ahh!" and runs at me with big stomps of his feet. I laugh and run away from him, picking up whatever beanbags I can find and tossing them at him. One hits him in the face, and then I trip and roll to the ground laughing.

Alex jumps in front of him with her fists up like she's a boxer. "Don't worry, Anna! I'll protect you!"

"You'll protect her?" Jackson says, incredulous. "I'm supposed to be the hero!"

"Why? Because you're the guy? No way. Besides, you

attacked. Heroes don't attack people."

He puts his hands on his hips, and I laugh.

"I don't need saving. How about that?"

"Deal," Jackson says and flops down next to me. Alex narrows her eyes, like she's not done playing their stupid game.

"You guys are seriously insane," Jen says.

"Yes, they definitely are."

They both shrug.

I look around, beanbags all over the stage, pages from the album twisted and ripped, photos and paper everywhere. Whoops.

"Well, we had a productive first day," I say.

Alex beams. "I could get used to this. You get extra credit for doing this all the time?" she asks Jackson.

"Pretty much."

"Damn, I'm doing high school wrong."

Jackson gives one firm nod.

I watch Jackson as he stands and grabs a big broom to sweep all the mess into a pile. What is it about him that makes me feel like a kid again? Like I really am innocent. Like I can have a normal, happy life.

And then people like Marissa and Brandon remind me that while a normal, happy life might be possible for other people, it's probably never going to happen for me.

Finally, I get up to help him clean, and Alex and Jen take my lead. It doesn't take long for us to get things back in order, except that some of the pictures from the album are irreparable. Jackson says no one will notice, and considering how bad some of them are, I believe him. No one should remember those horrible red bows.

Jackson's dad picks us up from school and takes us all home. Well, except that Jen comes to my house for our tutor session. I don't speak to Jackson's dad, but I try not to look at him like a cop. He's Jackson's dad, and that has to mean something, right?

I take a deep breath.

Unfortunately, trust is something you can't force.

I'm feeling about a thousand times better now than before our beanbag war. My heart is lighter, and even though I'm still scared and feel completely guilty for misleading Jackson, I know I made the right choice.

This is just something I have to live with.

As Jen and I study, Mom gives us Cheetos and chocolate milk for a snack. Weird combination, I know, but actually pretty good.

Jen finally asks me about what happened at school.

I shrug. "I just let Marissa and Brandon get to me." Which is true. I hate that I let them get under my skin…they just hit me with a seriously low blow.

Jen is still quiet, but she's opening up. She not the kind of person I'd usually be friends with, but we both need friends. We're both kind of messed up.

Mom invites Jen to stay for dinner, but she declines, keeping her eyes cast low.

I walk her to the front door, then tell her good-bye and watch her walk away, alone, down the sidewalk.

I wish she'd be more confident. Hold her head higher or something. But I kind of understand why she doesn't after what she went through with Brandon. You only have to be told once that you don't always have a choice before you realize the truth. You'll never have as much power as you thought you had. Not over yourself. Not over your destiny. Not at all.

Dinner's quiet, and I notice that my father still won't look at me. Mom is pretty good at faking nice-happy, but at least I can pretend our shopping trip made a difference, at least a little bit.

We're about to go our separate ways, Mom to do the dishes, me to my room, when my father clears his throat.

"We haven't had a chance to catch up," he says. "So you two enjoyed your little outing over the weekend?"

I don't dare meet his eyes. I shrug and pick at what's left on my plate.

"Darling?" he says, looking at my mom, and he frowns when she smiles but doesn't answer. "Not speaking tonight, are we?"

No choice now. Why couldn't he have stayed at work tonight?

My mother opens her mouth but then shuts it. I feel like I'm missing something here. Some part of an argument I wasn't in on.

"Go ahead. Tell me about it," he says, his hand clenching into a fist on the table—a show of power.

"I…took her shopping."

"*Shopping*, huh?"

"We had a nice time," I say, stepping in, unsure exactly how to help. My mother must not have told him about the shopping trip. Does he know about the dress?

"And what did you buy?" he says calmly.

My mother swallows and smiles. "We got Anna the prettiest dress." She glances at him. "It's very respectable. Modest." Then she glances at me. "But still beautiful."

My father slowly nods. "Beautiful. Well then, let's see it."

Mom freezes. "What?"

"The dress." He wipes his mouth with his napkin, a careful, deliberate motion. Controlled. "Let's see it."

The dress is in my room. I should have taken it to Jackson's. To school. Somewhere far away from here. Far away from him.

"I'll go get it," Mom says. She rises from the table.

"No," he says. "Let Anna."

I swallow. He rubs his napkin over his hands, as though wiping any hint of dirt away. Cleaning them for some special purpose.

My mom's eyes have gone wide. She wants to be there for me. And I guess I want to be there for her, too. We both know the only way out of this. We have to play along.

"It's okay," I tell her. "I'll be right back."

Three years ago, I would have taken my time going to my room and coming back. But all I can think of is my mom in the kitchen with him. Alone, under his cold stare.

So I go to my room and take the dress—hanging in its plastic garment bag—out from my closet. I go back down the hallway, the dress held close to me, and I hate that even now, telling him no isn't an option.

I hear his voice when I get close to the kitchen.

"Did you think I wouldn't know about it? Really, Nora? You used my credit card."

"I'm sorry, Martin. I just wanted to spend a little time with her. She's my daughter."

"She's my daughter, too! And she will do exactly as I say. And so will you. Or by God, I'll put you in line, too."

My hands and the dress they're holding shake. It would be so easy to drop the dress. To forget about all of this and run out of the house and back to the city. But then I hear my mom's voice.

"Martin, you know she's trying. *We're* trying—"

"I've got it," I say as I come into the kitchen. I stop by the counter.

My father straightens, then holds his hands out, gesturing for me to continue. "Don't just stand there. Take it out of the plastic."

I swallow and do what he says. I kneel down and carefully remove the dress from the garment bag, and then I stand up and hold the dress in front of me so that it can be seen unfolded to its full length.

It's more gorgeous than I remembered. That black and pink zigzag pattern on the top is perfect. Maybe not perfect for *Project Runway* or whatever, but absolutely perfect for me. And that's why I'm afraid.

"Okay, Anna," Mom says. "You should put it back so it doesn't get dirty—"

"Bring it here," Dad says. "Let me get a good look."

I step closer, the dress held to my chest, and stop a few feet away from him.

He wipes his hands again, lays the napkin down—

And snatches the dress from me so quickly, I can still feel its phantom weight in my hands.

"What are you—" I start to say, in such shock the words are out before I can stop them.

He raises his index finger. "Don't." He holds the dress with one hand, looks it up and down.

Mom says, "Martin, please. You're being—"

He slams his hand onto the table. The dishes clank. "I said don't!" His fist clenches around the waist of the dress. I wince just a little, knowing he's already wrinkled it and hoping he doesn't ruin it completely. Any second he could flip and rip it apart.

"Martin," she whispers, tears filling her eyes. "It's not her fault. I bought her the dress…"

"You think I don't know what you're doing?" he says to my mother. "The things you talk about when I'm not here? The things you do when you go out together?"

I don't know what happened to push him over the edge, maybe nothing, or maybe another argument with my mother. But I do know that he's close to his breaking point. He might already be there.

It takes everything I have not to leap forward and grab the dress from his hands, but the look in his eyes tells me today isn't the day to mess with him. I've been in situations like this before. Him. The johns. Even Luis. When they're angry, there's nothing to do but play along and hope today isn't the day they explode.

"Dad?" I say in a light tone, trying to pull him back. Trying to sound as innocent as possible.

"It is my fault," he says to himself. "My fault we're in this mess. If I hadn't let her coddle you"—he means my mom—"none of this would have happened. Well, you can be sure that's not going to happen again. I won't let you ruin this family."

"Okay," I say.

He cocks his head. "Okay?"

I nod. "Okay." He's never seen this trick before. Three years ago, I'd have shouted at him, run to my room, hidden until he came inside to unleash his fury. But now I know better. You don't want to get hurt? Then don't ask for it.

He shakes his head slowly, and when he looks at the dress again, his nostrils flare in disgust. "You're out of your mind—you're *both* out of your minds—if you think I'm letting you go to this dance."

My heart plummets, but I can't let him see. "Daddy." Sweat trails down the back of my neck, and my forehead feels cold. "I promise I'll be good."

"Good? You think you even know what that means?"

"I want to know what it means. That's why I need you."

His chest swells, like he's proud I see him as a source of wisdom.

"You're broken," he says. "Until you admit that, you'll never get better."

"I know I am," I murmur, I'm afraid too softly, but he must like what he hears. The quiet. The certainty. Because he's right. I am broken. "That's why I need you."

He looks at my mom, and I can guess what he's thinking. *See? This is how we get Anna to behave. This is how we fix her.*

"Please let me go to the dance," I say. "Let me…prove myself to you."

The words nearly choke in my throat, but now I'm thinking of everything I sacrificed to leave and everything I sacrificed to come back. I'm thinking of the dance. I'm thinking of Jackson.

After a long moment, I guess finally satisfied that we've been reminded who's in control here—who has the power—he holds out the dress.

close myself in my room. I put the dress back in its garment bag and shove it far under my bed.

I should feel terrified after what just happened, but instead I feel a quiet confidence. Maybe I learned a thing or two while I was away. Maybe now I know enough to get what I want and keep my father happy.

I pull out the book I'm reading for English. Jen gave me another one once I told her I couldn't do the first, and I've finally found a bit of a rhythm. This one's pretty interesting, anyway. It's called *The Catcher in the Rye*, and it's nothing like the kind of books I would have thought they'd have us read.

I've found that reading's not as bad as I thought. At least it gets me out of my own head for a while. I probably should have done more of it in New York.

But not long after I pull out the book, something distracts me. There's a strange tapping on my window. My heart pounds in my chest as I remember the last time.

Nothing happened then, but I do sort of wish I had Zara with me now. I take a deep breath and tiptoe to the window and peer out. A happy face peers back at me.

I blink and then slide open the window. "What the hell are you doing here, Jackson?"

His eyes are bright and alive, and I realize I'm very happy to see him. "I want to show you something," he says.

"Normal people come to the door, you know?"

He shrugs. "You told me your parents were strict—figured this was the safe way."

I shake my head. He's crazy. And sneaking around my parents with a boy, even a boy as innocent as Jackson, probably isn't the best idea in the world. Especially after what happened at dinner.

I narrow my eyes. "Is it important?"

He nods eagerly, and I sigh. Good thing I didn't change out of my school clothes yet. Besides, the chances of my parents coming to my room are nonexistent. After that big speech, my dad will want to bask in his own glory while he gives me time to think over his "lesson."

I grab a pair of tennis shoes from my closet, flick off the light so my parents think I'm sleeping, and climb out the window.

"Okay, what's so important?"

He grabs my hand and laces his fingers through mine, which makes my heart patter in a completely idiotic way. And then he runs, pulling me with him. I notice he's wearing a backpack.

We run down the street and behind one of the houses, back to the field with the honeysuckles and my mini Central Park.

Then we stop.

The sky is a dark blue, but there's still a little bit of light peeking out over the horizon. The field is right in front of us, with the little specks of lights flickering in the darkness.

"Fireflies," I say.

Jackson turns to me, his eyes bright. "You *are* human!" he says with a sly smile that makes my stomach tumble. At least my cheeks don't get hot. I do have some composure. "But they're actually called lightning bugs."

"What? You made that up."

"Did not!"

I laugh, and we both grow quiet and watch the little specks of light in the dark field.

"My family used to go camping in the summer when I was little," I say. "My mom and I caught fireflies together. But we haven't done it since I was eight or so."

"What happened after that?"

"I don't know. My dad started working more, we stopped talking to our cousins and even my grandparents for some reason, and my parents got stricter and stricter."

I shrug, wondering if that was actually the beginning of the end of my parents' relationship, and I just hadn't seen it. The same way they didn't see the way those changes affected me. "That's around the time that everything changed for me because they wouldn't let me out to play with kids my age, and they stopped playing with me, too." I'm telling him more than I'm supposed to.

"Loneliness sucks."

I nod.

He takes off his backpack and pulls out a jar. "Maybe we can make her a present."

"My mom? You don't think she'll say they're too…you know…childish?"

He takes my hand. "Maybe. But maybe she needs to remember what it was like when things were good."

"What do you mean?"

"Just some things you've said… It sounds like you guys haven't been happy in a long time."

He's right. It's been a long time since we were happy. Not just me. My mom. My dad.

Then he tugs on my hand and brings me into the field, thankfully saving me from having to confirm or deny anything.

I wonder why they're even still here, the fireflies. It's September; aren't they usually gone by now? There aren't as many as there are in the spring and summer, but there's enough for me to catch about ten in Jackson's jar. When we're finished, he pokes tiny holes in the lid of the jar and hands it to me.

We walk back to where he left his backpack, and I set my jar down.

"Is the night over?" he asks, his eyes alight with something else. Something very unchildish, and it kind of scares me.

My whole body feels alive. At his look, heat rises into my cheeks. Thankfully, it's too dark for him to see. I don't know what Jackson and I are, but I do know that I don't want to go home. Not yet.

"I'm not ready to leave if you're not."

His smile lights me up from the inside. He rummages in his backpack again and pulls out an iPod and little speakers.

"Some music?" he asks.

I nod. Is this how real dates happen? I've seen movies about these things, but it's safe to say I've never had anything close to a real date before.

He places the speakers down and lets the music play softly, enough for us to hear but not enough to bother the neighbors.

I don't know any of the songs, but they're kind of nice with their upbeat melody and acoustic guitars. Bugs chirp in the nearby woods, the tones mingling with our songs playing on his little speakers. We sit there in the field, just listening and watching the sky change.

But when a slow song comes on, Jackson stands and asks me if I want to dance.

"Seriously?"

"It'll be like practice for homecoming."

I raise my eyebrows. I hadn't really thought about the dancing part of homecoming. Maybe dancing here, with him, is a good idea, because no one else will be around to see me look like an idiot. It's just practice; at least, that's what I tell myself.

I get up but then just stand there awkwardly.

He wraps his arms around my waist, and I place mine over his shoulders. I'm not sure if that's right, but it *feels* right. He doesn't say anything, so I guess it's not completely wrong. We sway to the music. We're close, closer now than we've ever been before, and my heart pounds.

It's weird to like him. It's strange how good it feels when his hand gently touches my arm and sends a shiver all the way down my body.

This feels different. So different from all the other times I've been with boys.

I look into his hazel eyes, clear like crystal. They're actually a little like Luis's, only lighter…and kinder. Much kinder. Luis always looked at me in pieces—my boobs, my butt, my belly. It made me feel sexy at first, until I started to wonder if he only really saw me as a combination of sexy parts rather than a person. Jackson looks at me in a way I've never seen from him. Not from anyone. The looks that I've always loved getting from Jackson are still there, just different. More intense.

He's not looking at me as a way to get something he wants. That's what I'm used to, but he isn't like those other guys. I can feel it in his every movement. He wants me, but not like he wants to use me. It's like he wants to keep me.

Heat rushes to my face, and even though he's close enough now to see, I don't turn away. I want to soak up that look, remember it for the next time I feel myself slipping into the darkness of my past. I'll close my eyes and remember this. Remember Jackson.

He leans in closer and pulls me against him. The pressure of his body against mine awakens the memories of everyone who's ever done this to me before, whether I wanted them to or not. But one look at his face and those memories feel too far away to matter.

My stomach tumbles again; my heart pounds. I find myself wanting him to be even closer. I lean in, too, and I rub my thumb along the top of his neck, the feel of his skin there.

He presses his cheek to mine, his lips brush my ear, and he whispers, "You're so beautiful."

And now I'm lost. In this world of lights and music, everything else disappears.

My past, my future, all that matters is me and this sweet boy who thinks I'm beautiful.

We're alone in the middle of a suburban neighborhood, dancing like complete fools, but this feels so right.

It feels right in a way it never did with Luis, because with him, it was always about what he wanted. When what he wanted was me, times were good. But once he started wanting to pay the electric bill, buy a new television, get some new clothes, and wanted me to start working to afford those things…that's when things started to change.

Now, it's more. It's about what I want. And I want Jackson. It's about us. What *we* want. Each other.

My heart pounds. I close my eyes when I feel Jackson's fingers touch my ear and push a strand of hair away from my face. His hand lingers there, touching softly.

I pull away only enough to look at him. His eyes search my face.

I'm scared.

I'm scared of what I'm feeling, scared of what it means. Scared of knowing that I can never really be with him, so how can I want to now?

Scared of changing my mind and being trapped.

But as I look into his eyes, I know he's not like Luis. He's not like the older guys I dated before I left for New York. I know he's not like the man who raped me, or the dirty johns who only saw me as a pretty face and body they could buy.

I can trust him.

So when the song changes, we don't move, don't change our tempo or care that people might be watching us through the windows of their picket-fenced homes.

And then he does it.

He leans in. When he's close, my lips buzzing with anticipation, I lean into him. I can't stop myself. His hand comes up into my hair and gently pulls my face forward until his lips touch mine.

I don't pull away. I don't run.

This kiss is like nothing I've felt before. It's so simple and soft, but so very intimate.

My skin simmers. My heart floats.

His warmth spreads through me like a gift. Like he's giving me a piece of himself.

He pulls back for a moment and whispers, "Is this okay?"

I slowly nod, and he comes back in. When he opens his mouth, I'm delighted to find he tastes just like I expected. Fruit and brown sugar.

Then he releases me and backs away.

I don't want him to stop, but I'm too scared to pull him back in. Instead I look at him, hoping he can read my desire.

I feel silly, like this was my first kiss. How stupid is that? The whore is embarrassed to be kissed.

"I'm sorry," he says, and I blink.

He takes a step away, and now I'm confused. He's almost out of my reach, but I manage to grab his hand and stop him. He turns back to me.

"If…" I start to say, but I don't know what he needs to hear. "Why did you…" I begin, but that sounds just as lame.

He stands there, looking at me. "I don't know why. I'm sorry, I shouldn't have…" He runs his hand through his hair. "That was dumb, I shouldn't have pushed you."

"No," I say, shaking my head. "I don't mean why did you kiss me. I mean, why were you walking away? Why did you—"

"So you don't mind?" His eyes hopeful but scared. It makes my stomach flutter a little. Maybe I should mind, I don't know. But I don't.

"I didn't mind," I say softly. And then I remember what happened with his last girlfriend, so I tell him, "And I'm okay if you want to stop."

A look of relief comes over him, so intense that I realize I probably wasn't the only one nervous about tonight.

If my face wasn't already red, I'm sure I'd be blushing. He licks his lips a little, like he wants to kiss me again. I guess he and I are like each other at least in this way. A little freedom is all we ever wanted to feel okay.

I want more of his mouth. I press my lips to his again, mostly because I'm not sure I could resist if I wanted to.

When we're out of breath and finally pull away from each other, I don't know what else to do. What's the next step when the guy's okay drawing the line at just kissing? So I sit in the grass and lie back. The stars are pretty bright now. The sun's light completely lost to the other side of the world.

Jackson lies beside me.

"What about you, Jackson?" I whisper.

"What about me?"

"I've told you lots about me, but you've told me nothing about you. What are your deep dark issues? I mean, if you have any. You seem pretty perfect to me."

"Perfect? Seriously?"

I nod and feel a blush inching across my cheeks again. I'm not sure he sees me, though. I'm still staring up at the stars as they slowly grow brighter.

"I'm definitely not perfect," he says.

I don't speak, waiting for him to tell me something, anything.

"What do you want to know?"

I stop to think. "You used to date that Liz girl, right?"

"Yeah," he whispers, and for the first time, I wonder if he still loves her. If he's still upset about what happened between them. "That was a long time ago, though."

"Did you…love her?"

His head whips to me, and I look back at him. He's silent for a long time. What's he thinking?

"Maybe," he says finally. "But I was only fourteen. I don't think I really knew what love was then."

"Fourteen isn't that young," I say, thinking about how young I was when I met Luis. "Will you tell me what happened?"

He takes in a deep breath. "We dated in middle school and most of ninth grade. She was my best friend. But then things changed. She changed. She started lying to me about things and then eventually…she dumped me for some jock guy and became…well, not a very nice person."

"Why did she change, do you think?" I realize I'm pushing him in exactly the way I wouldn't want someone to push me, but I want to know more about him. This is making me hate those popular girls even more, to know how one of them hurt Jackson, but it makes me feel a little better, like I'm not the only one with a past we'd like to forget.

He shrugs. "She never told me this, but the rumor is that she slept with some guy at a party a few months before we broke up. It would make sense, because it was around the time things started changing."

"What a bitch," I say, but I didn't mean to say it out loud. "Sorry," I whisper.

Jackson laughs, a bitter laugh, one I haven't heard from him before. "People make mistakes, I guess. I just wish she'd told me. Even if it would never make things better... I just wish she'd respected me enough to tell me the truth."

I nod.

"I guess that's one of my issues," he says.

"What?"

"Liars. I hate liars."

My stomach drops.

Shit.

Why does it feel like he just told me he hates me?

He doesn't realize he's confirming everything I've worried about. Everything I've feared.

He'll never forgive me if he learns the truth.

"My mom lied to my dad for years about drugs and it destroyed her. Liz lied to me about whatever happened at the party. It destroyed me. If they'd just told me. If they'd just been honest..."

"Your mom was into drugs?" I ask, realizing I'm changing the subject, but I'm too shocked not to ask. He mentioned his mom had passed away, but drugs? Drugs don't seem like they fit into this world. They're for people lost in the gutters of New York, for the johns and the hookers with no hope left. The people with nothing else to live for.

"It's not something we talk about much, but yeah. She overdosed when I was twelve."

"So that's how she died?"

"Yeah," he whispers, barely audible.

"Wow… I mean, I'm sorry. I just didn't expect that. I… I've known some people who were into drugs. It's horrible."

"Really?" he whispers. "Who?"

"Oh, um, people in New York. It's just hard, because they don't realize how messed up they can get. The only thing that matters is the drug, and there isn't anything you can do to change that."

When he speaks, he sounds like his mind is a million miles away. "I always felt like there was something more I could have done… If only she had told us. If I'd been able to see what she was really hiding from us…"

I nod and try to hide my horror. I'm way more than just shocked at what Jackson told me about his past… I'm terrified, because tonight things changed between us. It showed me how good things could be.

And then he told me he hates lies. No, more than that…

He hates liars.

I've lied to him. If he found out the truth, it would be worse than him seeing me as a whore…he'd hate me. Because I didn't tell him the truth from the start.

I squeeze my eyes closed and hope he doesn't notice.

Shit. How long can I keep this from him?

CHAPTER TWENTY-SIX

I crawl back through my window and stand there, staring at my bedroom in the dark. Everything feels so quiet. So empty.

Tonight was incredible. Every time I'm with Jackson, things feel so right. Like I belong.

Except that I don't belong.

That's my biggest lie. That I could belong here. Belong with someone like Jackson.

I'm a liar. I don't deserve this, any of it. One day soon it's going to bite me in the ass and I'm going to lose it all. I know it. I can feel it.

The truth sits there in the shadows, watching, waiting for the right time to strike. Waiting for the moment I feel the safest, so it can take away everything I love.

My house of cards is going to crumble very, very soon.

I know I can't sleep here, not tonight, not with those thoughts floating around in my mind, so I head to the backyard, to the one person I know I won't lose.

I don't know if Zara loves me, but I don't need love. I just need someone who won't hate me for who I am.

So I sneak out the back door through the kitchen and into the backyard. It's so dark, the only thing breaking the silence are the bugs chirping in the darkness.

Zara's already watching me, bright-eyed, and I walk to her quickly. She climbs out of her doghouse and wags her tail in greeting.

"Hey girl," I whisper, and lean down to pet her. She licks my face, and I immediately feel better. I know I'll lose Jackson someday, but I won't lose Zara. Not to hate, anyway. I sit down, and she lies beside me. I lean over and lay my head on her back. Her long black hair tickles my ear.

This must be what unconditional love feels like. I wish I'd known that feeling before. I wish my parents had told me they'd love me no matter what.

Maybe I'd have come home sooner. Maybe I wouldn't have run away in the first place.

I wish Luis could have loved me without the money I brought him.

I wish any single one of my boyfriends before I left home would have loved me without the sex.

They all used me, every single one.

I was a hooker before I had a name for it. But I was just a child. I guess that's the thing I never really let myself understand. Those boys took my innocence when I was just a child. Even my first days with Luis…I was too young for all of that. Too young to understand, to say no when I needed to. Too pathetic, too naive, to really understand.

I learned the hard way.

I feel my mask slipping, old Anna drifting to the surface.

Marissa and her boyfriend see through me; they see the

truth. Whoever's leaving notes in my locker knows the truth.

Maybe I should beg my parents to take me out of school. I tried and it worked for a while, but I can't bear to watch it all crumble at my feet. If it falls, I fall with it. But then what would I do? Stay home with my parents?

Not go to the dance?

I came back to school sure it wouldn't work. And even though it feels now like it might crumble at any moment, I have to give it a chance.

I just wish I knew how this was going to all turn out.

CHAPTER TWENTY-SEVEN

I wake to my mother pounding on the door. "Anna!" she yells.

"What?" I groan.

The door opens. "You're late, you—" She freezes, her eyes stopping on the dog my arms are wrapped around. She doesn't speak, just stares at us.

I sit up. "I'll put her back outside," I say.

She still doesn't speak, just lets me pass. Zara doesn't follow at first. She's staring back at my mother. Guess I don't blame her. Zara's used to Mom or Dad punishing her.

"Come on, girl," I say, and Zara hops from the bed and follows me out, head low as she passes my mother. I put her outside.

My mother is waiting for me in the kitchen when I come back in.

"Anna, I've told you before, that dog isn't safe."

"Mom, I'm not going to fight about this. I need her."

She blinks but says nothing else until I head back to my room to get ready for school. "I'm going to call Sarah."

I shrug. "Do whatever you want." I'm really not in the mood

for this. Really, really not in the mood. Besides, I have a feeling Sarah will be on my side for this one.

I don't have time for a shower this morning, but I decide that's okay, because I still smell like Jackson. And even though I'm terrified of what will happen when he finds out the truth, he still makes me feel good.

Even without the shower, I'm about five minutes too late to make it to the bus stop, so my mom has to take me to school. When I come into the kitchen to let her know, she's hanging up the phone.

"Did you talk to Sarah?" I ask.

She nods. "She thinks it's okay. The dog. Just be careful, okay? She's nearly bitten a lot of people."

"Okay."

Zara wouldn't bite me, but I guess it's always possible, so I won't say that. Truth is, the risk is worth what she gives me. Comfort in a world of torturous and constant uncertainty.

Mom drops me off in front of the school. I watch the hundreds of kids file into the big brick building. Maybe I should have stayed home today. I'm so not in the mood for this.

When I don't get out of the car right away, my mom asks. "Are you okay, Anna?" She nods to the school. "Here, I mean. Or even just in general."

I shrug. "I don't know. Sometimes."

She clears her throat a little, and I wonder if she's holding back tears. "This morning, it seemed like maybe something was wrong."

I don't say anything.

"Was it what I said about Zara? It's not that I don't want her in your room. But if your dad finds out…"

Still nothing.

So she looks at me, like she's trying to see through my silent disguise. She can't see through it. No one can. But still, something seems to occur to her.

"Is it something else? If you want to talk…" she whispers.

I think of telling her about the notes. The ridiculous students who won't leave me alone.

I think of telling her about Jackson. Why going to homecoming with him is the best and the worst thing that could ever happen.

I think of telling her how exhausting it is to keep up this constant disguise, like the old Anna isn't still a part of me.

I know I should, but my mouth won't open.

My hands shake as I pop open the car door.

"Thanks, Mom."

I'll figure it out on my own, find a way to survive no matter what happens. I always have.

I take a deep breath and walk into the school.

open my locker and cringe at the folded piece of paper sitting there waiting for me. This is starting to piss me off.

i KNOW THE TRUTH. SEE YOU SOON, EXQUISITE.

Fuck. Another note?

This is not okay.

Who would do this? Is it possible one of these high school boys went to New York and slept with me once? No, I'd remember a boy that young.

Not knowing is the worst. If I just knew, I could deal with it.

I'm still looking at the note when someone taps me on the shoulder.

I jump and turn to see Jackson smiling at me. Shit. I crumple the note and throw it back in my locker.

"What's that?"

"Nothing." I fake a smile.

"You okay?" he asks.

I press my eyes shut. I can't hide this from him, not really. He'll know something's up.

"Not really. Someone's been leaving notes in my locker."

His eyebrows shoot up. "Like love notes or something?"

I can't help but laugh. "Jealous?" His cheeks turn red, and he looks to the ground. This boy really knows how to make me melt from the inside out. "No. Definitely not love notes. More like hate notes."

"Oh. I used to get those."

"Really?"

He nods. "Marissa and Elizabeth like to get under people's skin however they can. Don't worry about it, I'm sure it's nothing."

I'd believe him if only the note hadn't called me Exquisite. Though Marissa and her douche bag boyfriend did imply they knew more about me than everyone else.

"Anna?" Jackson says.

I look up, realizing that I'd completely zoned out there for a minute.

"I missed you on the bus," he says. "You weren't…avoiding me or anything, right?"

"What? No! I just woke up late. Mom drove me."

He nods but doesn't look completely convinced. "You sure

you're okay with last night?"

I grab his hand and intertwine my fingers in his the way he did last night, and his shoulders relax.

"It was perfect."

You know, other than the "you hate me but don't know it yet" thing. I can forget that for a little while, though.

And right now I really want to forget everything. Everything but the way Jackson makes me feel.

He bites his lip for a second and looks me in the eye. I think he wants to kiss me again, and honestly, there's nothing I want more, so I take a step toward him. He leans down slowly, and when his lips press against mine, the rest of the world disappears. I'm just Anna, and he's just Jackson. There is literally nowhere else I'd rather be.

Even though when we part, I notice that everyone within twenty feet has stopped to stare at us, I've never felt lighter. The light in his eyes melts me to the bone. This is exactly what I needed.

I forget about the note until fourth period, when I notice my phone has three missed calls from Sarah. Before lunch I go out into the courtyard to call her. I'd hate for her to get worried and call the police or something.

"Anna! Thank goodness. You wouldn't answer my calls. I was worried."

"Sorry, I'm at school. Couldn't really pick up the phone."

"What's wrong? Why did you call? Was it about the dog again?"

My stomach sinks. I can't tell Mom about the notes. They'd just make her worry for no reason. But Sarah's kind of like my therapist. Impartial yet supportive, no matter what, because that's her job.

"No," I say. "Not about the dog. I just… Well, someone's been leaving these weird notes in my locker, like threatening to expose all my secrets or something, and it was bothering me. But my friend Jackson told me he used to get them, too, so I'm sure it's nothing."

"Have you told the office about it?"

"No."

"You should. They might not be able to do anything right now, but it's best if they know it's happening."

"Okay."

"What about your parents? Have you told them?"

My breath catches in my chest. No. No I haven't told them. Is she nuts? How would that help anything?

"No," I say. "It's no big deal. I don't want them to worry over nothing."

"All right. Is everything else okay? I heard you're going to homecoming?"

"And decorating for it."

"That's great!"

I look over and see Jackson standing by the door, waiting for me.

"Hey, I've got to go."

"Okay. It was good to hear from you, Anna. If you have any more problems call me right away."

"'Kay." I hang up the phone.

Jackson steps outside and waves me forward. When I reach Jackson, I hold up the phone. "My mom. I told her about the notes, and she's, like, freaking out."

More lies. My stomach twists, but I can't really explain about

Sarah without making things that much more complicated.

He laughs. "Parents," he says with a shake of his head.

Lunch is fairly uneventful. Jackson and I don't kiss or hold hands, but things feel different. We hear a few whispered comments about us, and that honestly just makes me happy.

One, I don't mind people talking about us being together. I want to be with him, and I'm proud of it. And two, they're not talking about who I really am. One person calls me a slut—if they only knew—but whatever.

This new drama about Jackson and me is perfect for getting people to stop digging into my past. Who cares about who you used to be when the person you already are is so much more interesting?

Jen doesn't say anything about "us," but Alex keeps looking back and forth between us.

I ignore it at first, but eventually I'm fed up. "Alex! If you want to know, just ask."

She smirks. "It doesn't matter. Just curious."

"Curious?" Jackson asks. Is he really that oblivious or does he ignore it on purpose?

"You two really together?"

I look to Jackson, then to Alex, and I shrug, but a shy smile spreads across my face.

Jackson is smiling, too. "We're still figuring that out."

Alex rolls her eyes. "Well, figure it out quick."

"Whatever. Mind your own business," I say, and she laughs.

The bell rings, and the four of us walk into the lobby, where I see a group of kids staring at us. Marissa and Elizabeth included.

Awesome.

"First girl you date after me, and it's the whore. How much

did you pay her?" Elizabeth says. Well, isn't that just great. She sure seems like a keeper.

Jackson stops but says nothing. Their laughter fills the room.

I pull Jackson away from them. I'm not sure how much it bothers him, if he's embarrassed, or if he's still hurt by her. They dated longer than they've been broken up. Maybe he's still sad, or something. I don't know.

"You okay?" I ask him once we're free of the stares and laughter.

"Fine."

"I'm sure they're just jealous," I say. "Especially Elizabeth."

"Anna." He puts on his own version of a fake smile. "I said I'm fine."

I nod, but I'm not sure I believe him. Maybe he's hung up on her still. Maybe he's thinking about what happened between us and wishing it had happened with her. Maybe he's comparing us.

I have to get a grip. Why would I be jealous of her? She hurt him.

Me? I'd never do anything like that. I care too much about him to ever hurt him.

Even if that means keeping him from ever finding out the truth.

CHAPTER TWENTY-EIGHT

We stay after school to work on props again, and we actually start getting some things done. We've gathered a huge amount of white Christmas lights, so all we have to do is hang them the night of the dance. Mr. Harkins took our theme and ran with it, buying little fold-up cardboard Eiffel Towers for the tables in the lunchroom and the punch table, and even some of those fake candles to put all over the place.

All that's left now are the two big signs. One that just says WELCOME TO THE CITY OF LIGHT, which Jen and Alex are working on together, and one huge picture of the Eiffel Tower, which Jackson and I are doing together.

He got the theater director to let him use one of those huge plywood pieces they use for sets. It's already been used, but we're going to do the tower on the other side. It'll be like fifteen feet high and hopefully look amazing! Jackson found a cool picture for us to copy, and we'll use a projector to flash the picture full-size onto the mural board for us to copy. It's still kind of hard, but not as much as I would have thought.

Alex and Jen head home early, leaving Jackson and me

alone to work on our masterpiece. We get the outline of the tower completely sketched before we call it a night.

We've been here so long that now the school is completely empty, which should put me at ease, but something doesn't feel right. Our shoes squeak on the tiles and echo off the walls.

"This is cool, isn't it?" Jackson says.

"What? The creepy empty school that can only be out of a horror movie?"

"You're scared? I didn't think you were scared of anything."

I smile. "Oh, I'm scared of plenty."

"Coulda fooled me."

"What about you? What are you scared of?"

He blinks, more serious than I expected. "You."

"Me?" I whisper.

He nods. "Stupid, right? You terrify me because…I like you. A lot. It's the first time I've felt like this since Liz."

My lips twitch, but I don't smile, because there's too much bitter in this sweet. I look to the ground. He has more reason to fear me than he realizes. Maybe I'm better off leaving Jackson alone. The closer we get, the more I'm going to hurt him, eventually.

When I don't say anything else, Jackson picks up his phone and calls his dad for a ride, and we wait in silence.

The sun is already starting to set, we stayed here so long. Thinking back, maybe that wasn't such a good idea.

It's so quiet in the school. So quiet I feel like Jackson can hear my heart beating.

"I have to use the bathroom," I say. Not because it's true, but because I need a moment alone to pull myself together.

The hallway is, of course, empty as I walk down it. Except this silence feels thick. I find myself checking around every corner. I won't actually go to the bathroom. Just a few seconds out here will help.

Then a sound down the hall catches my attention, and I slowly turn to see a figure watching me. A broad-shouldered silhouette, just standing there.

My blood runs cold.

It's probably just a teacher, right? No reason to freak out.

So why is my heart pounding like it's ready to explode?

Instincts. Never ignore your instincts. My heart pounds faster, louder. My head buzzing.

The man steps forward, and the second I recognize him, I freeze.

Not him.

It can't be.

I saw him here once before. I convinced myself he was just the janitor. But now I see the truth. I should have known I was right all along.

His eyes are bloodshot, just the way I remember. Does his breath smell the same? A mix of something rotting and cigarettes? I want to throw up. But most of all, I want to—*have to*—run.

"Hey there, Exquisite." He slurs my name the same way I remember.

This cannot be happening. Not now. Not like this, not with Jackson so close by.

How the hell did he find me?

But then I see his janitor's uniform, and all of the pieces fall together. The notes. How whoever left them knew my name. And how he can be here.

He didn't find me. He works here. Maybe always worked here.

Westchester isn't that far from New York. Does he still go there on the weekends?

He always had a bizarre obsession with me and how young I looked. So of course he works in a high school, where he can get an eyeful before he goes to New York to take care of business without getting caught.

After he got rough with me, Luis said he was blacklisted from ever being with me again. So what if he paid for three sessions up front?

I thought that was the end of it.

My mind flashes back to when I passed out in the hallway and thought how much the janitor reminded me of this man.

I thought I was just being paranoid.

But he's here. In the high school.

I'm shaking now. I have to get rid of him, and fast. If Jackson comes out here and sees him…

"Hi, John," I say, hoping my voice doesn't sound as shaky as it feels.

"I always knew I'd see you again, Exquisite."

"That's not my name and you know it," I say, but this just makes me feel more like my old self. The old Anna—no, Exquisite— who would crawl into a car with this man. Who hated herself for every second she spent there.

He grins. "That'll always be your name. I know it. You know it."

Holy shit does this guy churn my stomach, and the sad thing is that he's exactly as I remember him. How in the hell did I get into a car with him…let alone what came after?

"Whatever," I say. "Leave me alone or I'll tell everyone about you."

He chuckles, like he sees right through my bluff. "How are you going to do that without telling everyone about yourself?"

"They already know."

"Not everyone." He points to the room I came from. The room where Jackson's waiting for me.

"How do you know?"

"Let me spell it out for you," he says. "You think he'd spend a second around you if he knew the truth? If he knew the things you've done?" He shakes his head. "I'm the only one who knows who you really are. I'm the only one who sees what you're like inside." He takes a step forward and raises his hands to embrace me, like I'm some old girlfriend he's happy to see, but I step back and cross my arms. He frowns. "I'm the only one who loves you for the truth."

"Don't touch me," I spit.

"Now, now, my Exquisite. You don't need that boy," he says. "You're better off without him. He can't love you for what you are."

"That just means he's too good for me," I whisper.

The john stands and places his hands behind him, like he's my principal ready to hand down some punishment. "Think what you want to think. Now, you and I have something to discuss."

I've dealt with guys like this for years. So I stop. I take in deep breaths until I'm calm enough to channel the old me. The hardened me. The me who was strong enough to deal with assholes like this.

I back away from him. "No, we don't."

"You and me have a debt to settle," the janitor says.

Of course we do. I'm just merchandise, and he prepaid.

But nothing in the world could make me crawl into a car

with him again. He will get nothing from me.

I came home willing to pretend to be someone I'm not. But now I don't want to pretend. I want to be that new person. I want to leave dirty, tarnished Anna back in New York. And now he wants to turn me back into her.

A police car's siren blares briefly, Jackson's father letting us know he's outside to pick us up.

"That's Jackson's father," I say.

The janitor stops, rubs his chin, and looks to the exit. "Maybe I'll say hello. I'm just the janitor."

"I'll tell him everything."

I pray he doesn't hear a single tremor in my voice. He can't think I'm bluffing. If Jackson's father knows, then Jackson will know. And I'll do anything to protect him from the truth.

The janitor frowns. "This isn't over." And he backs away, then disappears down the hallway as Jackson comes out of the room.

"Hey, did you hear the siren?" Jackson says.

I'm not looking at him. I'm still watching the shadows. Watching to see if the janitor is really gone.

This isn't over.

"We should hurry," I say. "Your dad's waiting."

He must hear something in my voice. He puts a hand on my shoulder. "You look freaked. You okay?"

"I'm just tired. Let's get my stuff."

He looks at me for a second. "If something's wrong, you can tell me." He hesitates, and that's all I need to know how much his next words mean to him. "Please tell me."

I know what he's thinking about. His mom. The lies she told him.

All the more reason he can't know about my lies. It would

destroy him. But how can I just say nothing? He knows something is wrong. And there *is* something wrong.

Maybe I need to tell someone. I need someone on my side. Is there a better option than Jackson?

There's my dad. But I can't tell him. If he knew what kind of terror I brought back with me from New York…

I'm doing well enough to convince him all of that's behind me.

Besides, he'd just blame me. Oh, a man once raped me? My fault for being a hooker. Oh, he wants to rape me again? I shouldn't have slept with him the first time.

I could tell my mom, but it would shatter her. The day we went shopping was one of the best days of my life. It's the first time in I don't know how long that she looked happy.

I can't take that away from her.

I could call Sarah, but that wouldn't help, either. She'd have to tell my parents.

Everything we've worked toward will be for nothing if they learn that my past isn't really behind me. That I'm not normal and never will be.

I'm not their little Anna. I'm still the hooker that girl became, and there isn't anything I can do to change that.

Red and blue lights flash again. Jackson's dad is waiting for us to come out, but Jackson is still waiting for an answer.

I think about my time in New York, my time with the police there. I've always been so good at letting half truths work to my advantage. It's a way to let Jackson help me without telling him the things that would just hurt him.

I swallow. "Umm, the janitor kind of freaks me out."

Jackson frowns and looks behind me. The hall is empty now. "He was here? Did he bother you?"

I shake my head. "No. No, he…he's been harassing Jen after school. That's why she won't stay, and today he was just here calling me beautiful and stuff. It's just creepy."

Jackson's eyes grow larger. "Where is he now?"

"Gone. He left when he heard the siren. You don't need to do anything, though. I mean, I'm sure it's nothing…"

"I have to tell my dad. He can do something about it—"

I grab his arm before he can run out the door. I know what happens if you talk to the cops, and I'm not about to make an exception for Jackson's dad. Even when they try to help, they just make things worse.

"No, please. Jackson. He's just a creep."

He looks at me, looks at the door, then back at me. "Are you sure?"

I squeeze his hand. "I'm fine. Promise me you won't say anything to your dad."

He takes a deep breath and clenches his jaw. I kind of like him being this way. Angry for my sake. Protective.

"Okay," he says. "I'm glad you told me, though. That means a lot."

I shrug. Unsure what else to say. It was a half truth, not exactly anything to be proud of.

Jackson leans in close, and his breath brushes my ear. "Are you okay?"

I nod and lean into him as he puts his arms around me.

I want to believe this is enough.

The janitor showed himself, but I got rid him of, and that's enough.

Jackson knows some of the truth, and that's enough.

So why can't I stop shivering?

CHAPTER TWENTY-NINE

The next morning, I stop at the front doors into the school. A sudden blistering headache pounds on my temples.

I shake my head and remind myself who I am. I'm just Anna. The girl pretending to be normal and so far doing an okay job.

My stomach twists.

The girl who actually has a few friends, as odd as they are. The girl who Jackson Griffin actually likes.

Why couldn't the janitor have shown himself when I first came home? It's so much worse now that I have something to lose.

I release a breath, and the tension in my stomach releases a little. My relationship with Jackson might be a time bomb waiting to explode, but I have it for now, so I might as well enjoy it while it lasts.

Jackson's not on the bus. What the hell? Where could he be? Maybe he got a ride from his dad, but it's not like him to skip the bus. Not since we've been riding together.

I walk inside school and find him sitting on the bench

reading something from his phone. I pull on one of my carefully crafted masks so he doesn't see how tense I am this morning, then kick one of his feet to get his attention.

He looks up suddenly. "Hey!" he says, his eyes bright with excitement.

My fake smile slips into a real one.

"What are you doing in the lobby?" I ask.

"Waiting for you, duh."

"Oh," I say stupidly.

He stands, grabs my hand, and pulls me down the hall. "Come on," he says.

"What's going on?"

"I took care of the janitor."

I freeze in my tracks. "You did what?"

He stops and turns around to face me. "Don't worry. I didn't tell my dad. I didn't tell anyone."

"Okay… Then what did you do?"

"I came in early this morning and found him. I told him if he ever comes near you again, I'll make sure he's fired. Or worse. I mean, that's kind of creepy that he's looking at high school girls. If he ever tried anything, he'd go to jail."

"Great," I say with a low voice.

Jackson doesn't seem bothered by my lack of enthusiasm, though. "That's good, right?" he asks.

I nod.

Maybe.

Maybe it is good. Jackson's on my side, and now the janitor knows he is. Maybe it'll be like when my dad tells my mom she'd "better do what's good for her." He doesn't always have to do anything. Just the threat is enough to make her hesitate.

So maybe the janitor will give up now. Cancel the debt.

Or maybe he'll take this as an act of war.

avoid going to my locker all morning, just carrying my backpack around school. The heavy weight on my back is a reminder of what I'm avoiding, but I'm doing a pretty damn good job of ignoring it.

What am I ignoring? Whatever might be in my locker. Those notes have been the janitor's weapon of choice, and I'm terrified of what I'll find when I finally have the guts to open my locker today.

When I join Alex at a lunch table, she smirks.

"So why do you still have your backpack, again?" she asks.

I shrug and take a bite of terrible mashed potatoes.

Jackson plops down with his usual excitement. A tater tot bounces out of his tray and flies into the middle of the table.

"Nice," I say.

He gives me a quick wink, and I find my cheeks turning red. Damn that effect he has on me.

Alex takes a bite of her sandwich "You know Mr. Dalton won't let you take your backpack into his class, right?"

"What?" I ask, sincerely upset.

"It's against school rules. Most teachers don't care, but he can be kind of a dick about that stuff."

"Great," I mumble, stirring my mashed potatoes around with the stupid plastic fork.

"Why? What's the problem? Forget your locker combination?" Alex asks.

I shake my head. "No, I'm just being lazy."

"Lazy?" Jackson asks. "That thing must weigh like twenty pounds."

"It's not that bad."

He shrugs.

I don't know if the janitor's left a note, but what am I going to do? Never open my locker again?

I end up just standing in front of the stupid locker, staring at it like a complete idiot. Finally, when the hall all but clears and I know I'm probably going to be late if I don't do this now, I spin the dial.

It clicks to tell me it's unlocked, and I pause again, then slowly open it.

My stomach drops.

The locker is empty.

Okay, not completely empty. It has my other schoolbooks and supplies and stuff. But there's no note.

Holy crap.

Is it really possible Jackson intimidated the janitor into leaving me alone?

The bell rings and I jump.

Well, so much for not getting into trouble.

I feel nauseous the rest of the day. I should feel calm. Excited. Hopeful. But this seems too good to be true.

The only thing that calms me down is seeing the smile of Jackson's face when he boards the bus and sees me. His whole face lights up like I'm the best thing he's seen all day.

God, how I don't want to lose this feeling.

My hands still shake a little as he sits next to me, and I grab his hand to steal a little of his confidence. We sit there, and his eyes glisten just a little. He squeezes my hand tighter. Is he afraid of letting go, too?

"Your hands are clammy. You okay?" he asks me.

I blink, but then nod. "I'm great."

For now.

CHAPTER THIRTY

My mother doesn't stop me from bringing Zara into my room that night, which is good, because I'm not sure what I would do without her.

She tells me to be careful not to let my dad find out. Right now, I'm her daughter, and she wants to be there for me. It should be a good feeling, but all it does is remind me why I can't open up to her. Not really.

I sit up and read through my old journals while Zara sprawls out on my bed. I don't know what I'm looking for, but I look anyway.

All I find are old pains, memories that leave me feeling even more numb. The beginning of the spiral that brought me here.

What I find the most surprising is that this—*this*—is my rock-bottom moment. That day that Luis left me in the street, beaten and broken, that wasn't the worst day of my life—not anymore. Right here, right now. Knowing my past could come back at any moment to slap me in the face and undo everything coming home accomplished.

Jackson stood up for me. The janitor didn't leave a note. I

didn't even see him today.

Please let that be the end of it…

I finally lie down next to Zara. She was very happy to have the bed all to herself, but she knows it's me. I guess she loves me. Because yeah, she grunts and huffs as I crawl over her and curl up in the few inches left open next to the wall, but when I stop moving, she shifts closer to me, maybe sensing I need her touch. Next to her, I feel safe. Comfortable.

When I close my burning eyes and channel the things that bring me the most comfort, it's not Luis I think of. It's fireflies and stage lights and honeysuckles.

The vibrations of Zara growling startles me awake. I jump up, heart pounding, and hear something tapping on the window. Zara doesn't move. The hair on her neck doesn't stand up. She just watches.

I take tiny steps toward the window and peek through the curtain.

I see hazel eyes and thick-rimmed yet sexy glasses. My shoulders relax, and I slide open the window.

Jackson stands there just inches away from me. I'm relieved for an instant, until I see the look on his face. Something's wrong.

My world crashes. What happened?

"Hey, want to go for a walk?" he whispers. "I couldn't sleep."

I swallow down my fear. "Um, I probably shouldn't tonight." I don't explain why, but I'm kind of scared to be out in the dark, even with Jackson. "What's wrong?" I ask, my tension relieved just a little bit. If he wants to talk, it's probably not what I think it is.

He shakes his head. "They just make me so mad. The things everyone says about you. It's not fair. If they just got to know you…"

If he only knew what he was saying. It's ironic that the people who don't know me at all are closer to the truth than Jackson.

"Who? People at school?"

He nods.

"People say a lot of stupid things." I shrug. "No point in getting upset."

I almost laugh at myself. Jackson's usually the one so calm about stuff. It's always me who's freaking out. What happened now that's got him upset?

"But now they're crossing the line," he says. "Do you know someone put a note in my locker today about you?"

My heart stops. "What?" If someone dumped a bucket of cold water on me right now, I'm pretty sure I wouldn't notice. The hair on my arms stands up, and my stomach drops to my feet.

I realize what happened.

The janitor didn't leave a note in my locker.

But that doesn't mean he didn't leave a note somewhere else.

Oh shit. Shit. Shit. Shit.

Jackson groans. "I probably shouldn't tell you. It's so stupid. Don't worry, I threw the note away."

I'm afraid to ask, but I have to know. "What did it say?"

"Anna—"

"Jackson. Tell me what it said."

He shakes his head. "It said, 'Your girlfriend's a hooker. Get the best price by calling her by her real name.' And then it gave some weird name."

I swallow. "Exquisite?"

He nods. "Yeah, that's…" Then seems to realize what I just said. "How'd you know?"

"It's an old joke…" I improvise. "Bullies in middle school used to call me that. It was the name of a hooker in some movie…"

His fists squeeze together. "It makes me so mad that people do that stuff! It's not fair."

"Shhh," I say, looking behind me to my shut bedroom door, hoping my dad hasn't heard. That's one more thing I don't need right now.

"Sorry," he whispers, and then he lets out a long breath.

I wish I could let him in. I wish we could cuddle up on my bed and fall asleep together. But it's not worth the risk of my dad finding out, and I'm not actually sure Jackson would say yes.

"I know you have a past, Anna, but seriously, prostitution? Did they think up the most horrible possible thing they could think of and say, 'Yeah, that's what we should call her!'"

"Prostitution isn't the worst thing, is it?" I ask. My blood drains further from my face. I'm not sure I can stay standing much longer.

"Can you think of anything worse? It's disgusting!"

I clench my jaw like I'm angry, but I'm not. He's right. It is disgusting. *I'm* disgusting.

I can't breathe. He might as well have slapped me in the face. I kind of wish he had. It would sting less.

Jackson might not believe the truth that's sitting right in

front of him, but he just gave me proof that all my fears are completely legit.

If he learns the truth, if he gets the proof that's now being hung over my head—he'll hate me. He'll think I'm disgusting.

I can't keep doing this. The lies. The deception. It's all going to fall apart. No, worse. It's already starting to crumble.

This is my future, I remind myself. I always knew Jackson was temporary.

"You should go, Jackson," I say.

"Oh… All right. Are you okay?"

Just one day earlier, his question would have made me feel warm and safe. Except now, his concern just makes me sick. When he learns the truth, will he care about me at all?

"Yeah. Fine," I say, but then I stop. It's not enough for me to know this was temporary. He has to know, too. If he sticks around…

He cocks his head and frowns. "What is it?"

This situation is only going to get worse the longer I string him along. As long as I have something precious, someone else can take it away.

"I just think…this is becoming too serious for me."

"What?"

"I still want to be friends." I wince. "But I just think we need to cool it and go our separate ways for a while."

"Cool it," he repeats. His eyes dart back and forth, like he's struggling to process what I said.

"Yeah." Careful to control my voice and not let him hear how much it hurts me to tell him. "I know it's short notice about the dance—"

"The dance?" he asks, like the implication hadn't occurred

to him. Like he's now starting to get how far I intend to pull back.

I wish I could tell him why, but it's better this way. Safer. For him. For me. For everyone.

"Listen, it's late," I say. "You should go."

"Sure." His voice sounds like it's coming from very far away.

"Thanks," I say, throat thick, and then I drop the window before he even walks away.

I close the window and curl up next to Zara again and think about the last few weeks as more and more tears fall. Such a short amount of time for someone to break through my walls, to make himself a part of who I am.

I'm still the same, really. Still dirty and scarred and broken. Still lost. But Jackson changed things. He changed the way I see things.

He has the strongest hope I've ever seen in someone. But he's not naive, not stupid. His life isn't so perfect. Maybe he's never been beaten and raped and hated the way I have. He's never had to lie to survive. But he's seen horrors in his own right, and somehow he finds a way to see the best in people. He still believes.

I can't destroy that hope in him. That's what would happen if he knew the truth.

As much as I want him—as much as I need him—I won't see him get hurt because of me.

CHAPTER THIRTY-ONE

When my alarm goes off and I roll over, my body feels like lead. Every movement is stiff, painful. It's not a feeling I'm new to, but it's strange that I'm feeling it now. It's not like anything actually happened last night, nothing physical, anyway.

Still, my head pounds and my body feels heavy. I drag myself out of bed because I refuse to feel sorry for myself. Step number two for surviving the streets is to keep moving. Keep fighting. Always, always fighting.

I have no idea what today will bring, but I do know that it will be one hell of an uphill battle. I'll feel better if I can get through it. If I let it stew, it will drive me crazy. The only way to move on is it to get the worst of it over with.

When I leave my room, I remember Zara, whom I fell asleep with, but she isn't in the room anymore.

Shit. I should have gotten up earlier. If my dad sees that I let her inside…

I walk out into the kitchen, bracing for the worst, but I see Zara scarfing down a bowl of dog food while my mother does the dishes. That's interesting.

"Oh, sweetheart. I was going to let you sleep in a little and drive you in myself."

I shrug. "That's okay. Where's you-know-who?"

"You know your father. Work, work, work. He left before the sun came up."

Yikes. I never even thought about that. Getting up early to let Zara out would have put me right in Dad's path. I should feel comforted that I got so lucky, but all I can think is how even that careful plan so quickly got away from me. I really don't know what I'm doing.

When Mom looks at me, her eyes are slightly creased, like she's trying to read my mind.

"I kind of just want today to be a good day," I say.

She nods. "Then let's make today a good day."

Maybe my mother really has changed. Maybe she doesn't see me as the hooker in her house. Maybe she sees me as the daughter she lost but got back.

Great. One more person to disappoint.

I'm so numb that I'm not even surprised when I find a new crumpled note in my locker the next day.

I knew he had more to tell me, more he wanted from me.

I knew this wasn't over.

It was only a matter of time before he made his intentions very clear.

The note reads:

YOU SEE WHAT HAPPENS WHEN YOU DON'T GIVE ME WHAT YOU OWE ME?

YOU'RE GOING TO GIVE IT TO ME OR I'LL TELL EVERYONE.

BUT I'M GENEROUS. I'LL TAKE HALF. ONE LAST TIME, THEN I'LL LET YOU GO. NOTHING IS TOO MUCH FOR MY BEAUTIFUL EXQUISITE.

I crumple the note and throw it back into my locker with the rest. I'm too scared to even throw them away in case someone reads them. They might be vague, but their words carry too much weight.

I let the numbness take over. I can't think about any of it. Not now.

I avoided Jackson on the bus by letting my mom drive me in, and now I avoid him at art class and lunch. He sits with his old friends, which, if I'm honest, kind of stings. But he's only doing what I told him to do. He's respecting what I want. And I told him to leave me alone.

His friends must be eating it up, telling him, *See? We told you she was bad news.*

Well, they were right. Being with me just got him hurt. My only comfort is that pushing him away will save him from even more pain.

Alex talks a mile a minute about some college party she's going to this weekend while both Jen and I sit in silence, pretending to listen.

"Okay, what's up?" Alex says, like she's accusing me of something.

"What?"

"Last I saw, you and Jackson were as chummy as ever, and now you're all solemn and he's avoiding us all."

I shrug and look over to his table. Our eyes meet, and he looks away like he's been caught doing something wrong.

"What happened?"

Jen perks up a little, like she's finally interested in something we're talking about. Great, even she's into my life drama.

"We got in a fight, kind of," I say.

"About what?"

"I don't want to talk about it, okay?" I grab my books, leave the table, and stomp all the way out of the cafeteria. I shouldn't start shit with the only friends I have left, but I can't handle being interrogated right now. Nothing good ever comes out of being questioned.

I head to the bathroom to hide out the rest of the lunch period, and when I shut the stall door behind me I realize I'm not the only one with this idea. The girl in the stall next to me is sniffling like she's trying desperately to stop crying.

I ignore it at first, 'cause it's none of my business, but even I can't ignore a poor person suffering.

"You okay?" I don't say it to be all warm and fuzzy nice, but it comes out softer than I expect it to.

"No," the girl whines.

I take in a deep breath and try to channel the people who have made the most difference in my life. People like Jackson and Sarah.

Except I have no idea what to say. *Do you want to talk about it?* is too cheesy, so what else?

But maybe it's not about being like Jackson or Sarah. About being like someone else. It's about being me. The me who has enough power to help someone else, even if I can't help myself.

"Whoever made you cry deserves to get the shit kicked out of them." Probably not the best advice in the world, but it felt good to say it. "You have to get your power back."

I don't know who this girl is, or what's making her cry. But there's truth in what I said. I don't have any more power. But I can help her get hers. I'll do anything to make sure no one else ends up as hopeless as I've become.

"How?" she whispers.

"Guess it depends. What is it that's making you feel so bad? So weak."

"My boyfriend…he's blackmailing me."

My eyebrows shoot up. "How?"

She pauses, and for a second I wonder if she'll tell me. Then she whispers, "A video on his phone."

Oh shit. I lean over and look at the shoes of the crying girl I'm giving horrible advice to. Sparkly black flats, probably stupid expensive.

"Marissa?" I ask.

The silence in the bathroom is thick, charged.

"Who the fuck are you?" she asks, her voice deep, no longer the sniveling weak girl I thought I was talking to. I sit still, frozen, as the girl slams open her stall door and stands in front of me, tapping her stupid sparkling shoe.

Slowly, I open my own stall door, a shy smile on my face. "Hi there," I say, a little nervous but mostly wanting to laugh.

This would only happen to me.

Her face fades from anger to surprise as she registers who I am. "How did you know?" she asks, her face blank.

I shrug. "I heard you talking about your boyfriend in that

bathroom once, remember? Wasn't hard to put two and two together."

I know a jacked-up relationship when I see one. At least, now I do. I've been there too many times now.

She takes a step back, almost stumbling like she's too tired to keep fighting. "You're the only one. I've been practically begging someone else to figure it out, one of my friends to tell me what to do."

"Guess I tend to see guys for the assholes they really are."

She leans onto the porcelain sink. "You got probably the only nice guy in the school."

"Got? No, I never got him, and if I did, it didn't take me long to lose him."

"Really?" She looks up, her eyes still bloodshot.

I nod. "But it's not me that needs the help now. What can we do about this douche bag boyfriend of yours?" Maybe I can't change my own past or fix myself, but if I can stop something bad from happening to someone else, I'm going to try. I won't be weak anymore.

"I don't know…" she whispers. "I've tried getting my hands on his phone, but he won't let me near it. Not like that would matter. He has it saved on his computer, too."

"Has he sent it to anyone?"

She shakes her head. "He likes to keep all the power himself. He shows his friends sometimes, though."

"That's good. We only have two places we need to get to, then. It's not impossible."

"How? I've thought of everything. I even thought about telling his mom, but he's told me he'd send it to everyone he knows if I ever tell."

"We'll just have to do both at once." I say it before I even really think about it. Truth is, I'm happy to have something to distract me. Something important.

She blinks.

I've known too many guys like Brandon, and I won't let them keep winning. This time, it's my turn.

"I've got an idea."

I know I only have a minute or two before the bell rings to end lunch, so I've got to work quickly. I rush into the cafeteria, and I swear a hundred sets of eyes turn to watch me. That's not awkward or anything.

Jackson watches as I run excitedly to Alex and Jen.

They're sitting there awkwardly, Jen flipping through a textbook and Alex picking at one of her fingernails. Have they been like this since I left?

"Whoa, what's up with you?" Alex says, looking up when I reach the table like I pulled her from something riveting.

"I need your help with something."

Both of them look at me expectantly but say nothing.

"It's going to sound crazy, but trust me, okay?"

"All right," Alex says. "Enough cryptic setup. What is it?"

I smile. "We're going to help Marissa."

CHAPTER THIRTY-TWO

The only time I see Jackson the next week is when I come by the art room to work on the Eiffel Tower mural. I've tried to time my visits with his schedule so that we're never in the room at the same time, but he must have gotten excused from class, because this time he's inside.

And he sees me.

I spin around to leave, but it's too late.

"Anna," he says.

I turn around and look at him. I want to tell him about Marissa, because I wish he were in on it with us, but a part of me knows it's better this way.

After another few minutes of silence, I guess he can't take it anymore.

"Are we ever going to be friends again?" he asks.

"I don't know," I say, my voice soft and broken.

I want to say something to make it better. Want him to look at me like he used to. But I know there isn't anything else I can say. Even if any words could take this back, no words should.

My mom is surprised when I tell her I'm going with my girlfriends and not Jackson, but she doesn't push it.

Dad, of course, is happy to hear the bad news.

"In the end, you'll see this was the right decision," he says.

Yeah. If he had his way, I wouldn't go at all. He's probably looking forward to me having a terrible time, coming home sad, and ready to never, ever do something like this again.

So screw it. I'm going to have fun tonight.

Jen, Alex, and I get ready in my room, doing one another's hair and makeup. Even Zara hangs out with us, watching as we goof around and joke about how to give each other the best makeovers.

Alex keeps trying to convince me to get a nose ring or cut my hair into a pixie cut, but Jen is actually beautiful when she's done with her. She pins her hair into a gentle updo, and after some serious peer pressure, Jen lets Alex take actual scissors to her and give her a side bang. She's softer this way, less plain. After a little mascara, eye shadow, and lipstick, Jen's ready to break some hearts. She looks happy, really happy, since the first time I've met her.

Homecoming might not be what I was hoping it would be, but this is pretty great, too. I have friends, and I'm helping someone have a little more power. And maybe, just maybe, help me keep a little of my own. As long as they're around, the janitor can't afford to show himself.

I just hope we can actually pull this off.

Once we're all dressed, Alex in her tight black dress with feathers hanging off the bottom, Jen in a long light blue A-cut dress, and me in my black strapless with the pink-and-black zigzag pattern at the top, we sit down to go over the plan.

I thought Jen might be hesitant to go along with this. But if nothing else, my plan brings a confidence into her that I've never seen her have. She doesn't want to hurt Brandon. She's sweet like that, desperate to not hurt even the bad guys who hurt her.

But she also won't stand by if she has a chance to stop him from hurting someone else. I just hope this helps her feel like she doesn't have to live in fear anymore. I hope this lets her know she still has the choice I never had.

Marissa can't be here because that would tip off Brandon, so Alex texts her to let her know the plan is on. Honestly, we're not asking much from her. She's to act normal. Do what she usually does, so Brandon won't know something is up.

Finally, my mom knocks on the door, tired of waiting for us to finish our powwow and way too eager to take pictures. When we leave the room, I feel like we're spies or something. This secret, it feels exciting, and I can tell the other girls feel the same.

Mom spends way longer than necessary, pulling us to five different places around the house, getting shots of us all together and each by ourselves, saying she's sure Jen's and Alex's parents will want some, too.

Even my dad stands behind her, watching. Quiet, seething, and always watching. He must be *thrilled* to see us having a good time, so I put on a big smile and laugh with my friends.

"It's too bad that boy couldn't be here," Mom says. "Are you ever going to tell me what happened?"

I groan.

"Don't worry, Mrs. Rodriguez," Alex says. "She won't even tell us." She sticks her tongue out at me.

I roll my eyes. "I don't need a date," I say, defiantly.

"Besides, Czar here is more handsome than any high school boy," Jen says, her voice light and happy.

"It's Zara, actually. But she is pretty, isn't she?"

Zara's eyes get big when we turn to her, like she's wondering what in the world we're talking about. I walk over and lean down next to her and scratch her neck. She lifts her head and licks my cheek.

"Wait!" Mom calls. "Hold that." She picks up the camera and snaps a shot of me hugging Zara, and I'm pretty sure that'll be my favorite picture.

Alex drives us to school in her mom's old Lancer. When we finally pull up to the big brick building, my palms are sweating.

I remember my first moments standing in front of these glass doors. It's dark now, but really, it's exactly the same as it was then. I'm the one that's different. Oddly enough, I'm more scared now than I was then. Because now, I have more to lose.

"I'm so nervous," I admit.

"I'm excited!" Jen says.

"Yeah, this was your idea. How can you have cold feet?" Alex says.

"I don't! I'm just nervous. What if it doesn't work?"

"Then everything will be the same as before. But it's going to work."

I nod. No matter what, I'm going to make sure Marissa isn't the one to blame if this goes bad.

But it has to work. It will.

The parking lot is already dark by the time the dance starts.

I watch the other students walk into the school with their fancy dresses and shirt-and-ties.

We walk through the parking lot, me much too comfortable in the high heels, and I march quicker than Jen and Alex, but I stop when I see a cop car pull into a parking spot. What the hell?

Three boys hop out of the back seat, laughing. The one who hops out first has those sexy glasses, and even from far away, I know it's Jackson. His father's in the driver's seat. I guess he came as a chaperone.

I turn away quickly and keep walking.

As soon as we enter the school building, all three of us stop and stare. Jackson recruited a few guy friends to help with the actual setup of the dance, so none of us have seen it all put together. Jen and Alex's sign hangs right at the entrance, candles light the path down the hall to the gym, and a little plastic runner leads the way all the way down.

It's pretty, but it's nothing compared to the way the gym itself looks. There are lights over both sides of the gym, covering the walls from ceiling to floor. I didn't even realize we had this many. The Eiffel Tower Jackson and I worked on sits behind the DJ, and it's beautiful. The background is dark, with hanging little twinkling stars.

We did an amazing job.

I just wish I could share this pride with Jackson.

From what I can hear around me, everyone else seems to admire the work done on the dance decorations, too. The only real proof this is the same sweaty gym we use for classes and games and prep rallies is the floor. There wasn't much we could do to cover up the basketball court.

"This is awesome!" Jen says, her smile stretching all the way across her face. I grab her hand, and she grabs Alex, and I feel so close to them at this moment. I've never been in this position, but now I see there can be safety in numbers.

As kids head out onto the dance floor to dance to the heavy beat music, we just stand there, watching.

Finally, the moment's over when Alex goes running into the crowd, pulling me and Jen with her. I laugh as I'm dragged onto the dance floor and start dancing with my friends.

It feels good. Surprisingly good.

We take turns gawking when Marissa and Brandon walk in. She doesn't even look our way, which is good. She's good at this faking thing. Guess she's been doing it for a while.

Everything has to seem normal, so our job right now is to have fun. The real mission doesn't start until a little later in the night. So we dance, and we laugh, and we have fun. Part of me is just pretending to complete the illusion and help Marissa, but it's not all fake. I'm actually having fun.

Alex messes up her hair by swinging her head around to every song. She's the kind of girl whose hair should always be down. It's so pretty anyway. Still, I can't help but give her a hard time.

"I put a lot of work into that!" I yell over the loud music.

She pulls out one of the bobby pins and flings it into the air.

After a few songs, I see Marissa and Brandon through the crowd, only a few random grinding dancers over. Brandon's hands are all over her. I hate the expression on her face, complete misery. There must have been a time when she loved him, wanted him, but that time is clearly long gone. That tends to happen when someone treats you like shit.

I don't know what Brandon deserves, but Marissa at least deserves better than this.

Marissa pushes through the crowd, and as she passes us, she stops to lean in and whisper in my ear, "The decorations are awesome." I'm careful not to smile at her kind comment, knowing Brandon needs to think it was something nasty. She gives me a wink and then pushes past us, pulling her boyfriend behind her. He gives me a smirk and a wink, and I shiver.

We stay and dance a little longer, and while this is fun, I'm starting to get restless. I want to get this over with.

"Want to get a drink?" I yell out to Alex and Jen, who both nod, and we head back up to the cafeteria. It's there that I see Jackson.

He's wearing black slacks, a white button-up, a checkered vest, and a bright green bow tie. Sticking to his too-attractive-for-true-geekiness geeky thing. It's weird, but it's so him. So Jackson.

He's with his goofy gamer friends. They're debating about something serious, but then again, knowing Jackson, it's probably about which food item or cartoon character is better. His head pops right up when I stop at the doorway though, his conversation forgotten, and we just stand there for a few seconds, watching each other.

I so wish I were with him tonight.

I shake my head. There's a reason I sent him away. Eventually, he'll find out the truth. And the closer we are, the more it'll hurt when he does. I could deal with it, but I'll do anything to save him from that pain.

There are a bunch of round tables covered in tablecloths

and little Eiffel Towers and candles in the center. We sit at one of them to catch our breath from all the dancing.

"The decorations turned out great, didn't they?"

I spin to see Jackson standing there, his hands in his pockets and a hopeful look in his eyes.

"They're amazing," I say.

Jen and Alex agree. Alex lifts up her cup and says, "Cheers!"

She's so weird sometimes. We all laugh politely, but there's nothing else to be said, so after another awkward moment, Jackson says, "I'll see you around," ending our conversation much too soon, and he heads back to the dance floor with his friends.

"Think it's almost time?" Jen asks as soon as Jackson is gone.

My eyes are still following Jackson, but I force myself to turn to Jen. "I hope so."

It's been about a half hour, enough for us to get kind of bored dancing, so maybe it's enough for Brandon, too. We head back into the gym and search through the crowd of packed bodies, hopping and bobbing and grinding to the heavy beats until we finally find them.

Marissa is dancing halfheartedly alone, eyeing up a blond girl now dancing with Brandon.

Yup, it's definitely time. I nod to Jen. She gets this look on her face like she's a lioness or something. Brandon is her prey. She hands me her phone and then pushes in.

I like this Jen. Powerful, confident, determined. I hope, after tonight, she'll be more like this. Happier, stronger.

Alex and I casually drift over to Marissa.

"Game on," she says.

I lean in and whisper to Alex, "You should probably get

going."

Alex nods and winks dramatically before pushing into the crowd toward the door. Jen has about ten minutes to get where she needs to get to. By the expression on Brandon's face, she might not need that long.

Marissa and I bob awkwardly and watch Jen work. She grabs Brandon's upper arm and pulls him down just enough to whisper in his ear. His eyebrows raise, confusion written on his face. Jen said she had this part under control, but I kind of wish I knew what she was saying. Last thing I want is for her to have to relive her own nightmare. But she was pretty damn adamant about being the one to take him down. I think she deserves the right. Even Marissa was okay with that.

The goal is to keep Marissa clean no matter what, just in case it doesn't work. I'll take the fall if I have to.

Jen manages to pull Brandon away from the dance floor and to a dark corner, then gets him talking about something. She's stalling, I know. We need to give Alex enough time to get to his house.

Marissa and I exchange a look and follow them, just far enough that we won't be noticed. Except someone notices.

"Hey!"

I spin around and nearly run into Jackson.

"Oh, hi!" I say.

"I just wanted to say…" He shifts on his feet, his eyes cast to the ground. Then he lifts his head and our eyes meet. My stomach flips. "You look really nice."

My lips twitch, fighting a smile. "Thanks. You, too."

It takes everything I have not to take his hand and go with him to the dance floor, where he could hold me, make me feel safe, wanted.

I glance over my shoulder to Marissa, who's watching me with impatience written all over her face. Right. Jen needs my help. I can't leave her to the wolves.

"I'm sorry. I'd love to talk and stuff but...I've got to..." How the hell do I explain this?

He takes a step back. "Yeah, no problem. See you around."

I take a step past him and then turn back, giving him a shy smile. Damn it.

I watch him walk away, back into the crowd. Once he's gone, I take in a deep breath and head back to finish what I started.

I check the phone, but no word from Alex yet.

Brandon already seems to be sweating this, running his hands through his hair and looking anywhere but at Jen. I take a step in front of Marissa, because I don't want him to see her watching. Then again, he'd probably think she's just jealous.

Jen looks at us over his shoulder and winks. We both stifle a laugh.

The phone in my hand vibrates with a message from Alex.

Talking to his mom now.

All of this is riding on Alex's ability to convince Brandon's mom of the sex tape on his computer and letting her in to delete it. We have a plan B, but I'd much rather not get into that one.

I make sure Brandon can't see me, and then I hold up the phone and wave it at her. She nods and pulls him out of the gym, and they walk down the hall to the nearest door outside. Marissa and I sneak down the hall after them.

"Keep out of sight," I whisper-yell at her. "Don't let him see you!"

"Shut up. I know what I'm doing!" she whisper-yells back.

Is this what they mean by frenemies? I ignore her defensiveness. That's just our dynamic. She knows the risks. She'll be careful.

We reach the end of the hall and stand next to the cracked door and listen to Jen and Brandon.

"Wow. It's so cold out here," she says.

"You kidding? It's blazing inside, this feels good."

"Give me your jacket then," she says playfully. I sneak a peek through the crack and watch him place his jacket over her shoulders.

"So what are you doing after the dance?" he asks her.

She casually reaches into the pockets of the jacket but comes away empty-handed. Strike one.

"Going home," she says, her voice flat. She's rocking back on her heels now, and I wonder if she's getting nervous.

"Can I come?" he asks.

Marissa pretends to stick her finger down her throat. I wonder if this is getting to her. Deep down, does she still care about Brandon? Does it sting every time he cheats on her?

It has to hurt. Maybe she'd still be with him if she had a choice. But there's no worse feeling in the world than feeling like someone's taken that choice away from you.

Tonight, we have to make this work and give her choice back to her. Back to Jen. Back to anyone Brandon would ever take that choice away from.

It's too quiet on the other side of the door. My heart pounds. I want to see what's going on, but I'm scared. I can't tell if he's still looking the other way.

But I have to take the risk, so I step over and peek through the cracked door. Brandon is leaning over her, pushing her toward the wall.

Not good. I know it's part of the plan, but it's all I can do not to run over and shove him off her.

"I know you're lying about the pregnancy thing. You just wanted to get close to me again, didn't you?" he says into her hair.

Damn. Telling him she's pregnant? That was pretty genius. But now what?

"No," she stammers, stumbling back, all confidence gone. "I'm telling the truth… I…you…"

He shrugs and leans into her, and when his back turns to me, I see it. His phone, tucked in the back pocket of his jeans.

Bingo.

I take a step forward. Enough of this. Time for a little improvisation. He won't make her feel weak again, not while I'm around.

"Hey, Jen, don't keep him all to yourself," I say with a light, flirty voice.

He looks up, interested. "The slut wants a piece?" He steps past Jen.

Good boy.

Just a few steps closer, buddy.

Perfect.

He's just inches from me now, and I stare up at his handsome face and smile. "Want to know what we do with guys like you in New York?" I ask him, still flirtatious. He raises his eyebrows, and I place my hands on his shoulders—

And with one quick motion, I push down as I thrust my knee up to his groin.

He groans and bends over. "You bitch," he says.

While he's bent over, struggling to contain the pain, I grab the phone from his pocket. I hold on to the phone for dear life and then grab Marissa by the hand and sprint down the hall and into the gym. We should be able to lose him long enough to delete the video before he finds us here.

Jen barely catches up before we push into the crowd of dancers and wonder what took her so long.

We push our way through the room and circle around the phone.

"Hurry," I say, then pull out Jen's phone and type a text message.

We have the phone. How's it going with you?

"I can't believe we did it," Marissa says triumphantly. "How's it going on their end? Did Alex do it?"

Only a few seconds pass before a reply finally comes from Alex, but it feels like forever.

His mom wants to hear it from Marissa.

I show the message to Marissa, who groans.

"I don't want anyone to know," she says.

What do I tell her? I had the same problem, and I chose to say nothing.

"What do you want to do?" I say.

She looks back and forth, then at me. "Let's do it. I won't be able to live with myself if he gets away with it. What if he does this to someone else?"

She starts forward, but I stand there, her words a heavy weight over me.

She turns back to me and says, "Come on."

I walk closer to her. The music is thumping so loud it's hard to talk to each other, let alone on the phone.

We'll have to find a way outside without Brandon finding us. That means splitting up, just for a minute. Long enough for him to be too busy with me to notice what they're doing.

"You and Jen go, I'll find him and distract him," I say.

I rush out of the gym, first hoping to catch sight of Brandon. He sees me, fire in his eyes, and I run down the hall, toward the door to the parking lot, hoping he'll follow me so Jen and Marissa can slip past and reach the lobby to make the call.

When I hear the heavy footsteps behind me, I rush faster, outside and into the parking lot.

The second I feel the cool air, I know I made a mistake. It's dark. I'm alone.

Even if it's just Brandon behind me, it's not like I'm exactly safe. So I keep rushing forward until I reach the brightest spot of the lot. All the kids are still inside, having the time of their lives. I should be inside.

I shouldn't be out here. But if I go back inside now, Brandon might reach Marissa before she can talk to his mom.

I stop to catch my breath, my chest heaving much harder than it should for how much I ran.

Screw this.

I turn—

And see a large figure in the shadows of the parking lot.

"Brandon?" I ask, my heart pounding. Hoping it's him and not someone else.

But I can't make out his face. Is it just me, or is that not a suit he's wearing? I'm imagining the ugly blue uniform, right?

The figure is tall. Brandon's tall, right? It's probably just him. Just Brandon. I can handle Brandon.

Then he calls my name, and a chill of the worst kind rushes through me. The kind that feels like a scream trapped inside.

Everything stops. Frozen.

That's not Brandon.

He comes forward, and I have nowhere to go but backward. Do I run and hide behind the cars? How long until he finds me? My feet feel cemented to their spot.

Now is not the time to panic, Anna!

"Exquisite," he says, slurring the name and making it sound even more disgusting than it already was.

"What do you want?" I spit.

"I told you I wasn't through with you. No one can keep me away from you. Not Luis. Not your new boyfriend." He tilts his head like a damn puppy dog, but I know he's anything but. Calling him a rat would be too kind to him and too mean to the rat.

"It's not a school night anymore, Sweet Pea."

I shake my head. "You won't have me again," I say. I wish I felt as confident as I sound.

He laughs. "Oh, I will. You've been a bad girl, Exquisite. But don't worry." He glances back to the school. "They'll all know your real name soon enough."

"What?" I ask.

"Unless you'd prefer to keep it between us." He grins. "But you have to stop running from the truth. It's who you are. No more pretending."

I shake my head. "It's not who I am anymore."

He laughs, like I'm a little child, then lunges at me.

I spin away, but he's too fast. His body slams into mine, and we both fall to the ground. Pain ricochets up my arm and head, making me dizzy, but I manage a scream. Not just a yell, but an animalistic scream that I swear should shatter the glass of the school. It doesn't.

My scream does nothing.

No one is coming.

He grabs my arms and pins them against the ground. Pins me.

"You can run from the cops," he says breathlessly. "You can run from your pimp, but you can't run from me."

"No!" I cry out. I can't go with him, I won't. I'd rather die now.

I claw at his face, tearing at anything I can get my nails into. Warm blood drips onto my face, but he doesn't stop pulling at my dress, doesn't even scream or groan.

Is this part of what he likes? Causing me pain? Forcing me to do what he wants?

Then I see the lights, hear the siren. I don't know how cops could be here so fast. How they could know I need help. A spotlight shines from the car and onto us. The janitor pauses. Through the bright light, a cop comes toward us.

Will they understand what happened? Or will it be like always? Will they blame me? Tell me I was asking for it?

The janitor's grip on my arm weakens a little as he looks up, surprised, and I manage to rip my arm free and push the base of my palm up to his nose. I hear a crack, a scream, and his blood splashes onto my arm. I spin away, but he grabs me.

"You tell them nothing. I have more. More I can tell them."

The cop comes to a stop in front of us. His face is obscured by the bright light.

"Step away from the girl."

I know that voice. He speaks with such confidence, such certainty, that a pulse of strength rushes through me.

"Officer, we were just—"

The figure doesn't let him finish. He punches the john in the face, which gives me a free moment, and I'm able to get away from him and stand beside my hero.

He's not a cop. It's Jackson.

"Get the hell out of here," he says.

He must have brought his father's cop car close and turned the siren on when he saw what was happening to me.

I take a few steps back, but I don't want to leave Jackson with the janitor.

The janitor chuckles as he realizes Jackson's real identity. "How cute, your boyfriend came to the rescue. Even after I told him the truth."

"Jackson, let's run. We can get away," I whisper, hoping he'll listen.

"No, I'm not letting him get away."

"Don't be stupid, boy." The janitor stands tall. "You can't compete with me."

He steps forward, and I know he's too big, too strong. I'm scared. Scared that he'll hurt Jackson. Scared he'll force me to admit to Jackson more than a hint of the truth. Scared that Jackson won't win this fight.

The janitor lunges at Jackson, and I yell, a desperate scream.

What do I do? Run for help? Join Jackson and fight the janitor?

Jackson takes a hit across his jaw, but he bounces back and tackles the janitor to the ground. They roll over each other, and then the janitor is on top of Jackson and raising his fist—

Someone reaches down and pulls the janitor off Jackson with more power and anger than I've ever seen, even from pimps. It's a man in a blue uniform. And not just any cop. It's Jackson's father.

"Get off my son!" He flings the janitor off Jackson, then pins him to the ground.

There are more red and blue lights, more cars, more men in uniforms. Everything happens so fast. Three men struggle with the janitor, and another rushes to help Jackson, who's bleeding from his lip but seems fine.

Then there's a crowd, kids from the dance filing out into the parking lot to watch the excitement.

"We had a deal, Exquisite! You owe me!" the janitor yells as he's wrestled and cuffed.

Two officers pull him toward a cop car.

Another to the side says, "You have the right to remain silent—"

"She's a whore!" the janitor yells. "I was just getting what I paid for!" He starts laughing as the cops shut the door on him.

I shiver and then collapse onto the ground, unable to stop the tears as they drift down my cheeks.

The police eventually come over to me, give me a blanket and ask if I'm okay, who they should call for me.

"My mom," I manage to squeak out.

Alex, Jen, and Marissa are the only faces I recognize in the crowd around me. I thought I understood them, but I can't read their expressions. After everything we went through together… Shit, was that just a little bit ago? I'd love to think my past doesn't make them hate me.

All I know is that everyone now sees me for who I really

am.

I don't expect them to understand. How could they?

Jackson stands beside me the entire time, and I can't even thank him for what he did, because I can barely keep up with the police questions. I'm not sure even I understand what I tell the police, but Jackson helps me to explain as much as he knows, and I guess what I say about the janitor makes enough sense, because finally they tell me it's okay. We're done for now. We can talk more later.

Jackson's dad doesn't seem too happy. His face is like cold stone, and then he rushes toward Jackson, and I almost leap forward to come between them, tell his father that it's not his fault. I can't stand him getting into trouble because of me.

But I find myself staring, surprised when Jackson's father wraps his arms around his son.

Finally, my parents come to pick me up and take me home. I wonder if they'll ever let me out of the house again after this. Guess I wouldn't mind if they didn't.

When we drive out of the school parking lot, there's still a crowd of about a hundred people, some parents, but mostly kids still in their homecoming finest. I see them whispering, some of them sad, some shocked, some excited, probably that they got to see something so dramatic in real life or that they'll have the best drama to talk about in school on Monday.

I can only imagine what they'll say. I don't know how much the witnesses heard, but I know it was too much, and soon the cops will know the full truth. Soon, they'll all hate me.

It's my fault for coming back here.

It's my fault for thinking I deserved a second chance.

CHAPTER THIRTY-THREE

When I finally make it home, my mom's worried gaze bores into me. My father shakes his head like he always knew I would end up in trouble. Like it was inevitable. It always is when I'm involved.

They talked to the cops, but they don't know the full truth. They know a man attacked me in the school parking lot after homecoming. They know Jackson tried to save me. They know the cops now have the man in custody.

But they don't know that this man wasn't just a creepy janitor. They don't know that I've slept with him before in New York and that he paid me. They don't know that's what he wanted from me now.

And it's probably best that I'm the one to tell them. I've lost every bit of power I thought I had. At least this way, I'm asking for whatever punishment I get.

I won't hesitate. I'll tell them before we even go inside.

But as soon as I'm out of the car, my mother wraps me in her arms and holds me all the way into the house. My father glances at us, his anger palpable, but my mother doesn't seem to care right now whether he's angry.

I want to stop her. I need to tell her what happened. She deserves the truth. But her arms around me turn me into a sobbing mess.

She helps me to my bedroom, like I can't walk or something. She does know I'm not injured, right? The blood on my arm is from the janitor. It's not mine.

"Lie down," she says. "Rest."

"Wait," I manage to say. "Mom. There's something I need to tell you, about tonight, about that man…"

She shakes her head and shushes me. "It doesn't matter, not right now. He's in custody, you're safe, and you need to sleep. We'll talk in the morning."

I swallow and let her tuck me in like I'm five years old, and then I let my body collapse in exhaustion.

As I'm falling asleep, I hear my parents whisper-arguing about letting the dog in to sleep next to me. Apparently my mother wins, because a few minutes later Zara is licking my face and trying to jump up on the bed with me.

She ends up jumping up by my feet, and I scoot to make enough room for her. She lays her head against my thigh, and that's the last thing I remember until morning.

When I finally wake up, I sneak down the hall to find my mother. She's rolling some dough behind the counter but looks up and smiles when she sees me. I don't know where my dad is, but it's better this way. I'll tell her first. And maybe then, when I tell *him*, it won't be so bad.

"Hi, sweetheart, how are you feeling?"

I attempt a smile. "There's something I need to tell you."

She nods and puts down the roller, then wipes her hands on the towel by the sink. "What do you need to tell me?"

"It's about last night. About that man."

I need it to be me that she hears it from first.

"Okay, sweetie," she says, sitting down beside me, brushing my messy hair down calmingly.

"He wasn't just the janitor. He…he was one of the men from New York."

She pauses, and I can feel her entire body tense up. "You mean…"

I nod, tears rushing to my eyes.

She takes her arm from around me and presses it to her mouth. Her eyes squeeze shut and push a few tears down her cheeks.

"I'm sorry, Mom," I whisper, but she doesn't respond. Maybe it's the first time that she realizes that I'll never be normal, not really. Because the horrible things in my past will never really go away. There will always be something coming back to slap me back to reality.

I'm a whore. That's all I'll ever be, no matter how hard I try to pretend—

Someone grabs me violently by the arm and whips me around. I face my father, terror rising in my throat.

"What did you just say?"

"Daddy?" I manage to get out through a sob.

"Martin!" my mom yells.

"You're telling me you *brought* one of those men back with you?"

"No…" I murmur, but there's no denying it.

My mother rushes forward. Zara barks and growls from the hall, and my father shoves me from him. I nearly fall into the corner of the wall.

"Martin, stop!" my mother yells again.

He pauses for only a moment, as though shocked that she said anything. "Don't you realize what she's done? I warned her what would happen. I warned *both* of you."

Zara's barking continues as he approaches me. As he unbuckles his belt.

I wince, already preparing for the blow.

He curls the end of the belt around his hand. "You brought this on yourself."

He raises the belt—

My mother screams and charges into him. She's not nearly strong enough to overpower him, but he's taken off guard, and he falls into the wall.

"Don't you touch her," my mother says just before he slams her into the wall and they both fall to the ground. He presses her down by her upper arms and pauses, looking at his wife openmouthed. He definitely didn't expect his obedient wife to fight back, like ever. He pulls back after a second and grabs the belt, tightening the end of the belt around his hand. "You brought this on yourself."

It happens so fast that I can't stop him, can't step in for her the way she did for me. The belt whips through the air and lands on my mother's forearm—which covers her face just in time—with a sickening crunch. Zara jumps forward, snarling and snapping at his feet. He kicks her away. I scream and throw all my weight into my father. Before I even know it, he slams me into the wall, and my head hits with a bang and a flash of white-hot pain.

Zara barks again and leaps at him. Her big jaws just barely miss his forearm as he twists out of the way. She stops and stands between me and my red-faced father. She barks at him, threatening him to try again.

"Down, Czar!" he commands, but Zara doesn't even flinch. Her bark turns to a snarl, and my father clenches his fist.

Then the doorbell rings.

Everything freezes.

My father pauses and looks to the door. My mother is still on the ground, tears in her eyes.

"Nora, get the door."

She wipes her face, then nods and pulls herself up to answer the door. She doesn't bother fixing her hair, and I wonder if that's on purpose. Zara licks my hand to see if I'm okay, her eyes still studying my father. I pet her head. She proved herself today.

"Hi. Are you Mrs. Rodriguez?" I hear a deep voice ask. "I just came by to see if Anna's doing okay."

There's a pause at the door, and my father and I look at each other. He waves his finger over his mouth, a gesture to stay quiet.

I wait for my mother to assure them everything is fine, but we can't take visitors.

This is just a temporary pause before I get my punishment.

I used to think it was punishment for being me. But now I see the rage in him. The desperate desire for control he'll never have. I couldn't control whether the janitor came for me. I couldn't control whether Luis wanted to sell me. And I can't control whether my dad wants to hit me.

"Not a word," my father whispers to me.

He stands to the side of the room, out of sight of Jackson's dad but close enough to hear whatever my mom says.

"Anna's…" Her voice trembles. She looks over and sees my dad, who wags his finger, and she gives a quick intake of breath. "She's not really up for a visit right now."

"Mrs. Rodriguez, is everything okay?"

She nods quickly. Too quickly, it seems to me, and Jackson's father must see it, too. He glances down, takes in my mother's full appearance. And that's when he notices the still-fresh mark on her arm from my father's belt.

"Mrs. Rodriguez, if there's anything wrong, all you have to do is ask me to come inside."

My mom looks at my father, and I think it will be like always. But then she looks at me, and her face hardens.

"Please come inside," she says. "My husband is—"

My father registers the betrayal she's about to commit and grabs her by the arm. "You bitch," he says, pulling her inside—

Jackson's father moves like lightning. He grabs my father, removes him from my mom, and pins him against the wall.

"You do realize I can arrest you for domestic violence, right?" he yells at my father.

"I wasn't doing anything!" My father's yells are muffled by the wall.

Is Jackson's father always like this? That quick to act? Or had he already suspected my father was abusive? Maybe all this time I thought we were so good at hiding who we really were, but the truth was obvious to everyone but us.

"Nora, do you want me to take him?" he asks.

She swallows and looks at me. Then she turns back and nods.

We watch as my father is cuffed and thrown into the back of Jackson's father's cop car. I'm not sure what to think about this. Does my father deserve to be arrested? I don't know.

As soon as the cop car is out of sight, I say, "Dad was right. It was my fault."

My mother turns and looks me in the eyes for a second. Then she wraps her arms around me again and squeezes me tighter than I've ever been hugged. I hug her back, even though I'm not really sure what it means.

She pulls away, not to retreat but to put her hands around my face. "Don't you ever say that again. You didn't ask for this." Her lips quiver. "You only wanted to be loved." She pulls me back into her arms. "I'm sorry, Anna. I should have been there for you sooner." Her voice falls apart, a quaking mess, and she sobs into my shoulder. "I should have done something. I should have…" She pauses, then simply says, "I love you." She presses her mouth into my hair and whispers it over and over again.

I love you.

I love you.

I love you.

And for the first time, I believe her.

My memories of New York will always be there, and they might always be stronger. But today, I sleep better than I ever have. My brain is on overload, shutting down to protect itself—it's about time.

A couple of times, my mom knocks on the door to let me know someone called for me. First Jackson, just to let me know he hopes I'm okay. Then Marissa, Alex, and Jen.

Oh, crap. I hope they're okay. I hope the plan went okay. I hope Marissa is free of Brandon. I hope Jen no longer feels afraid.

I hope they're all okay, even if I won't ever be.

I don't wake up in time for school the next day, but again, my mother says nothing. She just lets me sleep.

I put Zara outside, because I'm pretty sure I'd be torturing her if I didn't get her to the bathroom, then I head back to my room.

I'm not sure how much longer I'll stay like this, avoiding everyone. A few times, my mom lets me know my friends called to check on me, but I'm not ready to talk to them. I'm not ready to face their reactions to the truth.

The next day, the phone rings around noon, and my mother answers close enough to my bedroom door that I can hear her talking.

"She's fine. She's in her room."

My first thought is of Jackson, but he'd be at school now.

Then there's a light knock.

"I don't want to talk to anyone," I say, even though I'm not sure that's true.

"It's Sarah."

I open my mouth to yell something back, but that's not what I expected to hear, so I answer the door. "Sarah?"

Why do I feel like it's been years since I've seen her? It's only been a few weeks.

My mother hands me the phone.

"Hello?"

"Anna!" She sounds tired but happy it's me. "I heard about

what happened. Are you all right?"

"I'll live. I always do."

"I'm on my way there if you're up for a visit. We're going to have a long talk. It's been too long. I should be there in less than an hour."

"Oh," I say awkwardly. "You're already on your way?"

"Yup."

"Okay," I say, secretly happy she'll be here. As much as shutting myself off from the rest of the world is effective, I'm lonely and bored and starving. And at least I know Sarah doesn't hate me for the truth.

"Are you hungry? Would you like to get dinner when I get there so we can talk? Or is your mother cooking?"

"Um, I don't think so. Dinner would be okay, I guess." I don't tell her that I haven't eaten in days, practically.

"Good, be ready in about forty-five minutes."

My mother is very tense when I hand the phone back to her. There's more than one thick line on her forehead.

"Sarah's coming. She's going to take me to dinner. That okay?"

"Oh." She straightens. "Do you want to go?"

The question knocks me for a loop. What do I want? The very idea feels weird.

"Yeah. It would be nice to see her."

"Then you should go. Maybe she can help you talk about some of these things." She looks away, then turns back and quickly adds, "If that's what you want."

I go back to my room and search through my clothes for something to wear. Is it better to wear something Sarah bought me or some of my new things? I go for a happy medium, one of the tops my mom bought with a sweater Sarah bought over it.

Then I stand in the kitchen for a moment, trying to think of something else to do while waiting for Sarah.

I do want to talk to her. I need to. But what will I say? She's been okay with the truth so far, but there are some things not even she knows about.

Finally the doorbell rings.

My mother answers the door, and I notice she's put on fresh makeup. She looks much better now than she did when the call came. In fact, she looks better than she ever has. I don't know when my dad's coming back, but maybe that doesn't matter. Today, Mom seems truly alive.

Sarah and my mother exchange a polite greeting, then Sarah asks me if I'm ready. I nod and walk out with her, sending a smile to my mother as we leave.

The car ride is silent except for when Sarah asks me what I want to eat. The rest of the ride, I just watch the houses as they fly by. We end up going to Friendly's, which is a cheesy little restaurant. It's the place you take your little brats after soccer games, but it's good food, so whatever.

When we sit down, we don't start talking immediately. She orders some coffee, and I get a Coke. Then, once our drinks arrive, she starts asking me questions. Lots of questions. They start off small, simple.

"How has everything been?"

"What's your favorite subject in school?"

"I see you got a new top."

But when they don't get much out of me, she goes straight to the real things I knew she'd want to talk about.

"Your mother mentioned your father's not home right now."

I look at the table. "Is that all she said?"

"She said he has some problems. And the police had to get involved."

"Is that what she said? That they're his problems?"

She shrugs. "Yeah."

"What did you tell her? You've always got something to say." I know how harsh I sound, and I want to say I'm sorry, but she doesn't seem to take offense.

"I told her if she wants some help, I can put her in contact with a therapist. Someone to help her. You. Your whole family, if that's what all of you want."

"Great," I say. "More talking."

"What about you? How do you feel about him leaving?"

"I'm glad he's gone."

"Because of what happened after homecoming?"

"You know about that, huh?" I say, looking down at my sandwich. I guess I knew she would. That's why she came, right? That why I *wanted* her to come. It's just that now, I sorta wish we could skip that part of the conversation.

She nods, a sign for me to continue.

"Yes, I went to homecoming and had fun, up until the part when the janitor attacked me, and now everyone thinks I'm still a whore, and he came after me because I was asking for it, or something."

I can see the concern on Sarah's face, but she stays calm. "But you didn't. "

It's not a question, exactly, but she's clearly asking me to defend myself. Like she knows the answer, but she needs to hear me say it.

I swallow. "No. I didn't."

"The police have looked into his history. He's got a background of violent behavior, but nothing that indicated why he would risk coming after you where he works. It's unusual. Most of the time, pedophiles who actively abuse children have a history. Prior offenses. But he flew under the radar. To think that he was a janitor at a high school the entire time…"

It's now or never. "He wasn't just the janitor," I say.

She puts her hands around her coffee cup, like she's suddenly cold and needs to absorb its warmth. "Who was he?"

"He used to see me in New York. He used to…you know. That's why my dad was so angry. It's like I brought him back with me."

Sarah's gaze doesn't break, but she bites her lip awkwardly, thinking.

"How did you feel about seeing him here?" she eventually asks me.

"What do you mean, 'How did I feel?' He *attacked* me. What don't people get about this? They think I asked for that? That I asked for all of this?"

I know she doesn't mean any of that, but the words are out of me before I can stop them. Because people do blame me. Or they will. As soon as they know the truth.

"Some people might think it's your fault," Sarah says calmly. "I don't. But I need to make sure I understand it completely. I can't keep you safe until I know if this man was a friend or someone you might want to protect."

"Protect? He's disgusting. I'd lock the key myself if I could."

She reaches over the table and rests her hand on top of mine. "Actually, you can. If you really mean it."

"What?"

"If he was one of the men who paid Luis to sleep with you, your testimony can put him in jail."

I look up. "What about Luis? Won't they use my testimony against him, too?"

She takes a deep breath. "The way the system works is they need evidence to put people in prison. There's a chance they'll both go free without your testimony."

My hands start to shake. "Both of them? Even the janitor?"

She holds on tighter to my hand. "Even the janitor."

"But he came after me at school. Everyone saw it." For better or worse.

"Yes. They saw him come after you. But that doesn't prove that he was going to rape you. And it doesn't prove that he ever did before." She takes a deep breath. "It's the same for Luis. We've found that we don't have any proof that he's solicited sex for you, that he was your pimp. He's saying that the men you slept with, well, it was all your choice."

I look back and forth. It's like I'm pressed against a wall, nowhere to go. My choice? He's saying it was my choice for all of those men? All of the johns. Including the janitor.

I had to sleep with those men. We needed the money. But I didn't ask for the janitor to become obsessed with me. I didn't ask for him to come after me now.

How am I supposed to explain that to anyone? They'll tell me I asked for it. If I didn't want him to come after me, I never should have said yes. Not even once.

Luis knew that. When he saw what happened, how the janitor beat me up, he threw the janitor out and told him to never come back. Doesn't that count for something?

"Can't someone else testify against him?" I whisper.

"If you won't testify, they'll probably ask the janitor to. They'll offer him a deal. Admit his guilt, but get reduced time in jail for coming out against Luis and telling everyone what happened to you."

"So what does this mean? That I'll get in trouble?"

"No, no. You've done nothing wrong. You were—and are still—under eighteen and under the age of consent in New York. The trouble is, or should be, all on the men who've had any sexual contact with you. It's just that we can't give them justice without a little help."

The waitress comes back now to see if we want to order some food, and I use the time to let what Sarah's asking settle over me.

She wants me to testify against Luis.

My heart is pounding; my eyes are wide. I don't know what to do, what to say.

Sarah asks the waitress to give us some time alone. When the waitress is gone, Sarah turns back to me.

"Anna, listen."

I stand up and look at her. I like Sarah, a lot. But I love Luis, or I did, I don't know. He hurt me when he threw me out. But that doesn't erase everything he did to take care of me. He was good at first. He cared at first. Surely everything that came later doesn't erase how we were at the beginning.

I can feel the tears welling in my eyes.

She grabs my arm softly, which makes me feel like it's defeating the purpose. "No one is going to make you do anything, I promise."

She lets go of my arm, but I don't move. Finally I sit back down, but I'm still breathing heavily. Nothing about this is okay.

"It doesn't sound like you have a problem putting the janitor in jail," she says.

"He deserves it," I say.

"Okay. Why is Luis so different?"

I open my mouth to speak, but I close it. Now I'm afraid of what I'll say. If I say the wrong thing, they'll use it against me. Against him. He'll go to jail.

The only way to make her understand is to tell her the truth. Even if she'll find it impossible to believe.

"Luis was my boyfriend, not my pimp."

"But he sold you to other men, made you do…"

"No! He never made me do anything."

"But he pushed you."

"Please," I say, squeezing my eyes tightly shut. "Stop, I can't do this."

"Okay, I'm sorry," she says in a whisper. "I don't mean… I'm not trying to hound you, or question you. I just want to understand, Anna. The way I see it, he used you. You were just a child. I wish you could see that."

I shake my head. That was always the problem—everyone saw me as just a child. Luis was the only one who treated me the way I wanted to be treated.

"I'm going to ask you one last thing, Anna, and you don't have to answer if you don't want to."

When I don't speak she takes it as consent. "Did you want to sleep with those men?"

My heart drops. No. I want to yell it, scream it. *NO, NO, NO, NO, NO!*

But I don't. I can't.

I get up and walk out into the parking lot alone.

CHAPTER THIRTY-FOUR

I'm quiet when I walk into the kitchen, and I'm surprised when my mother isn't there. Zara stands at the glass door, watching me, so I slide open the door to let her in. She sniffs at my feet, her little stump of a tail wagging eagerly. I pat her head absently, knowing that's not the kind of attention she's looking for. I'm just not able to give her anything more right now.

It feels very different here today. The house is quiet, still. Like it's waiting. Holding its breath to see how the shit settles after hitting the fan yesterday. Zara eventually gives up with me and walks across the room to sniff her empty food bowl.

I take a step toward the hall, figuring I might as well retreat to my bedroom where at least things are the same kind of weird they've been for the last few weeks, but then my mother emerges from the hall looking tired.

"Hi, sweetheart," she says.

I smile. "Hi."

"I made some brownies earlier. Want some?"

I'm really not hungry, but for some reason I nod. Her eyes grow brighter, and I'm suddenly glad I didn't say no.

I sit at the counter and watch as she microwaves two huge pieces and pours two glasses of milk. She sets one plate and one glass in front of me, and I take in a deep breath and watch as she takes a small dainty bite of her brownie with a fork.

She looks up at me. "Are you all right? Everything okay with Sarah?"

I nod, not because things are actually okay—nothing is okay right now—but because there's nothing she can do, and I just don't want to talk about it.

"Is it about your father?" she asks me.

This time I look up and shrug.

"I keep running it through my mind," she tells me, dropping her fork onto her barely touched plate. "What happened. Why. What I could have done better. Did I make the right choice? I don't know if I made the right choice, having him arrested." She's talking so fast, her bottom lip trembling. I'm not even sure she's talking to me anymore. She's just talking. Thinking out loud.

It's the first time she's ever opened up to me like this.

"You did the right thing," I say.

She looks up, blinking back tears. "He had his accountant bail him out of jail. Now he's at a hotel."

I pause, knowing she's scared. Scared of not being the perfect trophy wife anymore, and I have no idea what to say to make it better.

"I'm glad he's not here."

She blinks, her face blank. "Me, too." Then her shoulders relax, like a weight was lifted from her. She smiles, her eyes still filled with tears.

So she wasn't afraid of losing her marriage or image…she

was afraid of admitting she's glad about it.

We quietly finish our snack, not knowing what else to say.

Finally, I stand. "I'm going to go for a walk."

"Okay, be careful," she says, barely looking up from the sink as she scrubs her few dishes absently.

I walk out into the brisk autumn air. Fallen leaves float past, and I try to clear my mind as I make my way down the street. I need to think about something good. Something that's not royally screwed up.

My feet move on their own, and I try not to think about where I'm going or why. Not until I'm standing in front of Jackson's door. And then I realize how stupid this is. I have absolutely no clue what I could possibly say to him now.

I just know that I need to say…something. Anything. I need to hear his voice.

My breathing quickens as I fight with myself. Knock on the door and face my worst fear and greatest hope—or walk away a coward. My stomach clenches, a sour feeling filling every vein.

I knock on the door and it swings open in just a few seconds. I swear, if it had taken any longer, I'd have turned and run. I look up at the tall, muscular figure that is Jackson's father and press a hand to my stomach, willing myself not to throw up on his doorstep. I keep my eyes steady and watch his face for signs of hatred, disgust. But Jackson's father's eyes are full of concern, sympathy.

"Looking for Jackson?" he asks nicely when I don't speak.

I manage a nod.

He smiles and turns away. "Jackson! You have a visitor." He turns back. "It's nice to see you again, Anna."

I blink, unsure of what to make of such kindness. Is he just being polite? He can't possibly be okay with his son hanging around with a hooker, can he? Especially after the danger I put him in?

After a few seconds, Jackson jogs down the steps and freezes when he sees me. For one second, all my fear, all my shame, is washed away. Whatever happens now, it was all worth it for the few weeks I spent with Jackson. To have someone like him on my side.

But then I notice the look on his face. He's not the same lighthearted boy I remember. His face is heavy, darker, somehow.

My heart stops.

There's a blue mark across his eyebrow and a scab forming over his lip, and as much as I hate seeing him hurt, that's not what stabs me in the gut.

That look, the look that I loved from the very first time I met him, the look that made me feel brand-new—it's gone. Replaced by something dark, and I can't tell what it is, but I'm afraid it's the emotion I've been dreading all along.

Disgust.

Oh God.

I knew Jackson would be mad at me. I knew things would never really be the same. But I wasn't prepared for this. Seeing it. Seeing him change. The boy in front of me isn't the same boy with the Weedwacker. This is a boy who's been ruined.

I ruined him.

Shit. What do I say to him?

He doesn't speak, he doesn't make it easy on me the way he usually does, always knowing exactly what to say.

"I…I just wanted to see you…"

He steps forward. "Are you okay?" he asks, his voice lighter than I would have expected.

I shrug and take a step back. "I guess…." I pause and look up at him again. This time all I see is confusion on his face. "I just wanted to say that I'm sorry."

"For what?"

"For homecoming. For the janitor. For not being who you wanted me to be."

Tears fill my eyes, and my voice cracks. His voice is light as he speaks, not harsh like I'd expected. Not angry like he should be.

"You don't get it, Anna. Those aren't things you should be sorry for. You couldn't help them. I'm not mad at you for having to save you from some dirtbag."

I shift on my feet, not understanding what he means.

"I'm angry because you lied to me." His voice is harder now. "You looked me in the eyes and told me lie after lie."

My blood turns ice cold, rushing through every inch of me. He's right. My crimes are a whole lot more than just what I did in the past, or even putting him in danger the way I did…

I lied to him. Even when I knew that was the one thing that would really hurt him.

"Do you have any idea how stupid I feel? I stood up for you, over and over. I believed you. I told you everything. I *trusted* you with everything. And you…you…" He shakes his head.

I swallow and look down at the ground. "I'm sorry," I whisper, then turn and sprint down the street, away from him. Away from the hope he gave me. I can't hear anymore, not right now. I can't face this. I'm not strong enough.

I rush all the way back to my house, but instead of going

back inside, I hop the fence and walk through the backyard. I run my hand along the prickly wooden fence that once separated me from the innocent suburban boy who believed I was normal.

Like my mother said, I don't know if I chose right. Back then he gave me hope. A hope I desperately needed. But it was false. Always just pretend.

Because what if I hadn't lied to him? Would he have even taken a second look at me? Would I even have those amazing memories to hold on to if I had told him who I was right up front?

Could Jackson Griffin have ever loved a hooker?

CHAPTER THIRTY-FIVE

The next morning, I decide it's time to go back to school. I can't keep running. I've got to face the truth. Face the hate.

Sarah stays in town overnight, and my mom's fine with her driving me to school the next day.

I'm scared of seeing Jackson again. The way he looked at me yesterday… What if he never forgives me?

If I thought the rumors and looks and whispers were bad before, they were nothing compared to this. It always felt like every set of eyes turned toward me before, that the world stopped. But it was just a feeling.

Now it actually does.

They all stop, literally, and watch me pass through the hallway. Even the teachers look at me with worried expressions.

News is out. I'm the town whore. Maybe I should take a bow.

Every class is torture. I can't even focus on learning, because all I can hear are the rumors.

"That's the whore. Yeah, I'm not even kidding, she really was."

It makes me want to scream out, tell them it's true and to grow up and get their own lives. Maybe I should make an announcement.

Hello, everyone. It's me, Anna. You know, the whore? Yeah, it's true. Get over it now, please? I'd love to move on now, thanks…

Then lunch comes. I consider skipping it altogether, but somehow over the last few days, my appetite has come back. I get my lunch and find a table toward the back that's mostly empty.

But then a tray clinks down in front of me and I look up to see Alex.

"Mind?" she asks.

I smile back. It's small and sad, but it's real. So I guess that's pretty good.

It's quiet for a moment, awkward. I wish she'd ask me something ridiculous, like which was better on a soft pretzel, mustard or cheese? She doesn't. Instead she looks right to the elephant in the room. "So. Homecoming."

I blink and watch as she shoves a huge piece of cookie into her mouth.

"Yeah. That was fun, huh?"

She looks around for a second, checking out all the eyes watching us.

"I did want to ask, how did everything go, you know, with Brandon?"

Her eyes grow wide. "That part actually was awesome. First Mr. Shelf slammed him into a locker when he tried to hit Marissa after she told him what we'd done. He flipped out, royally. We found out later that his dad flew home early from his business trip and yanked Brandon out of school. Word is his parents are sending him to military school. Good-bye football scholarship. Good-bye dreams of fame and sports stardom."

"Military school?" I think of the janitor. I think of Luis. I think of my father. "They didn't arrest him?"

Alex shakes her head, and now a flash of anger crosses her face. "No. They should. But at least he didn't totally get away with it."

"Well, that's good, I guess. Too bad I had to go and ruin our celebration, huh?"

"You ruined it? By what, just being you?"

I shrug. "Yeah, kinda."

"You're the only reason it happened in the first place. Marissa would still be pinned under that dick if you hadn't put it all together. You're a hell of a lot stronger than you think, Anna."

I take a deep breath. "I don't feel very strong."

Alex nudges my shoe with hers and smiles. "Life's job is to sit around and wait for the best opportunity to kick us in the balls. Our job is to get up and kick back. You helped Marissa do that. Now it's your turn."

My lips actually curl into an almost kind of smile. Life advice from Alex is much better than I expected.

Jen walks up and sits next to me without a word. I was her friend when no one else was; guess she's returning the favor. It does feel good to not be so alone. But the stares, the whispers, still close in on me.

"Besides, the only people who care about that shit don't matter," Alex says, winking at Jen.

I look to the empty seat at my right.

"He'll come around," Jen says.

My stomach twists. No one else speaks for a while. We munch on our food and listen to voices ringing around us. I don't hear anyone talking about me right now—there are too many voices for that—but I'm sure they are.

The question is, how in the world am I supposed to stand up for myself like Alex said? The janitor's gone, but the real enemy, the one that's haunted me every step of the way, still lives inside me. And it always will until I find the courage to face my fear.

I jump when a third tray clinks down. I look up to see Jackson. I smile at him, but he doesn't smile back. He just looks at me, like he's still trying to make sense of our conversation yesterday. Of all of this.

Well, that makes two of us.

A passing senior coughs out "whore" as he passes us, and I freeze. Seriously? We're back to that?

Jackson's out of his seat and about to go after the guy, but I take his arm, and my touch seems to shock him out of it. He still looks pissed, though.

"He can't talk to you like that," he says without looking at me.

I shrug. "He's just telling the truth."

Jackson glances at the rest of the group, not like he's looking to them for backup, more like he's making sure he has everyone's attention. Then he looks back at me.

"You're not a whore," he says. "I don't care what the janitor said."

He doesn't get it. But it's nice of him to stick up for me.

"Let him go," I say. "People can say whatever they want."

Jackson sits back down, and everyone at the table falls back into that thick silence.

"So are we going to ignore this the rest of our lives?" Alex says just before shoving a piece of a Fudge Round into her face. "I mean, that's okay if we are. I just want to be clear."

I actually smirk. Leave it to Alex to be the blunt one.

"Ask, if you want to know," I say in a flat voice.

Jackson meets my eyes. He knows some of the truth. But he doesn't know it all.

"The prostitute thing," Alex says. "You did really do it, right? 'Cause we heard the guy that attacked you, and it—" She stops, like she ran out of words or something.

I nod, but then I shrug. "It's complicated."

Jackson wants the truth, right? I guess it's time he got a bigger piece. That they all got a bigger piece. If there's one thing I've learned, it's that eventually the truth will come out. Hiding it just delays the inevitable.

"I don't understand what the big deal is," Alex says. "Isn't it just sex? What's wrong with you making a little money?"

"It's not just sex," I say.

An odd look crosses both of their faces. Jackson is still as stone. Did they expect me to defend it? Maybe. It's not like I've been afraid to call myself a whore. I guess they thought I was proud or something.

When they say nothing, I continue.

"When you're a prostitute, it's not like you get to choose who you do it with. Imagine being forced to do it"—I rack my brain for the most disgusting person in school—"with Mr. Pickering," I say. He's an old, fat math teacher I've seen walking the halls. "Then Mr. Schueller." Our science teacher. "Then Mrs.

Timmins." Our creepy gym teacher. "All in one night."

"Ew."

"Sex isn't simple. Not when you're a prostitute," I say, no longer looking at them. I stare out into the sea of teenage heads around me. "Even if you did it with just attractive men, you lose everything you are. You have no choices, and everyone sees you as sex, nothing more."

Apparently I'm on a roll. The words just fall out of my mouth, things I didn't even know I was thinking. They all stare like I've just grown another head and they want to study it.

"You become nothing. Because that's the thing about sex—it's part of you. Giving it away for the wrong reasons, against your will…it changes you. Not always for the better. Every time you do that, you lose a part of yourself until…you have nothing left."

No one speaks, and I look down at my hands. They're shaking, just a little.

"I have nothing left," I whisper.

They still don't speak. Jackson looks at me, but I can't read him anymore. I can't tell if he's furious at finding out the whole truth. I can't tell if he pities me. I can't tell if he hates me.

I take a bite of my gooey mac and cheese and then take a sip of juice.

"Then why would you do it?" Jen asks quietly.

Jen. After what Brandon did to her, she's probably the one who knows what I went through. But it's hard to tell how much she understands when I barely get it myself, and I'm the one who lived it.

How do I explain that I didn't choose it? That I didn't know how to say no? That I did it for Luis when I won't talk about him?

Does Luis even understand what he did to me?

I open my mouth to speak, but I don't know what else to say. And honestly, do I want to stick around and see them realize they shouldn't be friends with me? They will. Now that they have a taste of who I really am.

"I have to go," I blurt out, and then I walk out alone. I go outside to the picnic area, and thankfully since it's about thirty degrees, no one else is out here.

"Hey."

I whip around to see Jackson, his arms crossed.

"You okay?" he asks.

"Not really, no. How about you?"

He shrugs. "Not really."

He takes a step forward, then seems to understand that I'm about to say something and need a minute to get up the nerve.

Finally, I ask, "Do you hate me?"

He sits down next to me. "Of course I don't hate you."

"Even after I lied to you? Ever after you heard the kind of things I did?"

He joins me, shivering, but sits there with me. "I wish you'd told me the truth. Wish you'd trusted me with it."

I shake my head. "I couldn't, Jackson. I was so scared. How could I tell someone like you all the horrible things I've done?"

"Someone like me?"

"So good. You're too good for me."

He laughs. "That's definitely not true."

"If I told you that I was a prostitute…you would have run away from me."

"Don't think that. I mean, sure, it's crazy to even consider, but…I would have still been your friend. Or whatever we are."

"But I lied to you. And after everything you said about your mom…" I look down at the wooden table, handwritten notes scrawled all over it.

"Anna, I hate myself because I never got the chance to help my mom. She wouldn't let me. And I hate that you wouldn't let me help you. But I would never hate her no matter how many lies she told…and I will never hate you." He straightens his shoulders. "I'm just glad I followed you outside at the dance. If I hadn't…I don't want to think what he would have done to you."

After a moment, I ask, "You don't think I deserved it?"

"Are you serious?" I don't move, don't look. He puts his hand on mine. "Anna." When I look up, he's waiting for me to meet his eyes, so intense he actually looks angry. "No one deserves that."

Strangely enough, I believe him. Maybe that makes me stupid, or naive, but maybe that's okay for once. He chose to believe in me. Maybe now I need to believe in him.

"Telling the truth is harder than it sounds," I say, and I hope it doesn't sound like an excuse. I know I was wrong but I'm just not sure what I could have done any differently.

"I wanted to sleep with her," he says.

"Liz?"

He nods. "I just wasn't ready. And I guess I didn't mean enough to her to wait until I was ready, too."

I put my hand in his, intertwining my fingers in his gently. I've always wondered what really happened. The full story. But he held it back until now. I don't know what I did to deserve his trust, but maybe that's not the point. Maybe we can trust each other because we choose to be worthy of each other right now. One step at a time.

"If I tell you the truth now, will you hate me? Do you even want to hear it?"

He shakes his head. "I'll never hate you. And I won't lie, I'm scared. But yeah, I want to hear it, because otherwise, I'll always wonder. I'll never understand unless you tell me, and neither will they." He points into the lunchroom, where—I have to laugh seeing their faces up against the window—Alex, Jen, and Marissa are looking out at us.

The bell rings, but Jackson doesn't move, and neither do I.

"They want me to testify," I whisper.

He takes a deep breath. "Against that man?"

"No. I mean, yes." Here it comes. The big one. "But someone else, too."

"Who?"

"A man I lived with… He was my boyfriend." I swallow. "He was my pimp." The word feels so disgusting coming from my mouth. I hate it. I hate myself.

But I don't see hate in Jackson's expression, and there's some comfort in knowing that as much as the lies hurt him—maybe *because* they hurt him—he's ready for the truth, whatever it is.

He squeezes my hand. "And you don't want to testify against him?"

"I don't know. I mean, it's complicated. He helped me. I know he hurt me, but if not for him, I'd probably have been dead. How can I do that to him?"

Jackson winces, but he's calm. "You wouldn't be doing anything to him. That's not how court cases work."

"What do you mean?"

"They'll decide if he broke the law. They'll decide if he's supposed to go to jail. Not you. All they want is for you to tell the truth. I know it's scary, but it'll hang over your head forever if you don't."

"But won't it hang over my head forever if I do?"

He shakes his head slowly. "The truth is the only thing that sets you free. There are repercussions, sure, but you won't be trapped anymore. You'll be free."

I blink. Freedom. That's what I've always wanted. But will testifying against Luis really free me? I think about what it would be like to see him again. To face him.

I'm scared. Terrified. But I realize it's something I have to do. I'll never get the closure I need without it. I'll never be free of Luis.

After we head back into school, I tell Jackson I'll talk to him later. Then I pull out my phone and dial Sarah's number.

"Anna?"

She must hear me breathing, because she waits for me to speak.

"I'll speak…at Luis's trial."

"Oh, Anna. That's terrific. But I want you to know, if you're not comfortable with this, you don't have to. We'll figure something else out."

"But I want to."

"What?" It's the first time I've heard her sound this surprised. She's always so…calm.

"I want people to hear my story. I need to face them. To face him."

Jackson's right. Testifying doesn't have to mean condemning Luis. I'm just there to tell the truth.

CHAPTER THIRTY-SIX

I get a text the morning of the trial from Jackson.

Good luck.

It's small, but it's enough. Enough to give me a pulse of strength, just for a moment. It's an odd feeling, but those pulses have been coming more often.

Everyone knows today is the day. For the past week, the trial seemed to be all anyone talked about. Apparently everyone wants to hear my story.

I dress in an outfit Sarah picked out for me. Most of it is new. It's much nicer than the clothes she bought me when we first met. It's a pretty pink sweater that comes up past my collarbone, a pair of dressy black pants, and some low wedge shoes. She even does my hair that morning, pulling some of the strands back and pinning them with a flowery clip. I realize that the way she dressed me makes me look very young, and I guess that's the point.

Even though my mom's going to drive separately, she holds my hand and walks me to Sarah's car and lets me know that she'll be with me every step of the way, even when I can't see her.

It's a little more than an hour drive because we have to go all the way back to New York for the trial. A part of me looks forward to seeing my city again.

I look at the busy streets, shocked at how different they seem. They aren't as bright today. Today they look dark and scary, like they know what I'm about to do.

Or like I don't belong anymore. Maybe I don't.

We arrive an hour early, but already there are people standing on the steps of the courthouse, groups of teenagers and parents standing protectively nearby. Some I recognize, some I don't.

I'm actually surprised people really came. I mean, Westchester is only an hour from New York, but it still seems surprising that anyone came all this way to hear me talk about how I became a prostitute.

Sarah takes me in near the back.

"I don't like the idea of this being such a public trial," Sarah says once we make it inside and things quiet down.

She knows very well it's what I wanted, what I asked for. There was a motion to control the people who could come, something about the nature of the crimes and my age, but I'm glad to see it must not have worked out. I want people to hear me. That's the point.

I've been going over what I'm going to say. I will tell them about how Luis saved me, took me in, became my one and only friend. I'll remember his warm, dark voice telling me I'll be okay. I'll remember the swallow necklace. And then I will tell them how his friends pushed themselves on me, and how that eventually turned into sex for money. It wasn't Luis's fault—it was theirs.

But now I'm scared.

Scared of saying the wrong thing and hurting Luis. Scared that that's actually what I want.

I'm scared of exposing my deepest secrets and worst moments in front of a hundred people. Scared of what they will think.

But more than anything, I'm scared of seeing Luis again.

I sip water while sitting on the cold metal chair. I wish we hadn't come this early. It's given me time to think about what will soon happen.

I'm going to see Luis again for the first time in months, and I have no idea how I'm going to take that.

A man walks into the room and tells me it's my time to speak. I follow him down a long hallway. My feet echo on the concrete floor. He opens a door in front of me, and I see a police officer. I close my eyes for a moment and try to pretend this man is Jackson's dad, with his kind smile.

My stomach is somewhere in my feet at this point, but when the stiff air hits me and I see the faces, somehow my confidence comes back. Whatever happens, this is my chance to stop hiding from the truth.

I sit in a seat near the judge, kind of like on TV. I take a couple of deep breaths and manage to look up into the crowd. I see Sarah, who nods reassuringly. I see my mother, who smiles.

In the rest of the seats—I purposefully start toward the back—there are more strangers. Then I recognize a few. Lamont is there. And Charles. And Dez. All Luis's friends. All men who paid to sleep with me. They don't look at me very kindly. They shouldn't. I'm going to call each one of them out if I get the chance. They never held me when I cried, never gave me a home when I needed it, never loved me.

And then I see Luis at a table in front of a barrier separating the courtroom from the public seats. He's sitting next to his lawyer.

I don't know what I expected I would feel when I see him again. I tell myself he loved me. He saved me. But all I can remember is him giving me up. Telling me good-bye forever.

How could he say he loved me if he was willing to give me away that easily?

A woman in a suit stands and begins to talk to me, but I barely hear the words. I feel like my head is filled with water.

I'm looking through the crowd, but I'm brought to reality with the sharp, unkind sound of my name. "Anna," the woman says firmly.

I look at her, but I'm really just wondering how red my face actually is.

"I need you to focus."

I nod.

She starts out small.

"Do you know this man?" she says, pointing to the front row, on the opposite side from where my mother and Sarah sit.

She's pointing at Luis.

His face is thinner, and he seems more serious than I've ever seen him.

I nod and look away.

"Is this the man who solicited sexual favors to other men for money?"

I reply calmly. "No."

She looks frustrated. "Is this the man you lived with while in New York City?"

"Yes."

"And did he make you have sex with men for money?"

"No."

Now she spins away from me, but not before I see her cheeks tinting red. She looks down at her notes and then turns back to me, composed once more.

She thought she already knew the truth. She doesn't understand that it's not as simple as she wants it to be.

"Tell me about your experience with Luis Santino."

Here we go; much better. I'd rather do this on my terms.

"I ran away from home when I was thirteen." I say, and the woman nods, like this is a return to the black-and-white story she wants me to tell. "But I didn't have any place to go. I was lost in Grand Central, and an odd man was following me."

"Mr. Santino?"

I shake my head. "No. I don't know who the odd man was. I never found out, because Luis stepped between us. He saved me from him."

The woman pauses. This was not what she expected. I look over at Luis again, and his eyes look softer, but he's still tense. Still serious.

Still scared.

I take the moment to search the crowd again. I see a police officer in the middle of the crowd, and next to him I see a skinny boy with hazel eyes. Jackson.

His eyes light up slightly when I look at him. I give him the slightest of smiles, and he smiles big in return. Here is the guy who convinced me why I shouldn't be scared. Right or wrong,

I can't hide from my choices. All I can do now—all anyone can do—is face the truth.

"Then what happened, Miss Rodriguez?"

"He gave me a place to stay."

"With him."

"Yes."

"And did you sleep with him?"

I look over to Luis instinctively. Funny how easy it is to go back to old habits. I'm looking for him to tell me what to say. Should I answer this?

"Yes," I say, because there's no point in lying.

"And you were thirteen."

"Yes."

"He was nineteen."

I nod.

"Was this the first man you had sexual relations with?" she asks, pacing a little as she speaks. When she finishes, she pivots quickly to look at me. She's not very good at keeping me comfortable, but maybe she doesn't want to.

"No."

She cocks her head slightly.

"No?" she says. "Who, then, did you sleep with before your interaction with Mr. Santino?"

"I lost my virginity when I was twelve. Luis did not push sex on me."

My descent into prostitution started long before New York.

The woman's eyes narrow, but she keeps going. "Tell me what happened next. You say Luis Santino never pushed sex on you. But you do admit to having sex for money while living with Luis, correct?"

"Yes." This is hardly a question, everyone knows. There is no denying this anymore.

"So how did that happen, then?"

"You want the whole story?" I ask.

"Yes." This is the answer I was hoping for. This is the reason I am here. I want people to understand.

"Please tell us what happened," the woman says.

"I lived with Luis for a month or so. He didn't make me go to school. He didn't make me work. He didn't make me do anything, really. He was nice to me, fed me, showed me around the city. One night he brought a friend over to watch a movie with us." I swallow and look around the room again. Most of the faces are unfamiliar, but there are so many teenagers that I wonder how many drove all the way here from my school, just to hear my story.

This is what I want people to know, but now that the moment's come, I'm scared to death to say it out loud and relive the memory.

"After the movie, I went to my room. Luis's apartment had a spare room, which is where I usually slept."

I take a couple of deep breaths, imagining the moment. The dark room, the silence. The horrible sounds of creaking footsteps that got closer.

"I was in my bed, lying there, when someone came in."

My heart is pounding now.

"It was dark and I couldn't see much. I called out, thinking it was Luis. He got into bed with me and started touching me and pulling off my clothes. I realized quickly that it wasn't Luis."

The room is filled with at least a hundred people, but everyone is deadly silent. Not that they were loud before. It's just that now, the silence feels…louder. More complete. I feel like my voice is echoing. My heart, my labored breaths, I am sure, can be heard by everyone in the room.

I swallow again and realize my throat is dry.

"I tried to get away. I called out. But no one came, and the man didn't let me go. I don't know if I'd call it rape, he didn't hurt me or really even hold me down or anything, not the whole time."

"This man had sex with you, though, when you didn't want to?"

I nod but remember I'm supposed to speak my answers aloud. "Yes."

"And did Luis tell him to do this?"

"No. Afterward the man left and Luis said he was sorry, that he didn't know. But he told me that the man had paid us, he gave us money for the sex."

"What did you use the money for?"

"We went out to eat at a sushi place in Manhattan. It was my favorite."

"So, sex for a nice dinner?"

I shrug.

"Then what happened?" the woman prompts.

"More friends came over."

"That night?"

I shake my head. "That weekend."

"And what happened? Did Luis 'not know' it was happening this time, too?"

I take a deep breath. "He wasn't home."

"Then how did they know to come over?"

I don't know. I mean, I'm sure I asked at the time, I'm sure

Luis had a good excuse, but I don't remember it. He always sounded so mature, so reasonable.

"I don't remember."

"You're sure? Men just randomly came into your apartment to have sex with you against your will and you don't know how or why?"

I shake my head.

"And the next time?"

"The second night I made five hundred dollars. I was glad I made the money. I knew Luis needed the money to make rent. He had just lost his job. I wanted to stay with him. I couldn't go home. So the next time, I did it willingly."

"You did it for Luis?"

I nod. "Yes."

"So for the next three years you had sex with Luis's friends for money?"

"Yes, but it wasn't always Luis's friends."

The woman nods, but apparently that's not important for her purposes.

"And never, during this time, did Luis say anything to you to keep you working?"

I shrug. "We made plans about opening a shop, selling goofy tourist stuff. But we needed money to do it."

"But you never opened a shop, did you?"

"We never got the chance."

The woman walks over to a desk with papers spread over it. "Anna, what if I told you that Luis never lost his job?"

My eyes narrow quickly. I'm confused. I don't know what she means.

"The year you met, he was working for a construction

company."

I nod.

"And you said you had sex for money because you needed the money for the apartment."

I nod again.

"And you needed it because Luis lost his job."

"Yes," I say, waiting for her to make her point.

She holds up a piece of paper. "This is Luis's resignation letter. It's dated forty-two days after you were officially listed a missing person."

"That can't be…" I lean in to look closer at the paper. Luis needed me. If he chose to leave his job, did that mean…

"He quit his job just after he started selling you to his friends."

I see Luis's lawyer begin to stand, but I beat him to the punch.

"He didn't sell me," I say firmly.

"Right, since Luis's friends forced themselves on you without his suggestion. Well, he quit right after that. You don't think that's odd?"

I don't know, I don't know.

I shake my head slightly, fighting back tears. I came here to tell the truth, and now I'm finding out maybe I never knew the truth at all.

I remember the kind Luis. The funny Luis. The guy I was in love with.

I look into the crowd and see a girl from my health class. She's thirteen, the age I was when I moved to New York.

She's so young, so innocent. I think about all of the girls like her, their awkwardness, braces, acne, and stringy hair. Was I like them?

Could I imagine that girl sleeping with older men for money

on her own?

I can't. But that doesn't mean I didn't, right?

I take a deep breath.

But what if Luis really did use me? He suggested my name, Exquisite. He introduced me to Tamara, the hooker from the Bronx. He brought all his friends over.

He quit his job before I ever agreed to do it on a regular basis.

The woman puts down her paper.

"Anna, do you really believe it was your idea to sleep with men you didn't know to pay the rent?"

I shake my head.

"What was that?" she asks, wanting me to speak aloud.

"It wasn't my idea," I say, and it feels like the most honest thing I've said today.

"Then whose idea was it?"

Faces of men pop into my head, flashing like one of those stupid slide shows they use in school, all the men that paid me for sex, willingly or not. I hated it. I hated them all.

Luis was the only one I didn't hate, but was he worth it?

Was I just too young to see, to understand?

I gave him everything.

Now I'm nothing because of him.

A string of words ring through my mind. Tears roll down my cheeks.

"He used to—" My voice breaks, so I start again. "He used to tell me, 'Sex is a good thing. People would kill to be paid to have sex.'"

Maybe sex can be a good thing. But is it a good thing for a thirteen-year-old? Is it a good thing to have sex with people you don't know, men you could get diseases from? Is it a good thing to do it when you don't want to?

Would it have been good if I had gotten pregnant from one of these men? Would Luis have taken care of me?

I remember my last days with Luis. I remember how he brought home five guys to have sex with me.

He didn't ask.

And if I had said no, it wouldn't have mattered. Not to Luis, and certainly not to them. I would have just ended up with a bloody lip and more ripped clothing.

A few days later, he took me to lunch, met a "gang" pimp, the kind who owned and sold a bunch of girls throughout the city, sometimes even in more than one city. Those kinds of guys take away a girl's future forever. There's no getting away from them once they have you.

Luis walked away from that restaurant without me, a pile of money in his hand instead.

He sold me.

I always knew this, but right now it hits me like a subway train.

I've tried to tell myself that he cared about me. That maybe he sold me because he had no better option. Maybe he even thought it would be for my own good. That we had started out good, only to crumble with time.

I only had one chance to get away from the gang pimp before he could get his hooks in me, before Luis was gone forever.

Getting away was the easy part. The pimp was a huge guy

covered in red tattoos named Axel. He was cocky. He knew I'd try to run. He just thought he could handle it.

I remember that I started crying and pretend to have given up. Then, when he wasn't looking, I ran. And I ran fast.

Down the streets of New York, Luis the only thing on my mind. I had to find him, get to him. Convince him to change his mind.

He wasn't very far down the street, so I reached him easily. I thought I'd won. For one glorious second, I thought it would be okay, just like Luis always said.

I didn't notice the horror on his face when I wrapped my arms around him. Not until after.

He pushed me away, his words muffled and unclear through my sobs. The blast to my face, however, was crystal clear. In all the time I'd been with him, Luis had never hit me. Not once. Not until that day.

I backed away from him, pressing my back against the wall. Then, several things happened at one. Axel turned the corner, and Luis threw up his hands like he was surrendering. I'm pretty sure the fist that Luis took to the face was worse than the one I'd taken. But that didn't make it hurt any less.

The second I saw the flashing blue and red lights, I ran. Leaving Luis behind. The cops didn't find me until that night. Until I was broken beyond repair with nowhere to go.

I never saw that day coming. I thought he loved me.

Now I know it was never love at all. Forty-two days. That's how long he waited. That's how long our "perfect" relationship lasted, if it had even existed at all.

"I'm going to ask you again, Anna. Did Luis Santino ever force or push you to have sex with men?"

I guess she wants a direct answer.

I look at Luis, whose face is green. Does he know what I'm about to say? Does he know that his little hooker has grown up? Does he know that I can see through him now?

"Yes."

The room is no longer silent. I hear a few small whispers in the crowd, the rustle of paperwork as Luis's lawyer tries to find a way around this. And I hear Luis let out an angry, exasperated grunt.

Did he really expect me to fight for him?

I'm not here to fight for him.

I'm here to tell the truth.

And now it seems like the truth is clearer than ever.

His eyes meet mine, and I see anger in them. Betrayal. Like this is my fault.

But he made his own choices. Just like I made mine. Whatever consequences we have to face are our own fault.

CHAPTER THIRTY-SEVEN

I wait back in the cold room, sitting on the metal chairs, drinking water and laying my head on the wobbly table until Sarah comes in.

I'm not sure what to expect, but a part of me doesn't really care. I feel numb.

I pick my head up just in time for her to wrap her arms around me in a huge hug.

"That was incredible," she says, though I'm not sure what was incredible or even good at all.

She talks a little bit about the trial, the parts I didn't get to see and how things changed once I'd spoken. Both sides were supposed to question me, but Luis's lawyer said they didn't want to.

Apparently the truth was bad enough that his lawyer was afraid to let me say anything else.

Sarah says I was "that good." She tells me that she spoke to Jackson, who seems like "a nice young man." She says that he said to tell me he's proud of me and he'll see me as soon as I'm ready.

After a moment, I ask, "Is the trial over?"

"The hearing is, but the verdict won't be in for a little while. The lawyers are considering making some kind of deal for Luis to turn in some of his friends."

"Oh," I say. I wonder if he would really do that. I mean, they lied profusely to help him out, but maybe they were just trying to help themselves. Which is better, saying you had sex with a thirteen-year-old girl, or saying you paid to have sex with her against her will?

"What about the janitor?" I ask.

"Him, too. Are you willing to give some names?"

I nod. "But I don't know all of their full names. Some of them were there, in the crowd, though."

Her eyes grow a little bigger, but then she lets out a long breath, like she's just too tired. "We've done enough for the day. Your mom wanted to see you. Are you up for it?"

I'm not really sure, but my body seems to answer for me. After years of feeling like I can't rely on my mom, I suddenly need her. The feel of her arms around me. The quiet security of her love.

As soon as my mother sees me, she puts her arms around me. "I love you, Anna," she says.

"I love you, too," I say, tears stinging my eyes.

I'm not even sure what I'm crying about. Maybe I'm just too exhausted. My mother holds me tighter, rubs my arms, and whispers in my ear, "Everything's going to be fine. I love you, and I'm here for you."

This feeling is a strange one. Bittersweet. Almost like heartbreak… Somehow this feeling is painful *and* good. Like I'm raw but healing. Finally, I'm healing.

I know things between my mom and me aren't completely healed, but I'm happy to have this little piece of normal. A little bit of acceptance.

My mom drives me home, and we stop at a little truck-stop diner for lunch.

We both get a roast beef sandwich with chips. Once we finish, Mom orders an Oreo milkshake to split. I give her my first posttrial smile.

"Have you talked to Dad?" I ask as I take my first slurp. An awkward conversation, I know. But at some point it needs to be said.

She shakes her head.

"I wish he'd been there today." I say. "Maybe then he could have seen…"

Things won't ever go back to normal, but I've learned that even the worst of wounds can find their own way to heal, if you give them the chance.

She shakes her head. "I'm glad he wasn't there. He never would have understood. Not really…and you didn't need that extra stress."

"He's still my father."

She takes in a deep breath and slowly stirs the remaining bits of her hot chocolate. She doesn't speak.

"I don't want him to come back," I say. Honestly, I hope he doesn't. Ever.

"Will you forgive him?" she asks sheepishly, unwilling to look me in the eyes.

I shrug. "I don't know. Maybe one day."

She looks up, her eyes red. "But not today?"

"Not today."

She nods. "Actually, Sarah wants us to go to some family therapy."

I open my mouth to speak but close it, unsure what to say to that. I take another sip of the milk shake before I speak. "Does that mean she wants you to get back together?"

She shakes her head. "I think she just wants us to figure some things out. Like you said, he's still your father."

I nod. "That's good, I guess."

I don't know what will happen with my father, but knowing that my mom's there for me now—better, that we're there for each other—lets me know that whatever happens, we'll be okay.

She clears her throat suddenly and smiles, all trace of her emotions gone. "How about we go shopping tomorrow? Maybe get some lunch together."

I blink. "Lunch? You mean instead of school?"

"I figure you could use a day off."

I let out a breath, amazed at how relieved I am. At least I can let some of those rumors wind down before I face it.

I realize how silly I was to fear that knowing the truth would push her away. We didn't lose everything we've worked so hard to build. The truth made us stronger.

We talk about what we'll do now, and I'm surprised when she tells me she's okay with me dropping out of school.

"We can talk about it. I can't expect you to be a child forever."

I smile, thinking of Jackson.

"I think I'll finish out the year," I say. Which is surprising, even for me. But the truth is, the learning stuff isn't so bad, the looks are bearable, and I actually kinda sort of have some friends now.

Four years is a really long time, and I'd be insanely old if I went through high school normally. But maybe I can have one sorta-normal year of high school before moving on.

CHAPTER THIRTY-EIGHT

Just a few months ago, I was a prostitute. I feel like I should be in one of those support groups.

Hi, my name is Anna, and I'm a recovering whore.

Do they have recovery groups for hookers? They should. We're just as jacked up as anyone else, drugs or not.

Mom tells me I can take all the time I need before I go back to school, but after a few days hiding out in my bedroom, I realize I'd rather go back now than keep putting it off.

I'm not sure what I expected to happen when I go back to school. Once inside, I head for the bathroom, just for a splash of water to wake me up, but I stop when a rather large body blocks my path. When it doesn't move, I look up.

It's Eric, Brandon's old friend, the guy who asked me if he could buy my services.

Well, this should be good.

"Can I ask you a question?" he asks me.

I say nothing.

"How much money do you make sucking cock?"

I guess there's a reason Brandon got along so well with this guy.

A sly grin spreads across Eric's face. I guess he's going to milk this for all he has.

"So what's the going rate?"

I don't know how to respond. Honestly, the only thing going on in my mind is how much I'd like to kick him in the balls. But talk about making things worse. Instead, I twist away from him and disappear into the crowd.

I hide in the bathroom and wonder what's going to happen now as I work on a random sketch of a bush of honeysuckle. Will the whispers and stares ever calm down? Will Jackson forgive me for real? Will I ever escape my past?

I pause when I hear a set of slow footsteps enter the bathroom. They're too slow to just be someone coming in to use the restroom or "freshen up" or whatever girls do when they look at themselves in the mirror for thirty seconds.

I see a set of pink-and-white striped flats stop in front of my stall.

"Anna?"

It's Marissa. Even if I didn't recognize the voice, the flats are a dead giveaway.

"Yeah?" I say, making sure I don't show any weakness in my voice. I'm just tired of being looked at.

"You okay?"

"Maybe. Are you?"

"Kind of." She's quiet for a moment, then she sighs. "Winning one big battle doesn't fix all your problems. Guess that's a lesson we're both learning."

"Guess so."

"I don't know how to stand up to all of them, how to move

on from here."

I open the bathroom door to face her. "You need to get your power back, remember?"

"Yeah," she smiles. "But maybe you do, too." She takes a few steps back and then retreats out the bathroom. I'm not sure if we're friends now. I'm not sure where she's at, but I do know things are better than before. Maybe we're both still learning.

I take a deep breath and run her words through my mind. Didn't I already face my monsters? Wasn't that getting my power back? I faced Luis and his friends, the ones who pushed me to have sex with them and then paid me. Wasn't that enough?

Then again, if it were enough, would I still be hiding in the bathroom? Maybe I do have a few more battles to fight before this is completely over.

Class is...interesting. Even the teachers seem awkward around me now. I guess maybe they thought the rumors were, well, rumors before. Now it's pretty public knowledge. Shit, there was even an article about me in the newspaper.

Mr. Shelf can't even look at me now. Mrs. Robert's eyes just glaze over me.

Only Mr. Harkins seems unchanged. He keeps pushing me to get better and better at art, and it's kind of working. He posts my self-portrait in the hallway, and every time I walk by it, I feel a little bit better.

It's watercolor, mostly blues and blacks, like a bruise. But on the white background, it doesn't seem too somber. It's just a face, no connecting neck or whatever, like I'm floating. The girl is looking down with a hood up over her head.

It's me, I guess, though it doesn't look much like me anymore. The girl in that picture is hiding. But for better or worse, everyone sees me now. I'm exposed. Naked.

Then someone sits at my table. I didn't realize how much I needed to see him until he was here.

Jackson.

He smiles at me, and my heart stops. He sits beside me without saying much as we work on finishing our third-quarter projects. It's nice just to be near him, to know he doesn't hate me. But I still wonder where exactly we're at now.

I try to ignore my unresolved feelings with him and focus on my artwork. I'm drawing a black bird taking flight, except this section is on "pointillism," so it has to be drawn with hundreds of little dots. You get shading by putting more dots in one spot than another.

"Any idea what you'll do for your last project? It's a big one," Jackson eventually says.

I groan and press my head to the table. "No. No clue." I look up. "You?"

Mr. Harkins wants us to do something that "makes a difference." He tells us a few examples, like how last year one of his students brought in an old fuzzy picture she had of her birth mother whom she'd never met. All she had was the picture and a name. She painted the picture and posted it all over the internet with the first name, hoping to find her.

It took a few months, but eventually a friend of a friend pointed her in the right direction, and she found her.

Another year, a girl painted a picture of her father in his army fatigues hugging her little sister and sold them to raise money for a charity that supported veterans after their service.

Now she wants us to do something amazing.

I look to Jackson, sure he'll know something fantastic to do for this kind of project.

"I don't know," he says. "You should have something good, right? I mean, you've got a killer story."

I shake my head. "But I already told it and no one cares. I'm back where I started. Besides, who would that help but me?"

"I think people care more than you think. But if you don't want to do something about yourself, pick something else you care about. Something that bothers you."

I'm looking at him, thinking about what to say, when I realize something is different between us after all. Something's missing. And then I realize what it is. That cold, heavy fear I've lived with for so long. It's gone.

I take in a deep breath. "What about you? What 'issue' are you going for?"

His face turns a little red, and now I see the old Jackson. The one who blushed when he first saw me. I wonder if he could ever be that boy again. I wonder if I could ever be the girl he thought I was.

"I was thinking maybe drugs, you know, since my mom… Or I was thinking maybe something to support people who come forward as witnesses. You know, like you did. It was brave."

"Oh," I say, totally taken off guard. He thought I was brave? "I just told the truth."

He shakes his head. "Maybe you don't see it, but it was brave. You could have kept it inside yourself until…"

He doesn't have to say it. Until it was too late. He knows better than anyone.

"I think you should do the one about your mom," I say. "That's part of who you are, you know?"

I think about the Jackson I first met, seemingly confident and at ease but hiding his own fear inside…and then I think about the Jackson who came between me and the janitor. Defending me because of who I am, because I was too weak to tell the truth before it blew up in my face—again. Because I was too scared to trust someone to help me.

The bell rings a few seconds later, and I'm not any closer to coming up with an idea for this project. I don't even know what I want my project to be about. Do I really want to go the obvious route and make my life even more about my past than it already is? Seal my identity with the horrors of my past? I've faced them. Now I want to move on.

Does it make me selfish to want that?

I don't want to be a former hooker forever.

I enter the crowded halls, too distracted to even pay attention to the strange looks. They're just background noise at this point. A part of life.

But then I look up into the faces that surround me and I realize how many of them I don't know. I don't have any names to go with their faces, any memories of them. I don't know their secrets the way they know mine.

But they have secrets, too. Secrets they're terrified will destroy them if they let them out.

Jackson's mother overdosed on drugs years ago.

Marissa's boyfriend used a sex tape to blackmail her.

Jen was raped and called a slut for it.

I slept with men for money.

Most of those are secrets no one knows about, with the

exception of mine.

I look into the sea of faces and wonder: what are all their secrets?

Are we really all that different, after all?

I smile when I think about Jackson, before he knew the truth about me, before he knew I was lying to him, before one of my ex-johns threatened him in front of me, he told me something.

"Everyone's been through something... I mean, what's normal, anyway?"

How can I prove that Jackson was right all along? My story might be a bit more intense than theirs, but so what? I'm not normal, but neither are they.

I think I know what my final project will be.

I spend the next three weeks planning my project. Truthfully, it's not really that hard. Not now that I know what to do.

I don't know if this will turn out the way I hope, because it's not just about me. This is about everyone in the school and if I can give them the courage to admit who they really are. They don't have to tell me. They don't have to tell anyone they don't want to tell. But if I can use my past for something good, if I can use it to inspire people, maybe I can do more than make peace with what happened. Maybe it can become something I'm proud of.

I may end up looking like a fool—again. I guess I can't get much worse than the town whore who got attacked by the janitor after homecoming.

The point of this project is that I'm a freak, just like everyone else. If I'm not brave enough to risk more social embarrassment, how can I expect anyone else to be?

Mr. Harkins lets me use the theater stage again, partially because my project wouldn't fit on those art tables, and partially because I want to keep it a secret. Even from Jackson.

He watches me every day as I leave art class to work without him, but a quick smile from me lets him know I'm not avoiding him. He showed me a new life. He gave me hope. Without that hope, I don't think I'd ever have had the strength to let go of Luis, not for real, not for good.

Right now, I'm still stuck inside the looks and these concrete halls, but I'm not trapped anymore. I'm not chained. I can walk away from this school, these people, and live an actual life. I don't know what I'd do, but I could do it. I believe in my future. I believe in the people who love me.

Most of all, I believe in myself.

And I only know that because of the boy who danced in the park with me, who believed in me when he didn't even know me.

I finish the final touches of my poster…and decide that I'm not done yet. This isn't enough. I'm not so good at telling people how I feel, but maybe I can show them.

Maybe Mr. Harkins is onto something. Using art, any kind, can help me change the things I want to change.

I curl up my poster, ready to unveil it on Monday morning, and run back to the art room to ask for one more thing from Mr. Harkins. I'm going to write three notes, but I want more than just notebook paper. I want them to mean something.

He gladly gives me three pieces of thick parchment paper and a calligraphy pen. I put the pen into my purse and press the paper inside my history textbook. I'll write my notes at home this weekend. For now, I sit by Jackson and write a list of the objects I'll need.

1. A chain
2. A jar
3. A picture frame

Jackson looks over my shoulder. "What are you planning?"

I wink. "It's a secret. But I promise this is a good one."

CHAPTER THIRTY-NINE

Monday morning comes too soon. I'm nervous as hell, and not just about the poster. I'm nervous about all of it.

I drink a cup of coffee with my mom and pretend to be leaving for school. She sends me a quick farewell, and then she turns back to the magazine she was reading at the table.

My heart thuds in my chest, but I know I have to do this.

I place a picture frame, the glass jar—now filled with lightning bugs, lighting up and fading out—and a note on the kitchen counter, and then I walk out the door.

Inside the frame is a picture of her and me before I ran away. I was eleven, my unruly curls flying into my face, but in the picture my mother doesn't seem bothered by that. Our cheeks are pressed up against each other, and we're both smiling cheesily.

The picture doesn't take up the whole frame though, and below it is a piece of pink paper I cut out from my old journal. It has my sloppy bubble letters I used to think were cool in middle school, and in the entry, I talk about the trip my mom and I took to the fireworks over Inner Harbor in Baltimore one year. I talk about how much I loved spending time with her and how I wished we could do more things like that.

On the parchment paper, I wrote:

> Mommy,
>
> It might not seem like it, but I'm still your little girl. I want to start over and have the life we should have had together, catching fireflies and shopping and talking about boys. I did love you then, and I still love you now.
>
> I'm sorry for hurting you. I hope you'll forgive me, too.
>
> Love
>
> Anna

I stop at our mailbox and hold a gift for my father in my hand.

His gift was harder to come up with. It's hard to forget about everything he did to my mom and me. It's even harder to accept. I don't know if he'll ever change. But I know now that people can. If he ever decides to, I want him to know I believe in him.

So in the end, I decided the simplest gift would be the best. I wrote a letter.

> Daddy,
>
> I'm sorry I went away. I'm sorry I changed. I'm sorry I grew up.
>
> Sometimes you have to let the things you love be free or they'll suffocate.
>
> I hope one day you can accept me for who I am.
>
> Love
>
> Anna

I put the letter into the mailbox and then practically run to the bus stop. My heart pounds while I wait for the bus, and it hasn't seemed to slow by the time the bus arrives.

On the bus, Jackson flops down next to me, and I jump.

"Whoa. You okay?"

I laugh awkwardly. "Just nervous about today."

His eyebrows shoot up. "Do I finally get to see what you've been working on?"

"Yup. And this is going to be a looong day."

He laughs. "I'll be ready and waiting."

I hold back a groan. I am so not ready for this.

We pull up to the school, and when we walk inside, I feel like my skin is on fire. Do these kids know how much of an effect they have on people? On each other? Do they know they have the power to destroy me today?

I shake the feelings and head to my locker. Today, I refuse to hide.

I finally take Mr. Harkins up on his offer of an escape inside the school. All my projects are done now, so I sit down at a table and just sketch a random face. It's not very good, but it gets my mind off of what I'm doing today.

Because of Jackson, I'm going to wait until lunch to unveil my project, because I have one last thing to do during art class. I get permission to leave science a few minutes early, and I run into Mr. Harkins's room to drop off Jackson's gift and a note at his desk, and then book it down the hall to the theater room.

I hide out there for the rest of art period, where all I can imagine is Jackson as he sees my gift and reads my note.

Jackson,

I don't think you'll ever realize how much I needed you this year. You were the only light in the darkest time of my life. I have no idea how to thank you for that or how to make up for the horrible things I've let into your life. But I knew I had to tell you, somehow, how much you changed me.

You, Jackson Griffin, helped me break my chains, so I gave you some to remind you of how amazing you are and how much power you have to help people.

You believed in me. Now I believe in you.

Love

Anna

Next to the note, I left a tiny little bottle topped with a cork and filled with a silver chain connected to a key chain hook. The key chain is brittle, cheap. But it's supposed to be. I want him to always be able to touch it and feel how weak the chains we wear can be. All it takes is the courage to break them.

I end up lying back on the stage and staring up at the lights like I did that first day with Jackson. I was so different back then. So jaded. So lost.

Maybe I'm still lost, still pushing my way through a life I have no idea how to live, but I have my feet planted, and I'm moving toward something. One day, I'll figure out what that is.

After one more excruciatingly long class, it's finally lunch and time for me to sink or swim.

I leave my English class early—with the teacher's permission—to hang my poster (teachers seem happy to let me break rules if it's for another teacher). I want my poster ready before anyone arrives at lunch. Alex and Jen help me place it right next to the entrance of the cafeteria, where everyone will see it.

Mr. Harkins comes down to check it out himself before all the kids comes crashing down the hall. I'm very glad he did this, because I'm not positive it won't be destroyed within a few minutes.

Three big words are written across the poster.

WHAT'S NORMAL ANYWAY?

And to the side is a painting of a person with half her face covered with a mask. I thought about writing more words to explain what I mean, that secrets chain us and that we're all the same underneath those masks we wear. But I decided I wanted everyone to come to their own conclusions.

While Alex, Jen, and Mr. Harkins watch, I walk up to the poster with a permanent marker and write, I slept with men for money, and then I hand two more markers to Alex and Jen, hoping they'll take my lead.

Jen walks up to the poster and writes, I didn't want to have sex with him. He made me do it.

Tears fill my eyes at her honesty. Anyone could have written that note, so not everyone will know it was her, but it doesn't matter. When she turns around with a light in her eyes I haven't seen before, I know she's free of it.

The bell rings, and right away bodies fill the lobby. Alex

looks around for a second and then steps forward, in front of the kids now, stopping to watch before they enter the cafeteria. She writes, *My father used to hit me. Now he's in prison and I'm glad.*

Everyone stops. More kids fill the lobby and stop to look.

Alex shrugs and hands the marker to someone else. "What's your secret?" she asks the freshman boy. I want to hug her, for more than one reason.

Jen hands her marker to someone else, and I do the same.

"What's your secret?" I ask.

Soon the lobby is packed. A few kids move past the crowd and head into the cafeteria, but most of them don't. Maybe partially because the spectators are blocking the path for the rest. No one else steps forward to expose themselves.

Then I see Elizabeth, Eric, and the rest of their not-so-nice friends. Brandon smirks at us, our three secrets sitting there alone, exposed, in front of everyone.

Then Marissa steps forward. She practically rips a marker from the freshman I gave mine to and walks up to the poster.

She writes, *I had a sex tape and Anna helped me destroy it.*

I almost laugh out loud. Alex actually does.

Already the whispers are spreading, but Marissa is free of it. She walks right up to me and throws her arms around me.

"Whore!" someone coughs.

Marissa looks up. "Dick!" she coughs back, then winks at me and steps beside Alex to watch as more kids write their secrets on the walls.

Now more kids are walking up to the poster, hesitantly at first, but soon people are fighting for their chance to write something.

My parents hate me, one kid writes.

My dad is gay, a senior girl writes.

I make myself throw up

I gave my virginity to a boy whose name I don't know

I'm still a virgin

Secrets cover the board quickly, but just as quickly people head back into the cafeteria and back to their normal lives.

Alex picks up one of the fallen markers and walks back over to the poster. I thought she was done telling secrets. She writes, *I wish I were more like Anna.*

I blink. Me? Why would she want to be like me?

Alex smirks and hands the marker back to me. "You're stronger than you think," she says, and I want to say the same back to her, but she's already walking back into the cafeteria with everyone else.

There are only a handful of people left. They're reading the poster full of so many secrets, so many I doubt anyone will remember whose was whose.

Jackson walks over, and I watch him pick up a marker off the floor.

He finds a place in the corner of the poster and writes, *Heroin killed my mom,* but then he scoots a few feet over and finds another place right in the middle, underneath the word "normal," and writes, *My heart belongs to Anna.*

I don't know what to say. He smiles and crosses the room with big steps and wraps his arms around me. And then, in front of everyone, he gives me a kiss that feels like everything I've ever wanted and everything I'll ever need.

I decide that this is my new favorite moment. No matter what happens between us, this will be the moment I remember forever.

CHAPTER FORTY

Sometimes being interviewed is a chance to stop playing games. It's just you, them, and the truth.

My palms sweat as I shift in the metal chair.

The room is quiet. Just me and a gray-haired woman in a blazer, sitting at her desk as she flips through my portfolio.

Why doesn't she speak? *Say something!* I want to scream at her.

"You've had quite a life, Miss Rodriguez," the woman says, monotone. I can't tell if this is good or bad. She knows about my past. Will this mean she won't want me in her school?

"Yes, ma'am," I say.

She finally looks up, and I see a tiny spark of life in her brown eyes. "Will you tell me about it?"

I swallow. "I was a teenage prostitute," I say. It still sounds so strange to say, to admit out loud, but it's no secret anymore.

She looks down at one of my paintings. One I keep in my portfolio just because I know how many people find it interesting. It's of a girl sitting on the curb in a dark city, her arms curled around her legs, dark hair covering her face. She's hiding, even from the view of the painting.

She flips the page to another, one I like much better than the street picture.

It's a girl's face, screaming while the world whizzes by around her. Everything is blurry except the girl.

"Tell me about this."

"That's always how I felt before and after my time on the streets. Like I was screaming for help, but no one would stop to help me. Like no one cared."

"But you got out of that life."

"Yes, ma'am. There are hopeful pictures in there, too. I use both the light and the dark of my past as inspiration."

She nods. "You have quite a perspective, that's for sure." She pauses. "Tell me why you want to go to my school."

My heart hammers, head pounds.

"Art is my outlet. It's the way to express myself, the way I communicate with the world. I want to go to your school because I feel you can teach me the skills I need. Make me better. There's nothing else I want more than to be an artist."

The woman smiles. She actually smiles. I wasn't sure she was capable for a second.

"Anna, it takes a lot more than skill to be an artist." She folds her hands in front of her. "That being said, I'm hopeful that you have what it takes. I'd love an opportunity to see what else you have in you."

My heart stops. "Does that mean I'm in?"

"I can't make that call alone. It has to be decided by a committee. But they listen to my recommendations." She chuckles. "So while I can't guarantee anything, I'd be very surprised if we don't see you this summer."

She stands, and I stand, and she shakes my hand.

"Thank you," I say.

"Good luck, Anna. You'll hear from us soon."

My head's spinning, and I walk slowly toward the door. Once it's shut behind me, I turn to my mother and Jackson, who are sitting on a bench outside the room, waiting for me.

They both jump up and hug me. It's just a summer art school. Even if I get in, it probably won't mean that much in the long run, but to me, it means everything. It's a step toward a new future.

"I knew they'd love you," Jackson says as we leave the building side by side, my mother behind us, smiling.

"I don't have a yes yet. I won't find out for sure for a few more weeks."

"They're crazy if they don't let you in."

I roll my eyes. "Yes, but you're always optimistic. I'm a realist."

"A realist who was totally wrong."

I shrug. "They'll just hate me once I start taking classes," I say, but I can't hide my huge grin.

"Probably," he says.

I punch him in the arm, and he laughs.

Once we're outside, my mom says, "Anna? Where's the best sushi place around here?"

I stop at the corner of the street and think. Taxis fly by us; crowds of people walk past. I know New York better than my mother ever will. All of these places have memories connected to them. Not all of them the best memories. But today, the entire city feels like the place I always dreamed it could be. A city of hope.

"How about we try someplace new?" I ask. Then I remember one place I'd always wanted to try. "What about some Indian food?"

"Ooh! Sounds delicious," my mom says.

I'm not afraid of the past anymore, and I've opened up to Jackson and my mom more than I ever thought I could, but now I'm all about moving on. All about the new.

I have no idea what will happen now. If I'll get my GED and go to college in the next year. If I'll make it into this art school for the summer. But I'm not really worried about it.

I'm not perfect. I never will be. But I'm okay with that.

For once, I'm actually happy just being me.

Anna.

ACKNOWLEDGMENTS

I am incredibly blessed to have my name, my words, in print. So many people had a hand in helping me to get here, some more direct than others, but they all deserve a huge thank you!

First, I have to thank my amazing and supportive husband, Sean...who I will never forget to thank again! ;) You were my very first fan and biggest supporter! I love you!

Plus the rest of my insane family! Love you guys!

A big, huge, massive thanks to my editor Stephen. Without you, this book might never have seen the light of day. Thank you for seeing its amazing potential and being willing to do whatever it took to get it where it needed to be! Thank you for all your hard work and thank you thank you for believing in me!

Thank you to all the writing friends I've made along the way. Each and every one of you has made an impact on me and my writing. Some specific thanks go to: Stacey Nash—you're so giving and rarely ask for anything in return. Thank you! Naomi Hughes—thank you for your encouraging words and helpful critique when I was still just starting out on this crazy road to publication. Rebecca Yarros—I didn't know you personally when you helped a little newbie writer back in the day, but now that I do I know you are even more incredible than I thought back then (which is saying something!). Laura Timms—thank you for your encouragement and reading my revision before it went off to the acquisitions board. Thank you to all my friends involved in Unborn Writers, my old writing group. It was an awesome time with all of you. And of course, thanks to all the friendly folks who helped me with my query and pitch. You guys rock!

Thank you to everyone involved in the online writing community. You all amaze me every day. Thank you to Brenda Drake and Erica Chapman for seeing something in this crazy little story during Pitch Madness. You sincerely gave me the confidence I needed. Thank you to the folks at Query Kombat-Michelle, SC, and Michael, for involving me and being so supportive ever since! Thank you to Tamara and Jessa for running Pitchmas. Without you, Stephen may have never stumbled upon my pitch for NAKED. I owe you much, ladies!

I already mentioned this person, but she deserves a double thanks for all that she does. She is so incredibly modest about the impact that she has had on so many writers. The online writing community would not be the same without you! Brenda Drake—you are truly incredible!!

Thank you to the folks at Absolute Write. It's a roller coaster ride there sometimes, but I've grown exponentially by being a part of your totally insane community. And thank you to Victoria Strauss for being so giving to writers everywhere!

Lastly, I owe the thanks of all thanks to my God. This passion has been the most incredible gift I've ever been given. So THANK YOU, THANK YOU, THANK YOU, THANK YOU!! You are truly amazing.

NAKED

by Stacey Trombley

READING GROUP GUIDE

Prepared by Nancy Cantor
Media Specialist
University School of Nova Southeastern University

1. Before the first instance of Anna's father being physically abusive, Anna's justification for running away was that her parents didn't allow her to be herself. Did you "buy in" to this reason for a thirteen-year-old running away, with no plan and very little money? What do you think are the causes of teenage girls running away from home? Were Anna's experiences as a runaway realistic?

2. Are high school kids really as cruel to one another as they were depicted in this book? Is high school bullying as pervasive in your school as it was in Anna's?

3. Anna discovers her passion for art because of a supportive teacher. Have you had a similar transformative experience with a caring adult?

4. When Anna began her first drawing in art class, she looked at the blank paper as a "fresh start." Have you ever needed something to serve as a fresh start for you?

5. Early in the book, Jackson says, "We're all messed up in some way. You're not so different from the rest of us." Do you agree?

6. Almost every character in the book has secrets. How did revealing her secrets help Anna heal? Anna's mother? Jackson?

7. Anna and her mother are emotionally distant through much of the novel. Discuss how they repaired their relationship.

8. Anna mistrusts men because of how she has been treated by her father, Luis, Luis's friends, other johns. Have you ever felt this way? Are there good men and boys out there?

9. Anna thinks to herself, *I know all about doing things you don't want to do just because you can't see a way out.* Is this common for teens, especially girls? Do you think many girls (and women) stay in destructive relationships because of this? How can we help break the cycle of domestic abuse?

10. Marissa's boyfriend is blackmailing her because of a sex video. How can girls protect themselves from these types of situations in today's world of social media?

11. When did you suspect the janitor was the person leaving the notes in Anna's locker?

12. When Anna begins to trust her mother again, she states that

if she had received unconditional love from her parents, perhaps she wouldn't have run away. Is unconditional love possible for parents? How can they draw the line between discipline and love?

13. What are your thoughts on the romance between Anna and Jackson? Do they have a future? Was he a realistic teenage boy?

14. What is *normal*, anyway?

Check out more of Entangled Teen's hottest reads...

WHATEVER LIFE THROWS AT YOU

by julie cross

When seventeen-year-old track star Annie Lucas's dad starts mentoring nineteen-year-old baseball rookie phenom, Jason Brody, Annie's convinced she knows his type—arrogant, bossy, and most likely not into high school girls. But as Brody and her father grow closer, Annie starts to see through his façade to the lonely boy in over his head. When opening day comes around and her dad—and Brody's—job is on the line, she's reminded why he's off-limits. But Brody needs her, and staying away isn't an option.

MODERN MONSTERS

by kelley york

Last night, something terrible happened to a girl at a party. And now she's told the police that quiet Vic Howard did it. Suddenly Vic's gone from being invisible to being a major target. He's determined to find out what *really* happened, even if it means an uneasy alliance with the girl's best friend, Autumn Dixon. But while the truth can set Vic free, some truths can destroy a life forever...

LIFE UNAWARE

by cole gibsen

Regan Flay is following her control-freak mother's "plan" for high school success, until everything goes horribly wrong. Every bitchy text or email is printed out and taped to every locker in the school. Now Regan's gone from popular princess to total pariah. The only person who speaks to to her is former best-friend's hot-but-socially-miscreant brother, Nolan Letner. And the consequences of Regan's fall from grace are only just beginning. Once the chain reaction starts, no one will remain untouched...

SEARCHING FOR BEAUTIFUL

by nyrae dawn

Brynn believes her future is as empty as her body until Christian, the boy next door, starts coming around. Playing his guitar and pushing her to create art once more. She meets new friends at the local community center. Gets her dad to look her in the eye again…sort of. But letting someone in isn't as easy as it seems. Can she open up her heart to truly find her life's own beauty, when living for the after means letting go of the before?

LOLA CARLYLE's 12-STEP ROMANCE

by danielle younge-ullman

While the idea of a summer in rehab is a terrible idea (especially when her biggest addiction is organic chocolate), Lola Carlyle finds herself tempted by the promise of spa-like accommodations and her major hottie crush. Unfortunately, Sunrise Rehabilitation Center isn't *quite* what she expected. Her best friend has gone AWOL, the facility is definitely more jail than spa, and boys are completely off-limits…except for Lola's infuriating(and irritatingly hot) mentor, Adam. Worse still, she might have found the one messy, invasive place where life actually makes sense.